# THE IRON EARL

## A VALOR OF VINEHILL NOVEL, VOLUME 1

# K.J. JACKSON

First Edition: February 2019
ISBN: 9781723943829
http://www.kjjackson.com

# K.J. Jackson Books

## Historical Romance:

Stone Devil Duke, *Hold Your Breath*
Unmasking the Marquess, *Hold Your Breath*
My Captain, My Earl, *Hold Your Breath*
Worth of a Duke, *Lords of Fate*
Earl of Destiny, *Lords of Fate*
Marquess of Fortune, *Lords of Fate*
Vow, *Lords of Action*
Promise, *Lords of Action*
Oath, *Lords of Action*
Of Valor & Vice, *Revelry's Tempest*
Of Sin & Sanctuary, *Revelry's Tempest*
Of Risk & Redemption, *Revelry's Tempest*
To Capture a Rogue, Logan's Legends, *Revelry's Tempest*
To Capture a Warrior, Logan's Legends, *Revelry's Tempest*
The Devil in the Duke, *Revelry's Tempest*
The Iron Earl, *Valor of Vinehill*

## Paranormal Romance:

Flame Moon
Triple Infinity, *Flame Moon #2*
Flux Flame, *Flame Moon #3*

Be sure to sign up for news of my next releases at
www.KJJackson.com

# { PROLOGUE }

Late.

He was too late.

Above a rocky outcropping a mile away smoke snaked into the sky. The stream of blackened ash billowed into a ragged cloud, then vanished as the wind snatched it into oblivion.

Lachlan set his heels into his horse, thundering across the last field toward the small set of buildings just out of his view.

His brother and sister hadn't waited for him at Vinehill. Not as they should have. Not as they said they would.

*He* was the soldier. They should have waited for him.

But no, not his siblings. Jacob and Sloane had taken off, following their third cousin, Torrie, to get to her family's farm before the clearing men came.

How Torrie's family had put off the brutes that were clearing the Swallowford lands for as long as they had was a miracle.

A miracle that was ending in front of his eyes.

Baron Falsted's men were intent on removing one of the last families in the area. There would be no further reprieve.

The stench of the fire charred his nostrils long before he could see the blazes.

He crested the last hill.

Worse than he imagined.

Five buildings were now torches flaming from the ground, the air about them undulating with heat.

Yanking on the reins, Lachlan leapt from his horse before it stopped. He tore toward the hellfire, searching the flames. Searching for people in the sooty haze.

Three men. One far off on a horse, watching. One on the ground by the cottage with a torch in his hand. The third standing halfway between the two. None he recognized and all a distance back from the raging blazes.

His brother. Where the hell was Jacob?

Lachlan ran across the wheat field, flying straight between the barn and a cottage, both engulfed in fire. Heat singed his skin and his arm flung up, shielding his eyes from the heat that enveloped him.

There.

Far at the opposite end of the buildings, the main house. Two bodies sprawled prone on the ground in front of it, blood smeared across one man's face.

Not Jacob. Not Sloane. Not Torrie.

Lachlan spun, squinting against the embers spewing into his face. Where the hell were they?

He spun again. Movement out of the main cottage.

Jacob. Jacob carrying Sloane on his hip, her arms stretched out, dragging a screeching Torrie with her.

Flames engulfed Torrie's skirts.

Five steps from the cottage, Jacob dropped Sloane. She scrambled to Torrie's skirts, swatting at the flames with her arm, screaming as she tried to squelch the blazes.

"Jacob." Lachlan ran toward them. "Jacob." But his bellows didn't stop his brother—didn't slow Jacob one step.

His forearm swinging up to cover his face, Jacob plunged back through the flames licking out of the cottage door for air and he disappeared into the inferno of the house.

Hell, Torrie's family had to still be inside.

Lachlan ran past Sloane and Torrie. Two steps away from the door, a terrifying creak filled the air and the roof of the cottage collapsed inward.

The surging blast of heat and flames sent Lachlan flying backward and he landed on his back.

Seconds slowed to lifetimes. One after another.

His ears ringing from the blast, he managed to push himself up from the dirt as embers spun through the air, sizzling onto his skin.

No. Not Jacob. It should have been him. He was the soldier, dammit. His was supposed to be the expendable life.

Sloane. Where the hell was she? He twisted his body to see behind him. Where?

Onto his knees, stumbling to his feet, he searched through the choking smoke, nothing but pounding in his ears, reverberations shaking his skull.

Sloane.

She'd rolled away from Torrie, the flames on their cousin's skirt now dampened.

Screaming. Sloane was screaming. He couldn't hear her, but he could see her through the blackened debris floating through the air.

Screaming, she struggled to her feet and charged directly at the man holding a torch that stood just beyond the reach of the inferno.

The brute tossed the flaming stick to the ground a moment before Sloane blasted into him, her arms swinging in attack.

A blade. A silver blade flashed in the smoldering air, high in the brute's hand.

His brother dead and now Sloane—hell no—not Sloane too.

Lachlan found his feet and lunged at the two of them. Instinct from the years fighting on the continent engulfed him and his hands stretched out, reaching with one purpose. Stop the knife.

Lachlan crashed into his sister and the brute and sent all three of them sprawling, tangled, to the ground.

But the blade was in his hand—he'd managed that.

Red flashed in his eyes, taking his sight, taking his mind.

He rolled to his knees and plunged the dagger into the brute's neck in one quick motion. His arm lifted and drove the blade into him again. And again. And again.

And again.

Lost. Lost in a netherworld of rage, for how long he didn't know. A hell where he didn't know anything other than the blade sinking into flesh again and again.

"Lach."

"Lachlan."

The slightest whisper of sound broke through the pounding in his ears.

"Lach."

Something hitting his back. Pounding on him.

His hand on the hilt of the blade stopped, high in the air.

He spun.

Sloane. Her face terrorized. Her eyes tortured in pain. Her mouth screaming at him.

Her arm—hell—her arm was bloody, festering.

He blinked, shaking his head.

He was too late.

Again.

The purgatory of fire and ash surrounded him, swallowing him.

Swallowing him whole.

# { CHAPTER 1 }

The gravel granite of the pathway crunched under the heel of her slipper, betraying her presence.

Devil take it. Too soon.

Evalyn wanted the man further set into the secluded alcove ringed with tall evergreen hedges. It would be far easier if she cornered him. Far easier for her plan to work if she could hold him captive deep in the alcove.

Her heel lifted from the gravel as she stilled in place, steadily breathing in the crisp night air flush with the scent of recently trimmed boxwood hedges. He didn't move. Didn't turn around. She dared a long look at her prey, staring at the wide expanse of his dark tailcoat stretching snug from the twin boulders of his shoulders.

Never mind that the Scotsman was twice her size and could step directly over her if he so chose not to be trapped.

*Trap him? Hell, it'd be easier to trap a demon in a windstorm.*

His shoulders swayed slightly and his head cocked to the side, his left ear lifting to the moonlit sky. Brown hair curled about the curve of his ear and reflected a glimmer from the torch lit above her head on the pathway.

She turned into a statue, attempting to make him move his feet farther into the garden alcove by her thoughts alone.

Just three steps further, sir. Three was all she asked.
Three tiny steps.

The man turned fully around and the rage she'd
witnessed in him as he walked through the ballroom still
pounded deep lines into his forehead. His head tilted down,
his eyes pinning her.

Her lips parted, words lurching over her dry tongue.
"My lord, I was hoping to have a word."

"I don't think you want it with me, lass." The low
rumble of his Scottish burr shook through her belly.

The timbre of his voice was more than enough
warning. She should run and she knew it.

But there was nothing else for it.

She charged forward, straight at the impossibly wide
chest of Lord Dunhaven.

She'd barrel into him if she had to, but she would get
him deep into this alcove.

A step before she crashed into him, he jumped
backward one, two, three steps.

Far enough.

They were secluded, or at least enough so.

Her heels dug into the gravel, skidding to a stop, her
breath leaving her in a whoosh as she looked up at him.

The anger on his forehead relaxed, a knowing smile
curving onto his lips. "You're not out here for a word, are
you, lass?"

Before she could answer, his hand lifted, wrapping
about the back of her bare neck, and he descended, his
mouth meeting hers.

Warmth juxtaposed with the hardness of his lips as the
faint smell of brandy and spice filled her head. Without

thought, without resistance, her mouth fell to his—fell deep into a well of desire instantly out of her control.

*Blast it.*

She didn't know this man. Didn't know him at all, and he was kissing her?

Not only that, she was letting him.

The momentary loss of her senses sent a jolt of fear down her spine. She yanked her head backward, breaking the kiss, though she refused to let her feet retreat.

She had him cornered and she meant to keep him so.

He pulled up, his hand falling from the back of her neck as his eyes searched her face. A lascivious smile danced about his lips. "Why so nervous, dove?"

The murmur of far-off voices floated through the night air of the expansive gardens and over the evergreen hedge.

She glanced over her shoulder, her gloved hands settling across her belly and the golden embroidered silk of her gown. She would have to talk fast. "My name is Evalyn—Eva."

"Then my name is Lachlan."

Her head swiveled back to him and she met his eyes, now hooded deep in the shadows of the alcove. Shadows that masked whether the anger that had been palpitating from him just moments ago was truly gone. "You're also soused, Lord Dunhaven."

"Lachlan, sweet lass. I want to hear the name from your exquisite lips." His fingers lifted and his thumb settled onto the center of her lips, then dragged slowly across the delicate skin still pulsating from his kiss.

Her shoulders pulled back, her spine stiffening. "Lachlan then my lord. And it does not negate the fact that you're foxed."

"My lips and hands still work the same, dove."

She snatched his wrist, tugging his hand from her face. "No. I did not approach you for this, Lord Dunhaven."

"Lachlan."

She stifled a seething breath. "I did not approach you for this, *Lachlan*."

"No?"

"No. I understand you and your companions intend to leave the duke's estate tonight?"

"Aye. We are done with Wolfbridge." His head tilted to the side. "You said your name was Eva?"

"Yes. You are leaving posthaste?"

"In a number of hours. Aye."

"Take me with you."

He laughed, a low rumble that vibrated through his body and shook the gravel under her toes. "Take you with us?"

"Yes," she said the word with simple, unshakable determination.

"Forgive me, Eva, but do I forget making introductions with you?"

"No."

"You are serious?" The smile slipped from his lips and he straightened, sobering, all amusement at her request vanishing. "It won't happen, lass. Not how we travel."

"Why not?"

"One, I don't kidnap spry young chits from their marriage-mart-minded mamas. Two, I don't know you.

Three, I have a band of eight men with me." He leaned down, setting his lips next to her ear, his breath tickling her skin. "Eight healthy, virile, single men."

He stood straight, his mouth pulling tight into a smug frown.

Smugness that didn't give her even a moment of pause.

She wasn't afraid of eight virile men. She couldn't afford to be. Not with what awaited her in the Duke of Wolfbridge's ballroom not but a hundred steps away.

"You won't be kidnapping anyone, Lord Dunhaven. I swear it. I will be joining your traveling party of my own free will."

"You don't even know our destination."

"I heard you say you were ready for the journey home. Your home is in Scotland, correct?"

His dark eyebrows drew together, sending the shadow deeper onto his face. "Stirlingshire. You were eavesdropping in the billiards room? What else did you hear?"

"Nothing. I was standing in the ballroom near the entrance to the room and I heard you speaking with your companions inside. I only overheard that you would be leaving this very night and to a place far, far from here." She braved her hand upward, her fingers grasping onto his arm. "And Scotland is a place I can disappear into. A place I *need* to disappear into."

His stare skewered her for a long moment before his gaze moved to her fingers gripping his forearm.

Too forward—far too forward, she knew. As an earl, she couldn't imagine he would be accustomed to strange ladies grabbing him. Then again, the man had had no problem grabbing her neck and kissing her—a complete stranger—only a moment before.

He shook his arm, flinging her fingers from the sleeve of his dark tailcoat. His look lifted to her face. "What are you running from, lass?"

"My reasons should be of no bother to you."

"You think an incensed suitor of yours chasing me through the English countryside with a bullet meant for my chest not a bother?"

Her hand flitted in the air. "That is dramatic. There will be no such threats upon your person."

"Then you won't mind telling me what you're hoping to escape." His arms drew up, crossing over his wide chest.

"Please, my lord, I will do anything. I need to leave and you are my only chance for a true escape."

His left eyebrow shot upward, the devil pulling his lips back in a terse line that curled up at the corners of his mouth. "Anything, dove?"

Her breath caught in her throat. The man was dangerous. How had she not seen that?

More dangerous than just his brawn, his thick arms that could pop her neck in an instant and not think twice on it. Dangerous in how the wicked gleam palpitated in his eyes—hazel eyes, if she could trust the flicker of moonlight catching his irises.

She wasn't trading one malicious monster for another, was she?

What had she heard Lord Dalton call him—whisper to his companion as Lord Dunhaven had passed by them? *The Iron Earl.*

That was it. And that was dangerous.

The man was an iron wall, hard from the tips of his toes to the unyielding glint in his eye.

She started to take a step backward and the lecherous sneer of Mr. Molson's lips flashed in her mind. The way his fingers had ground into her sides when he'd caught her alone in the south corridor. His whispered words of blades and blood and sinking into her, splitting her in two.

A shudder, and her heel dropped to the ground, digging in.

No. She couldn't let Mr. Molson happen. She couldn't let the nightmare of that man and his twisted world capture her.

For a long breath, she stared at the glowing white of Lachlan's loose cravat. She'd seen this man with his sister, the new Duchess of Wolfbridge. She'd seen the care and adoration he had for her well-being. He was a boulder of unmovable granite with everyone, everyone except his sister. Evalyn had witnessed that in the last day and a half since he'd arrived at the duke's castle.

This man—Lachlan—he had it in him. Kindness. She'd seen it. No matter what he was to everyone else at Wolfbridge, with his sister he was loving.

Plus, he was an earl. A Scottish earl, but still, he had to adhere to some sense of propriety—including knowing how to leave his hands off her person. How to keep his men's hands off her person.

Her feet solidly in place, she tilted her chin upward. "Anything your household requires, I can do it, my lord. I can join the kitchens, I can sweep, mop. I can sew. I can contribute, my lord, I swear it."

He stifled a guffaw. "Now why would a fine lass of the ton be willing to trade in silks and madeira for a scullery maid's life?" He grabbed her wrist, stripping off the glove from her right hand. He flipped it palm upward and examined her skin in the moonlight. He snorted. "Soft. This hand has never once felt a scrub brush in it."

She yanked her hand away. "Looks can be deceiving, my lord."

"Can they?" His eyebrow had not fallen from its high perch.

"The fortitude of my will is able to see me through anything, my lord. I can and I will do whatever is necessary. No matter how dirty. No matter how low. I swear upon it. I need this. I need to leave with you tonight."

"Yet your will cannot see you through whatever it is you are trying to escape?"

The murmur of the voices grew louder, footsteps crunching on the gravel pathway coming their way.

Time was running out.

She exhaled through gritted teeth. "My will is smart enough to know what I can and cannot survive. And I cannot survive what is ahead for me if I stay."

His folded arms lifted slightly. "Why would you choose ruin, as that is surely what you are hoping for by asking to leave with us?"

"If ruin alone would help me, I would have done that the first night of this affair with a random gentleman. Ruin will not help me escape what is ahead."

He stared at her blankly, his eyes still edged with skepticism.

He wasn't taking her seriously—nothing of what she'd said had filtered through his brandy-soaked brain with any sense of urgency.

The footsteps drew closer.

Only a few precious seconds left.

Desperation sent her hand flinging out and she drew the dirk from the belt about his waist. Her hands in a flurry, she shoved the blade of the dagger between her breasts and yanked it downward, slicing open the gold embroidered bodice of her gown.

Her mother's gown, the only thing she had left of her.

For how the sound of the fabric ripping sliced Evalyn to her soul, it was a sacrifice she had to make. She needed to leave. Tonight.

Her breasts half spilling forth, her nipples only barely concealed by the tattered gold and white fabric, she held up his dirk between them. "Don't make me trap you, Lord Dunhaven. Give me your word I can come with you tonight, or I throw this dagger out into the pathway. I scream. They find us together like this and you are going to be bound to me in ways you would never want to be."

That threat made it through his brandy-addled mind.

The fury on his face was instant and his lips pulled back as a low growl shook his chest. Shook the air around him. "Brutal little harpy."

Without breaking eye contact, she threw the dirk behind her. It hit the ground, skidding into the granite gravel.

His next breath seethed from his mouth, his eyes skewering her.

But his ire didn't bother her. It couldn't. Not with what awaited her.

Her words slowed, softened to the slightest shaking whisper. "My stepfather is Baron Falsted and he will demand satisfaction." She grabbed his forearm, the cords of muscle under his coat sleeve steel against the grip of her fingertips. "But I don't ask that of you. I only ask that you swear you will take me north. Far away from here where I can disappear. Please. I am begging you…begging you, my lord. Please."

His cheek twitched and his slow burr deepened into a rage that sent her legs trembling. "Baron Falsted?"

Her head bobbled in a frantic nod.

He sucked in a breath through gritted teeth and his arms fell to his sides. "Aye, then it seems I'm saddled with extra baggage on the journey home." He glanced up at the night sky. "We leave in two hours, lass."

"In the darkness—in the middle of the night?" Her look flew up to the stars above. "But—"

"Two hours and we meet at the stables. If you are there, you can come. If not, we leave without you."

He stepped around her quickly, disappearing out past the evergreen hedges that lined the entrance to the alcove.

She heard the scrape of the dirk across the gravel as he picked it up.

His footsteps retreated and a low, murmured acknowledgement floated over the tall hedge to her as he passed the people that had been walking on the pathway.

Her hand clasping the front flaps of her ripped dress to cover her breasts, she exhaled, sinking down onto the wrought iron bench nestled along the wall of evergreens beside her. Deep in the shadows she waited for the people passing to vacate the area. Her eyes lifted and trained on the stars above her. They twinkled especially bright tonight, the full moon lending shards of hazy light to make them bigger than usual.

Stars she had stared at her whole life, wishing upon.

Stars that had finally delivered.

A way out.

Finally, a way out.

# { CHAPTER 2 }

"I thought we'd be traveling by coach." Trying not to choke on the dust kicked up from the horses and wagon in front of her, Evalyn looked to the mostly toothless elderly man next to her.

Rupe had hopped off the back of the wagon to walk as they ascended the last hill and had introduced himself. More curious than kind, she was nonetheless relieved that someone had finally uttered a word to her.

"Coach?" He chuckled, his lips drawing up along his gums. "Nae, lass. The journey down to these forsaken lands was riddled with stringy and rotten meat at the coachin' inns, and the earl's not looking to be repeatin' that. We have wares to pick up along the way, so we be travelin' like the almighty intended us to. On our feet and far from the inns this time."

Evalyn gasped and dust flew into her throat, gagging her until she coughed it clear. Her hand to her mouth, she stared at Rupe. "Our feet? But that will take…" Her voice trailed, her look swinging to the rear wheels of the wagon in front of her, already piled high with supplies. She had no idea how long it would take to walk to Lachlan's lands.

"Two weeks if the luck be on our side." Rupe jabbed the long walking stick he held into the dirt of the road. "Lach's got plenty o' peers with land along the way and business with them all. Though the master likes to sleep outside like the rest of us."

Evalyn had to swallow back the dry dust in her throat. "We…we sleep outside?"

"Course, lass."

She nodded, trying to keep her chin up when the whole of her felt like sinking down along the side of the rutted road. She'd been awake since yesterday morning and the brisk pace they were traveling at didn't look to slow anytime soon. Of course, aside from Rupe and the man leading the reins of the draft horse pulling the wagon, Lachlan and his men were all on horses—fine, healthy, well-bred horses that had energy to spare. She would have no hope for sleep for hours.

It had seemed like such a good plan last night. The perfect plan. A plan that would permanently get her away from the terror of her life.

A plan with a thousand gaping holes in it, now that she looked at it under the grey light of the day.

She'd thought there would be other women in the party moving north. Someone, at the very least, to connect with. She hadn't imagined she'd be in the back of a pack of men, on foot, eating dust for hours on end.

But at least she was walking away. Every step was another step further from her stepfather and Mr. Molson.

She lifted her chin a notch higher, searching the wide, swaying backs of the eight Scotsmen in front of the wagon.

Heaven help her, all of them were huge, the breadth of their shoulders two-wide filling the roadway. She had noted the wide shoulders of Lachlan when he'd first been announced in the great hall at Wolfbridge castle two days past. But she hadn't expected all of the men around him to contain his same sense of presence. It was hard to ignore any of them, to pretend they weren't in her space as she was accustomed to doing with all men she encountered.

The only one that even came near to her stature was Rupe, and he was still a half head taller than her, though he had a wiry frame.

Lachlan had said he traveled with eight healthy, virile men, and he hadn't been deluding her.

A shot of fear skittered down her spine.

She shook her head. Lachlan had promised her safe passage away from Lincolnshire.

Safe. She was safe.

She searched her mind, racing to remember his exact words on the matter of her safety.

Nothing.

Her head tilted down as her mind flew into a frenzy.

Had she forgotten to extract that very important promise from him?

~ ~ ~

Lachlan gave himself leave to look back over his shoulder. A clear sign to his men where his considerations were set, he'd focused his attentions forward for the better part of the day, paying no mind to who trailed them.

It had been long enough now that he could afford a backward glance.

His look traveled back past the staggered men on horses at his height, to the long wagon pulled by a draft horse, to Rupe sitting on the back of the wagon.

He paused for a moment before he let his gaze fall upon the last person in the party. The peculiar enigma tacked onto their journey north.

A cloud of dust flitted to the air in front of Evalyn and she waved it away, coughing.

*Hell*, he'd made a grievous mistake last night. What had he been thinking?

His head turned forward for a few strides of his horse, and then he looked backward once more, his look intent on her.

She'd managed to keep her feet moving the entire day, not straying behind—he gave her that. Especially when even he was tired, and he'd been on a horse all day.

Her auburn hair remained swept up into the style she wore last night. The only difference about her appearance was the hastily sewn bosom of her dress that she had sliced through with his blade. When he'd left her in the garden, her breasts had been spilling forth, milky white globes in the moonlight that begged to be caressed.

The nymph wavered back and forth in her steps from directly behind the rear left wheel of the wagon to the center, seemingly trying to find the least offensive air.

He'd noticed her in the Duke of Wolfbridge's ballroom while she stood near Lord Dalton, and not because of her insatiable need for attention like every other chit in the room. He'd noticed her for how she shrank into the wall, desperate for no attention to come her way.

Lachlan had thought she had flattened herself into the wall because of her odd dress—the last thing he did was monitor the fashionable frocks of society—but even his eye could discern that the gold and white concoction she wore was twenty years past its prime.

Yet her beauty was unmistakable—gold-green eyes that glowed canny behind her dark lashes. Auburn hair that swept in a long sweep across her brow, the locks shiny and smooth, and pinned back into a simple chignon. Fine cheekbones and a delicate nose showcased flawless skin that was only interrupted by a dusting of freckles across her nose.

The woman would have been the envy of every chit in the room if she'd had a proper dress on and managed to utter a word or even a smile.

Beauty that he'd now have to manage every step along the way. It'd be easier if she were uncomely, drab. Even average would have been preferable. But including Rupe, he had nine men with him. Nine men with eyes and cocks.

At least he'd predispositioned everyone in the party against her. That'd been easy enough. All he had to do was tell them she was the daughter of Baron Falsted. That was enough to keep their eyes locked forward as well.

Lachlan shook his head to himself. The daft lass hadn't even had the sense to change out of her dress. Or her damn slippers. She wouldn't last another day without the soles wearing through.

And her bare arms covered only by a thin shawl would be freezing once darkness descended. In Lincolnshire they'd had unusually warm September days that had spilled into October, but they were traveling north and the heat wouldn't hold—especially into nights.

Dammit. This was a bloody mistake.

Even if her stepfather was Baron Falsted. Even if stealing away the man's stepdaughter was sweet revenge upon the blasted blackguard. This was a mistake. And he'd been too soused hours ago to realize it.

She looked back over her shoulder. Too long. As though she was searching the empty road behind them.

What in the hell was she running from?

Some ill-mannered suitor, determined to make a match of her? A loveless groom? Silly wench. If she was out to teach a lesson to whoever drove her out into the gardens last night, she was the one about to learn a brutal reality about the way the world worked. Protected young chits of the *ton* dare not wander too far from the castles they tread in and expect to survive unscathed.

But for the fact that her stepfather was Baron Falsted, he'd have sent her back to Wolfbridge hours ago when day broke.

But now…now he'd resigned himself to keep her.

Not that anyone would be coming for her. Even if someone managed to attach her disappearance to their departure, no one other than his men knew which little-used roads they were traveling north upon.

Lachlan shifted in his saddle, facing forward.

He'd keep her until they reached Stirlingshire. She was beautiful, and if it suited her, he'd entertain the idea of making her his mistress at Vinehill. Or she could work in his kitchens. Whatever suited her sensibilities. Either way, stealing away Baron Falsted's only kin had turned the entire disastrous trip to Lincolnshire into sweet revenge.

Justice.

Justice had appeared in the most peculiar of places.

In the most peculiar of women.

# { CHAPTER 3 }

Her shoulders dragging, Evalyn picked her way over the long legs stretched out toward the fire, balancing three wooden bowls in her hands.

Rupe had sent her scurrying the moment they broke for camp for the evening—gathering twigs for the fire, running to the brook for bucket after bucket of water, and then cutting the potatoes.

She'd never cut potatoes before—any food for that matter—and potatoes were slippery and hard to send a blade through. The knife had slipped and sliced into her forefinger three times, slashes of blood stinging her skin.

It didn't help that she'd been blurry-eyed and half asleep since the moment they stopped. Not hungry, not even feeling the chill of the air on her bare arms as the sky darkened to night, the thought of crawling under the wagon and sleeping was all that consumed her mind. But Rupe kept barking orders at her, jarring her back awake.

Her head down, she'd stiffened her resolve and did everything bade of her. She'd sworn to Lachlan she would do anything to escape. So she had damn well not break her promise on the first day of the journey.

The stew Rupe had concocted finally complete, he'd sent her running with full, steaming bowls to the men gathered around the roaring fire.

She'd already delivered three bowls and the second set of three bowls were balanced in her arms as she stepped past the men—men that decidedly ignored her except for the food she set into their hands.

If anything, there were glares of death and destruction in her general direction.

She didn't talk to them. They didn't talk to her. She was perfectly fine with that arrangement.

What had Lachlan told them about her presence in the traveling party? When they had left from the stables in the dead of night, not one of the men past Lachlan and Rupe had acknowledged her presence. And the most Lachlan had given her was a curt order from high on his horse to move to the back of the wagon at the end of the trail of men.

Rupe had been the only one in the group to acknowledge her presence with actual words since they left Wolfbridge.

The second set of bowls delivered, she hurried back to the cooking fire where Rupe was fishing through the pot of stew with a ladle.

"Rupe, why did so many men from Lachlan's lands travel with him to Wolfbridge for the wedding? It is slow to travel with so many. I would think only Lachlan would have made the journey to attend the event."

"They didn't travel to Wolfbridge to attend the wedding, lass." He filled a bowl and handed it to her. "They went bearing swords and pistols to stop the wedding."

"To stop it? Whatever for? It is a splendid match for Lachlan's sister. And the Duke of Wolfbridge is well respected."

Rupe snorted. "English bastard." He turned his head and spit on the ground. "Ye don't know much about his grace, then."

Her head snapped back. "Oh, I did not know. Is the duchess in danger?"

"We left Sloane there, per the master's orders, so she must be fine enough."

Evalyn nodded and glanced over her shoulder at the crew of men surrounding the large fire. The size of them made much more sense. These men were not made for diplomacy. They were made for fighting. She'd begun to think all Scotsmen were built like Lachlan.

Lachlan was absent from the ring of warmth around the blazes. She'd seen him leave on his horse once they settled into the clearing along a grove of trees near the stream. A full day on the roads and he didn't look the slightest bit weary. His hand running through his devilishly rumpled brown hair, he'd ridden off high on his horse, his back straight, his irked eyes fixed solely ahead. She heard him say something about visiting the local landowner and then he disappeared out of the camp.

Rupe shoved the last bowl into her free hand. "Deliver these two and ye can eat and rest, lass."

She turned back toward the men, her steps heavy as she moved toward them to find the two with empty hands she'd missed. Her mind muddled thick with exhaustion, she couldn't even keep track of the murmured conversations of the men around her as she searched for homes for the bowls in her hands. The low burrs of their voices only lulled her more into weariness. Just as her eyes slipped shut against her will, her toe nudged a lump and her look slipped downward, finding a black boot blending into the ground. Her eyes snapped open.

Two more bowls to deliver and Rupe would let her sleep. Two more.

The boot at her toe didn't move and she stepped carefully over it while trying to swing her skirts away from the blazes of the fire. It wouldn't do to have her only dress—her mother's dress—set aflame.

"Hurry, lass, I'm ripe hungry here." A Scotsman at the far end of the fire grumbled her way.

Her head snapped up at the sharp words and she jumped, moving forward quickly. She knew what would happen if she didn't move fast enough—she'd lived a life of not moving fast enough and being punished for it.

The next black boot in the shadows of the fire she didn't see. Her toe caught on the edge of a heel and she flew forward, sprawling, a gasp escaping her lips.

Two bowls of soup flew through the air, spinning, tumbling, crashing into the Scotsman nearest to her.

Two hot, steaming bowls of soup.

She landed with a hard thud on her side, the impact taking the wind from her lungs.

"Bloody hell, ye stupid little wench." The Scotsman shot to his feet, sloughing off the scorching liquid from the front of his shirt and wool waistcoat. "It's fucking burnin' me, ye wee bitch."

Evalyn scrambled to grab the upside-down bowl closest to her, then clambered to her feet. "I'm so sorry, sir. So very sorry." Her fingers lifted out to try and help brush the scalding stew from his chest.

Mortified, her head bowed, she didn't see the slap coming. Didn't brace herself.

The back of his hand hit her. Hard. The force of it wicked across her cheek, it sent her sprawling onto the ground—sent her body into a panic that seized her nerves, her blood pumping fast.

She curled up into herself, her limbs dragging through the dirt. Her head hidden under her arms. Small. She had to get small.

If she was small, there was less to hit. Less to kick.

Her body rigid, holding tight against the oncoming pain, she held her breath.

But no additional blows came.

No hits. No kicks.

Just silence.

Silence around her. Silence echoing, pounding in her skull.

Silence was what she waited for. Silence meant she could escape. If there was no raging voice, there was no fist on the way to her head.

She moved her upper arm covering her eyes and saw the man that had smacked her walking away from the clearing in the direction of the brook.

Terror still fully gripping her body, Evalyn struggled to her feet, her slippers loose on the dirt, haphazardly catching ground as she ran past the men still sitting, watching the incident with indifferent looks on their faces.

Escape. She had to escape.

Her body moved on instinct, begging for it.

Escape.

Her eyes frantic, she spun, searching.

The woods. The woods opposite of the stream. Opposite of the man that had just hit her.

Escape. She needed to escape.

~~~

He'd wanted to make it farther.

Farther from Wolfbridge. Farther from the possibility of Lord Falsted sneaking up upon them in the middle of the night and capturing back what he just took.

He'd had to acknowledge the possibility, however slight. The ongoing festivities at Wolfbridge were his salvation. With the hunting parties during the days, the majority of the men would be separated from the females during the daylight hours. With any luck, the blackguard was just realizing now that his stepdaughter was missing. Maybe he wouldn't realize it for another day or two. Evalyn's disappearance wouldn't be tied to him.

Not until he wanted it to be.

Yet he still would have been happier to be another twenty miles up the roads.

He didn't have another twenty miles in him. Neither did his men. Exhausted, he wanted nothing more than Rupe's stew and his eyes closed.

Leaving Wolfbridge in the middle of the night hadn't been the best plan, not that he would have slept another wink the previous night in the duke's castle. So it was just as well that he was traveling away as fast as he could from those blasted lands. At least they could pick up goods on the journey home, so the trip wasn't a total loss.

Lachlan tied his horse off next to the stream and walked through the swathe of trees toward the camp. Baron Rogerton hadn't been in residence, so he'd alerted the steward of their presence on the lands, arranged to have a barrel of spirits delivered to the wagon in the morning, and then had hurried back to his men.

The second his feet crunched onto the fallen leaves at the edge of camp, he knew something was amiss. The way his men suddenly sat straighter, their eyes flickering to him and veering off.

He looked around at the faces around the low fire just starting to die off. He'd thought they'd all be asleep by now, for they were as exhausted as he.

His head swiveled. Rupe was busy poking into his black pot over the cooking fire, his head down.

He stepped into the circle of his men. "Where's the lass?"

Silence.

Every man in the group stilled at the one question, their eyes either sheepish as they glanced at Lachlan or looking off into nothingness.

Lachlan's look morphed into a glare, pinning them, until he saw Rory break and glance at Colin.

Lachlan moved to his left, stopping in front of Colin's outstretched legs. He waited until Colin ceased averting his gaze and looked up at him. Lachlan leaned forward, his voice turned to iron. "What happened, Colin?"

For a moment, mumbled rationalization came to his lips, but then Colin shook his head, the words spitting from his mouth. "I hit her."

"You what?" Lachlan seethed. The blasted man never could control himself. Not since they were five—Colin had never learned how to curb his anger.

Colin scrambled to his feet. "She scalded me with the hot stew. Dropped it all over me."

Lachlan's look dropped. Stains of Rupe's stew streaked down the front of Colin's white shirt. His hands balled into fists at his sides. "Tell me she did it on purpose."

Colin exhaled, his look flashing up to the night sky. "Not exactly, she tri—"

Lachlan's fist into Colin's jaw stole the word from his mouth and sent him reeling backward.

Lachlan glared at Colin bending over, his hand rubbing his jaw. Colin had the good sense not to look up at him.

His voice lethal, his stare didn't leave Colin. "Where is she now, Rory?"

"Don't know, Lach. She took off into the woods."

"And no one followed her?"

Silence.

He tore his glare off of Colin and he looked around at the faces of his men. "Which direction? How long?"

"Half the hour," Rory said. His head swiveled and his eyes landed on the trees across from Lachlan. He inclined his head toward the forest. "Into the woods there."

"So Colin strikes her and you all sat around here this entire time and ate and drank and not one of you thought to check on her?" The words fumed through his teeth as he sent a sweeping glare across the lot of them.

"Yes, that be the way of it," Rory said, his always unhurried voice not speeding in the slightest. "We figured she would come back soon enough. There isn't anywhere for her to go. Not for miles."

"Blasted imbeciles." His head shaking, Lachlan stomped away from the fire, going to the brook to retrieve his horse.

# { CHAPTER 4 }

This was a mistake.

No, not just a mistake—a sweeping error of judgement sure to sink her into the blazes of hell.

"Well, now, Kitty, what be it that ye be running from again?" Mr. Fitzgibbon shifted on the wagon's bench seat, the bones of his hip jutting into her side.

Evalyn bowed her head, refusing to utter a word as she watched the grey rump of the mule pulling the wagon in front of her.

"Well, never ye mind. A fine lady like ye needs to be taken care of. All will be well once we reach our house. A nice warm fire will open yer mouth." Mr. Fitzgibbon patted her knee through her skirts, his hand landing on her leg and not moving off.

Evalyn jerked her knee away, not that it did much good. His fingers had clamped onto her leg and weren't budging.

She knew it the minute she let this tall skinny man— Mr. Fitzgibbon—grab her wrist and haul her up onto the bench at the front of the wagon. The bones in his fingers, the way they slithered around her wrist—it was as though the cold clasp of death had cracked through the frigid ground and come for her.

She should have jumped and run then.

But she'd been too consumed with terror from the camp—consumed with the fear in her bones that demanded she find a way to escape. And they had appeared out of the darkness—Mr. Fitzgibbon and his cousin—and offered her help. Why had she not been immediately suspicious?

So there she found herself, running from Lachlan's camp and the behemoth that smacked her with all the thought of swatting a pesky fly, only to land herself sitting captive between two strangers. Both Mr. Fitzgibbon and his cousin were tall and thin with pasty skin stretched tight over their cheekbones that glowed in the moonlight. Lewd grins danced about their lips as they ogled the haphazard stitching on the bodice of her dress where she had sliced the fabric open the night before.

Heaven only knew what Mr. Fitzgibbon and his cousin thought to do with her.

The giants that Lachlan traveled with were beginning to look much more attractive, even if they intimidated her at every turn. Even if one of them had struck her.

She closed her eyes, trying to not let the swaying of the wagon bump her into Mr. Fitzgibbon every other second.

She had to be smart about this, this plan for her escape. She still wasn't far enough from Wolfbridge—far enough away to get lost and never be found.

And she'd probably just foolishly run away from the one man that could get her that far away. No matter the knuckles on her cheek, she'd survived worse. She could again. Again and again and again until she was free.

Whatever it took.

But she had to rein in her instincts. She couldn't react with fear as she had done at the fire. Fear fed malevolence. Fear excited. Fear made weak men feel like gods. She knew that. Knew that too well.

And she had sworn to never feel fear again. Not once she escaped.

Not that the vow did her any good by the fire.

Instinct had won out. Fear had won out.

Her hands clasped together in her lap, she tried to move her arms inward as much as possible to avoid rubbing shoulders with the lanky men on either side of her. Every modicum of space she achieved was quickly stolen away, the both of them squeezing closer and closer to her on the bench.

She stared at her entwined hands in the moonlight, in disbelief that her escape from her stepfather had fallen apart so quickly. She hadn't thought it through—none of it—but what choice did she have?

The fear that the behemoth, Colin, had struck into her was nothing compared to the blood freezing in her veins in imagining what Mr. Fitzgibbon had planned for her.

How could she have been so stupid—why had she run?

Her head bowed further, her chin touching her chest as she tried not to smell the rank odor of the men flanking her.

She needed to request to be let off. The sooner the better.

Or jump. Her look veered to the dark shadows along the passing trees. She could always jump and hope for the best. The mule kept up a quick trot, so she would most likely roll, but hopefully not injure herself. But she first had to make it over Mr. Fitzgibbon's lap.

The thundering of horse hooves striking the ground behind the wagon reached her ears.

A full breath of air finally reached her lungs—thank the heavens, a passerby she could beg assistance from.

Evalyn spun to look behind her.

The figure approached from deep in the shadows of the forest and it took a moment to see it was a lone rider on a horse. It took several more seconds before the rider was close enough that a shaft of moonlight hit his body.

Lachlan.

*Hell.*

Evalyn whipped forward, her shoulders hunching, trying to make herself invisible. She wasn't sure if she should be distraught or elated.

Her choices were very few at this point.

Moving onward with Lachlan's giants that would beat her.

Or stay with Mr. Fitzgibbon and his cousin who would probably rape her—and much worse if she judged by the look of their leers.

What was she willing to do for her freedom?

The thundering hooves on the roadway went past the wagon and Lachlan moved his horse in front of the mule pulling the wagon, blocking their path.

"Good eve, gentlemen." Lachlan nodded to the two lanky men sidling Evalyn.

Mr. Fitzgibbon's cousin pulled back on the reins of the mule and his head inclined to Lachlan. "Good eve, sir, might I ask why ye be blocking our path?"

Her face angled downward, Evalyn watched Lachlan with upturned eyes. His gaze locked onto her. "It would seem, good sirs, as though you have kindly found and assisted with something I have lost." His voice was soft, almost congenial, his Scottish burr rolling over the words with placid nonchalance. Nothing as she had ever heard from him. Even with his men, his voice was direct with a constant edge to it. And with her, it had been nothing but stony, anger palpitating in every word he spoke to her.

To the left of her, Mr. Fitzgibbon lifted his thin left leg and propped it on the front of the wagon, leaning forward on his thigh. "Now what would that be, sir?"

"The lass."

"The lass?" Mr. Fitzgibbon drew out the word, his look turning to Evalyn. "Well, now, she didn't look the least bit lost when we happened upon her. She looked happy to see two such fine gentlemen such as ourselves happen to come by her and offer a cozy spot to sit."

Lachlan nodded, a cordial smile on his face. "Nonetheless, she was mine to lose and now she is mine to retrieve." His look pierced her. "Evalyn, you must have gotten lost from the camp in the woods, but I am so relieved these helpful gentlemen found you and offered assistance. I thank both of you." His gaze moved to Mr. Fitzgibbon, then his cousin. "But it is now time for us to take our leave of them."

"Well, no, sir, how do we know the pretty kitty be wanting to go with ye? She got into our wagon on her own accord, seeing as how we're two fine sirs offering her right helpful aid."

Lachlan's head cocked to the side. "Evalyn, I imagine you got lost in the woods?"

Her chin lifted slightly and she met Lachlan's eyes. The glint in them, the inherent command lacing his soft words was unmistakable. Listen to him now or this was going to get ugly. Brutally ugly.

She nodded. "I had lost my way, Lachlan, and these two were very kind to offer assistance." Her breath held, she looked at Mr. Fitzgibbon. "Thank you again for your assistance. I do appreciate it."

Mr. Fitzgibbon didn't move, his bent leg blocking her path off the side of the wagon. He stared down his long thin nose at her, his jaw shifting back and forth. Then he looked over her head at his cousin and nodded.

Out of the corner of her eye, she noted his cousin lifting his leg just the same as Mr. Fitzgibbon had, effectively locking her into the middle of the bench.

"Again, thank you for your time and generosity." She conjured the widest smile she could manage and took a deep breath, moving to her feet. She'd jump onto the back of the mule—or climb over Mr. Fitzgibbon's lap—if she had to.

Any way she could, she was getting off this wagon.

"Not so fast, kitty." The cousin's nasally voice sneered into the night and the tip of something sharp jabbed into her side just above her hip.

Her look whipped to him. Even though she stood and he sat, she was eye level with him. He sneered at her, the tip of the dagger clutched in his hand twisting harder into her side, close to breaking through the silk of her dress.

"Why ye be wanting to leave us so soon, kitty?" Mr. Fitzgibbon drew her attention to his side of the wagon. "Ye think yer man be willin' to fight fer ye?"

Panic sent her veins aflame. She should have known. She should have run into the woods the moment she saw this wagon crest the hill in the moonlight. Instead she had stood there like an idiot, waiting for the wagon to approach.

She looked to Lachlan.

He stared at the three of them in the wagon, his eyes slightly squinted, bored by the tiresome scene. His chest lifted in a heavy sigh and his look met hers.

She couldn't be any more beholden to him than she already was. And she couldn't have him hurt on her account. She would just have to conjure up another way to escape these two.

One that didn't involve Lachlan.

"He's not my man," she said, looking down at Mr. Fitzgibbon. "I am to be part of his household, that is all."

Mr. Fitzgibbon nodded and a bright smile strained the tight skin across his face. He looked to Lachlan. "Well then, that settles it. Ye won't be mindin' if we take her for a spell? We can bring her to yer camp come morn."

"I'm afraid we'll be long gone from the area by then." Lachlan's hand slapped onto the pommel of his saddle. "So unfortunately, no, that will not do."

"An hour then?" Mr. Fitzgibbon jabbed his thumb in the air over his shoulder behind him. "Yer camp must be back there? We can deliver her right quick."

Lachlan shook his head, a frown crossing his lips. "Regrettably, that will not do either. I will just be taking her now, if you please."

"That don't please us none, sir." The cousin jabbed the tip of the blade into her side with the words.

She twisted, trying to avoid the dagger from impaling her and she fell back against the jutting bones of Mr. Fitzgibbon. He'd moved closer, securing the trap. And the blade hadn't moved from her side.

In a flash of sparking fire, Lachlan kicked his horse into motion and aligned himself next to the front right side of the wagon, his broadsword drawn and the tip of it pressing into the cousin's neck. "Well, it would please me. And I am the one with a longer sword." His words still nonchalant, he could have been talking about buttering his toast.

The cousin grabbed Evalyn's forearm, twisting her closer into the blade.

Lachlan's sword jabbed inward, the tip indenting the skin on the cousin's neck. "You are positive you would like to try me, sir?"

A grimace crossed the cousin's face, breaking through the mottled red outrage splotching across his pale forehead.

Lachlan's sword jabbed further into the cousin's neck. "This is about a wench, nothing more, sir. Make sure you're willing to die for it."

A long, breathless moment passed. Not a muscle by any party moved.

The cousin's hand dropped, the tip of the dagger slipping from Evalyn's side. He released her arm.

"Get on my horse, Evalyn." Lachlan held the sword hard against the cousin's long neck.

Evalyn scrambled across the cousin's lap, under the long sword, and awkwardly threw her leg up and parted her skirts. She slipped onto the saddle in front of Lachlan.

Once she was seated, Lachlan pulled the reins, nudging his horse away from the wagon with his sword still held high. His eyes never left the cousin.

Ten long strides of his horse and Lachlan set the steed to a trot.

He didn't look back.

Evalyn attempted not to be mortified by her legs spread wide, her calves fully exposed, and her backside jarring into the rock hard torso of Lachlan with every jostle of the horse.

But even through her humiliation, relief swept into her bones.

For what she had been facing with Mr. Fitzgibbon and his cousin, she recognized full well she was in safer hands with Lachlan.

At least for the moment.

Ten minutes passed and Lachlan yanked up on the reins.

She looked around at the surrounding trees and the unearthly shadows from the moonlight making the forest glow. Not the slightest whiff of campfire in the air. They were nowhere near the camp yet.

"Get off the horse." Lachlan's words were low, simmering with rage.

"What?" She twisted in the saddle to face him.

A mistake, for the full blast of the fury seething on his face hit her. "Get off the blasted horse or I'm going to push you off."

His palpable rage stunned her, freezing her in place.

"Stay on, Evalyn, and I just may beat you myself."

That jarred her into action. She jolted, swinging her leg over the pommel of the saddle, and slid down the side of the horse. The impact of the hard ground on her cold heels jarred her bones up to her skull. She swayed for a long second, fighting for balance against the pain reverberating along her nerves.

"Now walk." Lachlan nicked his horse forward.

What she wanted to do was collapse to the ground. Shrivel into herself for the night. Become nothing, if only so she could rebuild her spine and spirit in the process.

Three steps away from her and he looked back at her from high on his horse. "Move."

His anger prodded her forward.

There wasn't time to rest. To muster up energy. To steel her spine. Not when this man was her key to escape.

She forced her legs—both of them lead weights—to move.

He waited until she was next to his horse, her feet moving forward, before his low voice blasted into the night air.

"I don't want you with us anymore than you want to be here, Evalyn, but that was the bargain we struck. And I abide by my word."

Her head whipped up to him. "Then I am freeing you from your word, Lachlan. Leave me be."

"I said I would give you safe journey and that is what I intend to do." His gaze stayed forward, locked on the road ahead. "Those men that picked you up were not safe. Tell me you are not so daft as to believe otherwise."

"They had done me no harm other than to offer me a ride."

"A ride to where?"

She shrugged. "A ride."

"And you thought it wise to just hop onto a random wagon with random men without any questions—why?"

"I…I…" Her cheeks started to burn. A modicum of distance from those ruffians and she realized how insane her actions had been. But it couldn't be helped. The terror that had seized her when Colin hit her demanded she escape. Escape by any means necessary.

She shook her head. "I did not leave Wolfbridge to trade one brutal existence for another."

"Brutal existence?" His head snapped back. "One day with us and it's a brutal existence? You realize you almost welcomed with open arms a true brutal existence with those blackguards back there? What the damned hell were you thinking, getting into a wagon with those highwaymen, Evalyn?"

She started, craning her neck to look up at him. "Highwaymen? No, they said they were farmers."

"Yes. I was just talking to the steward of Baron Rogerton's lands and he warned me on two men of that very description that have been a scourge on these roads for months."

Her head dropped, her look going to the rutted dirt of the road in front of her. "Oh."

"Oh? That is how you defend yourself against idiocy?"

"I didn't know they were highwaymen."

"Did you not recognize they were two lecherous ruffians that could overpower you in a mere second?" His low voice pitched louder, almost to a boom. "Did you not see that? Did you not see that it is the middle of the night and no respectable gentleman would be out in a wagon at this time looking to pick up a stray woman?"

"I…I…"

He yanked on his reins to halt his horse. "I what, Evalyn? What?" His head shaking, a low breath seethed out. "How you've managed to stay alive this long with that lunacy in your brain is a blessed miracle."

Her feet shuffled to a stop as her shoulders pulled back, her spine stiffening as her lips drew inward.

He glanced at her, looked forward, then his gaze fell back to her, his eyes piercing. "Now you are silent?"

Her fingers curled into fists, her nails digging into her palms, and she turned her head, determined not to let the tears brimming in her eyes fall.

He was right.

She should be dead. Should be dead a hundred times over. She'd been told it her whole life.

Yet there she stood, alive.

She turned fully to him, but she couldn't look up at him. Only his boot. His well-worn black boot tucked into the stirrup.

She found her voice, feigning her own ire. "I had to escape—I could not help it. After I dropped the soup on him, Colin struck me and I—I panicked. I ran." Her chest started to shake, the air vibrating in her lungs as she tried not to get swallowed again by the rash of terror she'd felt by the fire. "I ran and then I was on the road and they passed by. Mr. Fitzgibbon offered to bring me to the nearest village, so I went with them. I knew full well the danger, but I...I could think of nothing but escape..." Her voice petered, dwindling to a whisper. So much for her false chagrin.

A frustrated growl shook from Lachlan's chest.

Her head bowed and she turned from his leg.

For whatever she'd thought she'd gain by escaping her stepfather's tyrannical eye, she realized in that moment she had nothing.

She was still just as powerless as she'd always been.

But now powerless in an entirely new way she had no inclination as to how to navigate.

Nothing to do but walk.

She picked up her heavy legs, starting forth on the road again.

Lachlan sighed and slid off his steed, his feet thudding onto the ground and shaking the dirt beneath her toes.

Before she took two steps, he grabbed her arm, stopping her and turning her toward him. He stood in silence, his fingers digging into the muscles of her upper arm. Silence until she lifted her chin, braving her gaze upward.

She looked up at him, the moon high in the sky above his head casting a glow about his wild brown hair, a rich deep color, like fresh bark pulled away from a tree—alive, deep. He looked like a fierce Viking she'd once seen an imprint of in a tome she'd snuck from her stepfather's library.

A warrior, meant to intimidate.

His mouth opened. "Once we reach my lands, lass, you are free to leave, free to find a different path in life. I'll not hold you to my household. But until then—until you are in safe lands where you can, as you say, disappear—I stand by my vow. I will get you there without harm."

His eyes caught the light of the moon, reflecting sparks of blue as his words lost all anger, his voice oddly soft. "You need to know I have already set the way of things with Colin. With all the men. No one in my camp will ever hit you again, Evalyn. No one."

The words stole the breath from her lungs.

He wasn't a fierce Viking. Not at all.

An angel warrior, meant to protect.

She nodded.

She believed him.

# { CHAPTER 5 }

Evalyn stared at the dead rabbit in her hand, its belly cut half open.

She swallowed down the gag in her throat, her tongue curdling.

Rupe had knocked the berries she'd collected from her hands when she'd arrived back in camp, grinding them under his heel. He'd shoved the rabbit into her left hand, his gutting blade into her right just before he'd grabbed the torch angled out from the wagon and stomped off, grumbling about how it would be impossible to find the right berries now that dusk had settled.

*Trying to poison the whole camp.*

He'd spit the accusation out at her and the look he'd given her would've melted steel.

She'd failed him again. He'd sent her out to collect the red berries that they'd passed a half mile back, and she'd come back with reddish-pink berries. Poisonous reddish-pink berries.

Rupe was her only ally in the camp, for she eased his job by little bits here and there, but she would quickly lose the only person that talked to her if she kept erring like this.

She'd bungled it three days ago when Rupe had taught her how to gut and skin rabbits, her vomit just missing the full cauldron of stew.

The day before that she'd botched it with all the men when they had to take turns staying up on watch instead of sleeping because of the highwaymen she had entangled Lachlan with.

She was no longer Evalyn. No longer the extra baggage that hitched herself to the rear wagon. *Wretched wench.* That was how she was now known.

Lachlan had ensured they couldn't hit her, but everyone addressed her as a wretched wench every chance they got.

Everyone except Rupe and Lachlan. Lachlan never addressed her. Never looked at her. And Rupe just liked her name, rolling his tongue along the V every time he said it.

Rupe was likely to join the lot of them dubbing her a wretched wench after her latest misstep.

Trying to poison everyone in the camp endeared her to no one.

Evalyn stared down at the drops of rabbit blood oozing over her hand. Bile chased up her throat. The scarlet drips fell, almost landing on her skirt and she jumped back.

Dirt, she had chance of removing from her mother's dress. Streaks of blood, not as much.

She looked at the men in the camp, standing and sitting about the main fire, cups of Scotch whisky to their faces, the low rumbles of their laughter and conversation filling the night air. Lachlan and two of the men were absent, gone to speak with the local landowner. Everywhere they stopped, bundles were either added or subtracted from the wagon per Lachlan's orders. Rupe had said Lachlan did a fair bit of trading everywhere he traveled.

The men still in the camp all looked at ease, the wide fire lending light to the cloudy night and bathing their hulking forms in the warm orange glow of the flames.

She gagged down the bile that stained her tongue and moved toward the back of the wagon where Rupe prepared the food. She had to gut this rabbit. If she didn't, he would banish her as his help, and then where would she be?

At least Rupe offered her an existence. A reason for being in the camp.

She set the knife down on the wooden planks folded flat from the rear of the wagon and began to stretch the rabbit out when a scream reached her ears from behind.

A scream of terror.

Her head whipped up, searching the faces of the men by the fire. None paused in conversation, none looked as though the scream had reached their ears.

"Did anyone hear that?"

The closest man to her, Colin, looked up from the fire. "Get to that rabbit wretched wench."

Scattered chuckles floated through the air.

Her head dipped and she looked down at the rabbit clutched in her fist, trying to set her hands in motion while disengaging her brain from what she had to do.

A muffled fresh scream echoed through the trees behind her, then abruptly cut off.

Her head snapped up.

Rupe. *Hell.*

Not the one person in this blasted camp that had made the journey bearable.

She glanced at the men. Not a one paused at the sound.

Her feet started running before her mind caught up and she dashed into the woods, aiming as straight as she could to where she thought the scream had come from.

At least she was fast now—Lachlan had procured boots for her from Baron Rogerton's household when they had set up camp the first night.

The pair of brown boots had been sitting under the wagon when they had arrived back in camp. Well worn, the leather on them soft and supple, they were slightly tight but entirely comfortable as opposed to her mother's silk slippers she'd been hobbling along in.

Lachlan had deposited her that first night at the wagon, walking away without a word, his anger still simmering. Rupe had been the one to point out the boots to her. And Lachlan hadn't so much as glanced in her direction in the last three days.

She had a hard time faulting him for it—she'd run away while he had been busy procuring her a pair of walking boots.

The screaming had ceased, leaving her with only the sound of leaves crunching under her feet. Evalyn's steps slowed. Her eyes searched the darkness and she realized how quickly it got dark in the forest away from the camp. Damn. She still had the rabbit clutched tight in her hand. She'd run without thinking and her hand had stayed clamped on the animal. Now she'd have to carry it until she got back to camp or risk Rupe's ire at tossing away a quarter of the stew.

A gargled scream cut into the air and she shifted her direction. She was close, close to the sound. Close to Rupe.

A light flickered through the brush. The torch burning along the ground fifty strides away.

She ran, weaving through trees.

Her feet skidded, sliding through dead leaves as she stopped just beside the torch on its side, sputtering to stay alive.

Her look went frantic, searching for Rupe.

She heard a growl a second before she spotted him. Propped back against a tree, blood cut across his cheek, his hands blocking in front of him.

Blocking what?

She searched the shadows, her eyes flying wide open before she squinted, disbelief taking a hold of her.

No. It couldn't be. Impossible. Not here.

Another growl, low, almost a furious purr.

A shadow moving in darkness, a black jaguar took a step forward, its yellow eyes reflecting the light of the torch with the eerie glow of a demon. The huge cat looked to her, taking one step toward her, then reversing course and moving toward Rupe.

A demon cat that had cornered its prey—Rupe—and was stalking in for the kill.

Evalyn surged forward, jumping in front of Rupe before the hunter could pounce.

A meow—tiny but loud—left her lips.

The cat stopped in mid-stride.

She meowed again. Louder, more plaintive—a kitten searching for its mother.

The sleek black head of the panther tilted.

Her heart thundering in her ears, Evalyn stepped forward, slowly lifting her hand, palm up. She meowed again.

The panther took a step backward, its thick paw crunching leaves as it bared its teeth and it seethed out a low growl—a warning.

Evalyn meowed, shuffling another step forward. Another meow, and she lifted the dead rabbit she still clutched in her right hand.

The black cat took a tentative step forward, its nostrils flaring as it sniffed the blood of the rabbit.

Evalyn meowed again, this time holding the sound as long as she could as she moved forward. Her open palm next to the jaguar, she extended her arm, her fingertips just brushing the slightest fur under the panther's chin.

The cat didn't move.

She meowed again and stretched the rabbit onto her palm.

For a second that lasted a hundred years, the cat stared at her with its yellow eyes.

Then it looked down, sniffing the blood of the rabbit.

With the gentlest of teeth, it bowed its head, taking the rabbit from her hand.

In a blink, it was gone. Silent as it disappeared into the blackness of the night.

Leaves crunched. Twigs snapped. Then nothing.

She exhaled, terror she hadn't felt a moment ago rolling into her limbs, sending her hands to shaking.

"Hell and damnation that demon beast near to had me, lass. The torch kept it away until it knocked me back and I fell with me bum leg and it was going for the kill just before ye appeared." Rupe's words flew fast, tumbling over one another. "Ye bloody well saved me life, lass. What was that demon cat?"

She couldn't turn back to Rupe. Couldn't breathe. She just needed a moment. A breath.

Rupe walked around her, his eyes wide as he looked to her face. "Are ye a witch, then, lass? That why ye can talk to the animals?"

She almost snorted a laugh and the back of her hand went in front of her mouth. Air sank into her lungs enough to breathe again. "No, nothing of the sort, Rupe."

She looked to him in the flickering light of the torch on the ground to her right. The jaguar's claws had made three deep gouges along his cheek. They would need to be tended.

"What of ye, then? If yer not a witch, what be ye? A druid gone to live with the English folk? A fairy?"

This time the snort of laughter did escape. "Again, nothing of the sort, Rupe. That was a jaguar, from the Americas, maybe. Though what a black jaguar would be doing in an English forest is beyond me."

"A jaguar? How do ye know that? How did ye know what to do with the blasted beast?"

Her lips drew inward for a moment and she couldn't stop her head from shaking. "My stepfather oftentimes had odd animals—predators—shipped from the far corners of the world. Lions. Wolves. Alligators. He once had two jaguar brought to his estate—one spotted and one black. I thought they were beautiful, especially the black one. It was just the same as that one tonight, with its black fur reflecting the light. I would visit them in their cage every day, and I learned if I meowed like a kitten, they would pay attention to me. Let me pet their snouts. I would feed them, of course. Fresh meat from the kitchens. They were majestic—proud—but with my mewling I could get them to come to me."

"Blasted me, I never heard of such a thing, lass." Rupe scuffed the wiry hairs on his chin. "Why'd he do that—bring the scourge of that beast upon this land?"

Her shoulders lifted as she drew a deep breath. "My stepfather liked to kill them. He liked me to watch. Would force me to do so." She said the words fast, factually, to avoid Rupe's pity.

"Hell, lass, a demon of his own kind, then?" Rupe's weathered face scrunched into disgust.

Her right cheek lifted in a forced smile. "Yes, one of his own kind."

"But a jaguar, lass—I never heard of such a thing as a jaguar." Rupe shifted, agitated, hopping from one foot to another. "Ye sure that be what that was?"

Her head swiveled around and she searched the shadows of the trees around them. "Yes, or some animal very similar. And we best not dawdle here in the middle of the forest. I don't imagine the rabbit will keep it occupied for long."

"Best idea I've thus heard from yer lips, lass." Rupe bent to pick up the torch and they started in the direction of the camp.

Three steps and both of them jumped.

Lachlan stood with two men flanking him, all three had swords drawn and at the ready. They had appeared out of nowhere, silently lurking in the shadows.

"Curse me bally, Lach, ye going to send a man to his grave popping out like that," Rupe grumbled. "Where were ye when that beast was ready to nibble on me arm?"

Lachlan kept a wary eye to the darkness past their heads. "We arrived here just after Evalyn jumped in front of you, old man."

"And ye didn't kill the beast?"

"You both were too close to shoot it and Evalyn appeared to have it well in hand—so to speak. There was no need."

"And if it had swatted her out of the way and come to eat me?" Rupe's arm swung back toward the tree he'd been pinned against.

Lachlan shrugged. "I would have killed it if it had raised a paw to Evalyn." He sheathed his sword and took the torch from Rupe's fist, walking toward camp with everyone following. One of his men trailed them, sword still at the ready. "It didn't. Beast that it is, it didn't need to die. Viscount Larring warned me earlier today when I stopped by his manor house that the jaguar had escaped from the menagerie he keeps on his lands. He has hopes of capturing the cat alive. So I deferred to his wishes." Lachlan looked back over his shoulder to Evalyn. "And to Evalyn's mewling."

Evalyn blinked, her eyes squinting in the darkness. Was that a smirk lifting the left side of Lachlan's mouth? It was hard to tell as the torch was on the other side of his face. His voice had maintained the same low, even rumble as always, so she couldn't be positive.

Rupe snorted. "Ye could have warned me what be in these woods before I went off searching for berries for yer supper, Lach."

Lachlan sighed. "I didn't know a warning was necessary, Rupe, as I had no idea you'd be straying from camp."

"Aye—I wouldn't have 'cept for the lass grabbing the wrong berries from the path." He shook his head. "Red berries, I said, not pink." His hands flew up, his grumble reaching a higher pitch. "And now we have one less rabbit fer the stew."

Evalyn's chest deflated.

She'd saved Rupe's life with that rabbit, but that wasn't what the cook would see. What the men in Lachlan's camp would see. One less rabbit for them to eat. A stew lean on meat because of her actions.

And it was her fault. She was the one that had mistaken the pink berries for red in the waning light of the day.

Another failure to add to the tally.

Her head bowed.

The rest of the walk to the camp was in silence.

~ ~ ~

He could feel it around him.

The shift in the air. The air around Evalyn.

It hadn't taken but minutes back in the camp for word of Rupe's altercation with the jaguar and what Evalyn had done to reach every ear of his men.

With the story spreading, curious glances were rampant to the back of the wagon where Rupe had Evalyn gutting the other three rabbits.

Lachlan didn't care for it.

His men had done what they could in the last three days to break her—save for another hand across her cheek. Did what they could to send her running back to Wolfbridge. They despised her, just the same as they despised her stepfather.

Or at least, they had.

She hadn't broken, the chit. The sneers and jeers. The laughter at her expense. The constant demands for her to serve them. Gutting rabbits. Crawling through the brush for berries. None of it sent her feet to halting. None of it sent her running.

If anything, the tilt of her chin, the raw determination in her gold-green eyes had intensified.

He didn't care for that, either.

He'd ignored her the best he could for days, but that was waning.

Lachlan took a sip of ale from the tankard slung along his hand as his look dipped to the main fire in front of him. This journey would be immensely easier if his men continued to hold dismissive contempt for her. With that, he didn't have to worry about one of them drowning too far into their whisky that they thought it was a good idea to approach her.

To proposition her.

She was a beautiful woman.

He'd seen that the first night in the gardens when she'd cornered him. Even through her facade of angry demands, he could see how her gold-green eyes sparkled under the torches of the gardens. How her smooth skin and fine features lent an ancient world elegance to her body. How her carefully styled hair swept low along her right temple, highlighting the silky smoothness of the auburn locks.

The last thing he needed on this journey north was the headache of keeping his men's hands off her person.

He glanced at her out of the corner of his eye.

Even with her silly gown on, now stained and wrinkled to hell, and her hands deep in the blood of the rabbits, she held herself with an odd modicum of grace. Maybe it was how she held her bare arms up and out, attempting to distance her dress from the blood of the rabbits.

Why would she bother? The gold and white concoction was now so dirty, there would be no saving it.

Her elbow lifted and she tried to force back a thick lock of her auburn hair that had fallen in front of her right eye. Unsuccessful.

He stifled a sigh.

No. He didn't need his men shifting their focus to her. Didn't need their curiosity. She was no longer extra baggage they had to haul across the land. She was now interesting and brave—not a despised silent tail to their traveling party. He'd hoped that's what she would remain when he ordered Rupe to take her on as his helper.

Lachlan's gaze dropped back to the fire as he inhaled a long breath of the crisp air. The days were getting chilly, the nights brisk. Cold he loved.

He couldn't help his eyes from lifting up to her once more.

He was dressed for the weather. She was not.

Procuring the boots for her at Baron Rogerton's estate had been easy enough, so he'd have to remember to ask the steward at Lord Jameson's estate for an extra wool dress and a heavy cape when they arrived there in a few days.

Maybe with dull clothes and the slope of her bare chest hidden away from sight, she could fade into the trail of the party once more.

# { CHAPTER 6 }

She'd harbored the smallest hope the derogatory comments would stop after the incident with Rupe and the jaguar. Saving a life had to be worth something, she'd presumed—it should temper in some fashion the general disdain Lachlan's men had for her.

It did not.

In the days since the Rupe incident, it was as though a dam had been opened. Leering looks from every direction. Propositions for tumbles behind the bushes. Hand motions that she didn't quite comprehend but understood the intent of them perfectly well.

Through all of it, she'd set her head down and moved through every task with as much grace as she could muster.

Not that it did much good.

She helped Rupe with whatever job he put in front of her. Cooked their meals. Brought them their food. Washed their bowls. Gathered firewood. With every task, she took their insults on her person. Insults on her body parts. She'd done nothing but serve their needs as best she could and all she got were leers.

But they had removed the word "wretched" from the "wench." A small favor.

With heavy feet, Evalyn picked her way over the legs that were always sprawled in front of her as she moved through the camp. A shiver ran across her back. Near to dusk, the evening air was decidedly cold now.

"Blast it, ye wench, watch yer bloody hands."

Evalyn jumped, looking down to see Finley wiping off remnants of stew from his shin. Stew dripping from the mostly empty wooden bowls she had stacked in her arms.

She tilted the stack of bowls to the left, careful not to let them slop onto her dress. "Apologies." She stepped over Finley's legs.

"Bumbling wench."

She avoided Finley's glare, moving to the far end of the camp past the supply wagon. If she washed the bowls quickly tonight, maybe she would have time to warm her blanket with hot rocks from the fire before she crawled under the wagon. Lachlan and one of his men, Domnall, both had tents, the rest of the men slept by the fire, Rupe included. While they were all within a realm of warmth by the main fire, her designated spot under the wagon kept the mist off of her, but offered little warmth as the cooking fire usually died out by the middle of the night. The last three nights had been particularly chilly, and she was determined to wake up tomorrow without her muscles aching from shivering throughout the night.

"Rupe, I'm going to the river to wash the bowls."

Rupe grunted in her general direction, not looking up from the cooking fire.

Evalyn made her way through the edge of the forest to the river that ran near where they had set camp that night. On her knees at the edge of the water, she was rinsing the third bowl, scraping at a hardened chunk of meat with the edge of her thumbnail when she heard twigs crunching behind her.

The hairs on her neck pricking, she scrambled to her feet and spun around.

Lachlan.

The held breath in her chest exhaled. Of all the men, it was Lachlan she trusted the most. Not that he'd bothered to curb his men's tongues during the past days.

He looked to the stack of bowls on the flat rock beside her and then lifted a bundle of cloth tied with twine in his arms. "I've brought you a more suitable dress and a woolen cape courtesy of Lord Jameson. They should keep you warm as we travel further north."

"Oh." Her wet hands went to the front of her gown, smoothing the gold embroidery along her belly. A small smile breached her lips. "That is most kind of you, Lachlan. I will change into it posthaste and bundle my dress to put in the wagon."

His eyes ran down along her body and back up again, then he lifted the clothing for her to take. "No, lass, you misunderstand. We'll be leaving that bundle of rags you have on now behind. There's no room for extra weight in the wagon, as it's stocked full of goods we're bringing back to Vinehill. The roads get much steeper and rockier from here on."

Her fingertips brushing against the dress and cloak he held up, her hands froze in midair. She took a step back, her palms drawing to her torso and splaying wide in front of her dress. "I'll do no such thing."

"You won't change?"

"I won't leave my dress behind."

He exhaled a long sigh. "Evalyn, I don't think you understand. If it doesn't have value, we don't bring it with us on these roads. There is no margin for extra weight." He lifted the bundle of clothing to her again.

Her hands waved in front of her. "Thank you, but no. I am perfectly content in my dress." Her bottom lip slipped under her teeth. "Might I take the cloak, though?"

Lachlan took a step toward her, thrusting the bundle toward her. "You'll take them both and change into the wool dress."

"No." She hopped another step backward, the heels of her boots teetering on the edge of the wide, flat rock she'd been washing bowls from.

"No?" His head cocked to the side and a lock of his brown hair fell across his brow as his eyes narrowed. Almost as though he'd never heard the word no before and was trying to place its meaning.

Her brow furrowed and she clamped her arms across her ribcage. "No."

"No? Stubborn wench." He shoved the bundle of the clothing into her body, leaning over her, his teeth bared. "You'll put this dress on or I'll do it for you."

Her head snapped back. "You wouldn't."

"I'll do whatever I damn well please, Evalyn." His words were slow, darkened with threat.

Fear snaked down her spine and her limbs started to tingle. She darted to her right.

Lachlan took a wide step to his left, cutting off her path.

She withdrew a step, lurching to her left. He jumped in front of her, his body a dark shadow smothering her.

"There's nowhere to escape, Evalyn. You'll put the damn dress on."

She backed up a step. Then another. And another.

Her heel dropped off the edge of the rock, slipping to shallow pebbles under the water that lined the edge of the river. She glanced over her shoulder. Several large boulders that were too far away. Water running fast. Cold.

He stalked a step toward her. "There's no escape, Evalyn. You'll change into the dress or I will tear that gown off of you with no regard to propriety."

Her head shaking, she looked at him as all feeling left her limbs and her throat started to constrict her air. "No. You can't."

"I can and I will." Another step to her and he shoved the bundle of clothes into her chest. "There's no escaping this."

*No escape.*

Hell. No escape.

Her mind went blank to all thoughts except for the terror slithering from her spine to her belly, to her neck, across her chest—all of it strangling her.

*No escape.*

She glanced over her shoulder again. The nearest boulder wasn't that far away. *Maybe…*

Lachlan was too close, his breath seething, his body raging.

The icy panic choking her cinched across her throat.

Her boot in the water slipped backward and she spun, running.

She made it three steps.

Three steps, and the shallow rocks in the water dropped out, plunging her into the current.

Freezing water blasted onto her face, swallowing her whole.

She gulped in water, her legs kicking. Kicking. Kicking. Her toes searched, not touching anything.

It hadn't looked this deep. This torrential a current.

Her arms flailed, reaching up.

The tips of her fingers breached the surface to touch air. Just a fleeting touch.

The current yanked her down, pulling her deeper. Deeper.

More water down her throat. Filling her lungs. Sinking her.

With the last of her strength, she pushed her right hand up through the water, grasping, grasping at air, at anything.

A brutal clamp locked onto her wrist and she was yanked upward. Upward to the air. To the land of the breathing.

Her head crested the surface and in a blur of water stinging her eyes and Lachlan's body banging into her, he dragged her to the river's edge and flung her onto the rocks.

The impact of a large rock into her belly sent her rolling onto her side, the gulps of water that filled her lungs expelling as she gasped for breath. Water out. Air in. Water out. Air in.

Heaving, she collapsed on the bankside, her body spent, her mind spinning, pulling her to darkness. The rocks that had been chilly to kneel upon five minutes ago were now warm stones against her frozen cheek.

"Dammit all to hell, Evalyn."

Her body lifted, flying through the air and her stomach landed hard on Lachlan's shoulder. It sent another wave of water spewing from her lungs, and she fell into a fit of coughing exasperated by her chest banging against the back of Lachlan with every step he took.

She couldn't speak, couldn't yell, so she slammed her fist into his back, trying to get him to stop, to set her down.

His hold across the back of her thighs and her sopping skirts only tightened.

Five more weak hits and she realized he wasn't going to set her down.

Her coughs ceased and the true state of her humiliation washed over her.

She was being hauled back into the encampment like a felled deer. Backside high in the air. Her head pounding for all the blood pooling in it. Her body so frozen she could barely move.

All noise, all conversation stopped the moment Lachlan broke through the woods and walked into camp.

Lachlan didn't slow, didn't say a word.

Evalyn curled her face into his back, eyes shut tight. She didn't want to see their faces. Didn't want to hear the jeers.

He stomped through the camp, bent, and in the next moment she was flipped off his shoulder, tossed to the ground in his tent. She landed on her backside, her fingers setting into the wool of the blanket covering the ground.

She leaned to the side, flipping away a long strand of wet hair that had fallen across her face, blocking her view. Her glare instantly found him.

He stared down at her, his breathing heavy—or seething. Yes. Definitely seething.

With her body no longer draped over the heat of his, the cold attacked and she tried to battle away the frozen shards taking a hold of her limbs.

It didn't work. The shaking started almost instantly, her muscles trying to warm themselves against the freezing wet cloth of her dress.

"Now will you get out of your damn dress?"

Her arms pulled inward, clamping against her torso as her legs drew under her. "I…I…"

His eyes narrowed at her. "If you say no again, I might just throw you back into that river."

The muscles along her back tightened into a thousand vicious knots and she shook her head, words sputtering out through chattering teeth. "I—I don't—th—think—I—c—can."

Lachlan exhaled a long breath through gritted teeth, his eyebrows drawing together. He stepped forward, moving to the side of her. His thick hands came down, landing on her shoulders.

Warm. They were warm, almost hot on the spots where his thumbs met skin.

In that moment she wanted nothing more than those hands to stay on her, to expand and warm every inch of her body.

He twisted her, spinning her in place so she faced the rear of the tent, and then he dropped to his knees behind her. Her hair had long since lost its pins in the water and he twisted the sopping strands into one long lock before setting it over her shoulder. Cool air hit the base of her neck.

Clearing his throat, his fingers started to untangle the knots in the ribbons that laced up her spine and secured her dress.

His rough, but warm knuckles brushed against her spine, his deep voice tempered with his next words. "Why did you jump in, Evalyn?"

"I did—didn't jump—I was running—I thought I could make it to that boulder."

"Running across water?" He jerked on the laces, yanking her torso backward.

She nodded.

"You felt the need to escape from me so desperately you were willing to drown yourself?" The exact opposite of the current of ire running through his words, she could feel his fingers soften to pick delicately at the knot at the top of the laces. "That's a better alternative?"

"N—no."

"It's a damn dress, Evalyn."

"I—I know."

"Did you think I was about to beat you?" The knot free, he started loosening the laces, working down her spine.

Her head dipped forward for a long breath as she tried to control her clattering teeth. She lifted her head slightly, looking to the back corner of the canvas tent as she tried to draw warmer air into her lungs.

"Esc—escape. When I cannot escape—" Her words cut off as her teeth went into a spastic flurry of clanging. She grinded her molars together in an effort to control them. With another deep breath, a sense of normalcy came over her tongue, enough at least to talk. "When I'm trapped and cannot escape—I cannot think—my mind goes blank—and

I do whatever it takes, Lachlan. I just—I just react—escape in my mind or in my body. And at the river my body could still flee you, so that's what I did. I turned and ran."

He grunted. "That's going to get you in trouble someday."

She smiled, a half chuckle breaching her lips as she glanced at him over her shoulder. "It just did. Again."

He didn't chuckle, but the smallest smile curved the hard lines of his lips.

Her gaze went forward. "I know I am on tenuous footing with you, Lachlan, and I fear my confidence is not bolstered by being regarded as the designated wench in the camp—and the adjectives that accompany it being constantly hurled at me."

He was quiet for a long breath, his fingers working the ribbon. "They call you names, lass, because they don't know what to do with you."

"They don't know what to do with me?"

"You're not what they thought and they are still trying to figure you out."

He pulled free the last loops of the ribbon along her spine. Silently, he moved away from her for a moment, returning to drape a wide fur-lined blanket across her shoulders. Heaven. Soft and dry against her skin, it coddled her in instant warmth.

"Are your hands thawed enough to move down your dress?"

She lifted her right hand, going to the strap of her dress. Her fingers still could not bend, not find a way through their shaking to grip the cloth from her damp skin.

More humiliation.

Not able to look back at him, she shook her head.

A sigh, and he bent forward, snaking his hands up under the blanket from behind her. His fingers found the top straps of her gown and he wedged the sopping cloth down her body, past her trembling arms, and then he settled it around her waist.

Without asking, his hands moved back up under the blanket, making quick work of loosening her short stays and then stripping down her stays and chemise.

"You—you are quick with that."

"I've had some practice." He was close now. So close his warm breath caressed the bare skin on her neck as he spoke.

He said the words with enough hint of pride that she couldn't help but wonder how many women he'd stripped like this. Probably too many to count. The man was so handsome Lucifer himself must have smirked when he set Lachlan onto this world. Women were entranced by him—she'd recognized that in the ballroom at Wolfbridge.

Hell, she'd probably be as delighted as the next woman at his touch if her circumstances weren't so dire. At the moment, she could only afford to concentrate on her last chance for escape.

Escape from her stepfather. From Mr. Molson. And for that she had to disappear far, far away.

She nodded, jerking slightly at his touch as he wedged the cloth from where it was clamped tight between her ribcage and arms.

The fabric peeled down her skin and she was naked from the waist up. Naked, but shielded by the heavy weight of the blanket. How he'd managed to keep it in place about her as he stripped the wet cloth from her torso she didn't know.

He was taking care not to strip her bare in front of his eyes. A kindness he didn't need to extend to her after her utterly foolish actions.

His hands left her hips where the mass of her dress, chemise and stays sat rumpled and he shifted away from her.

She tightened her hold on the edges of the blanket against her bare chest and glanced back at him.

He started to stand behind her, but then stopped on one knee, looking at her. "What would have happened if you would have had to escape in your mind?"

"What?" Her forehead crinkled.

"If you couldn't have escaped me with your body? You said you would have escaped with your body or in your mind."

He had understood her fully, her mad words, her weak explanation. Her lips drew inward, her breath quivering in her throat as her look dropped. "Then I would have gone limp and closed my eyes and imagined I was elsewhere."

"Where?"

"With my mother. We're walking together outside in the sun. She's picking flowers. I'm helping her. Lavender sprigs. It's simple and so long ago. But I was safe, so that is where I go."

She dared a glance at him.

The blue streaks in his hazel eyes flickered in the light of the lantern by the tent's entrance. She couldn't read anything in them. Stoic. Stoic as always when he looked at her. He offered a slight nod. "That is a good place to go. Lost memories."

For a second, he looked to say more, but then he stood abruptly, moving to the flap of the tent. He stopped at the entrance and picked up the dress he'd brought to the river for her. She hadn't even seen him carrying it back with them.

He turned and brought it to her, dropping it to her side. "Stand." He held his hand down to her.

She managed to unwedge her left arm from her ribcage enough to squeeze her wrist out past the fold of the blanket. His big hand enveloped hers and he pulled her to her frozen feet—so numb, she thought her toes would splinter under the pressure of her weight. It took her a long breath to catch her balance.

The wet mess of clothing surrounding her waist slipped, slapping to the ground in a wet thwack.

Lachlan bent, gathering up the clothing on the ground as she lifted her feet so he could slide them away to the side. He moved toward the flap of the tent, then stopped to point at the bundle by her toes. "Put that dress on." He stepped out of the tent.

Evalyn sank to her knees, then sat back, huddling the blanket close about her as she threaded her hands out to loosen the twine around the bundle and pull the grey dress onto her lap. The wool of it would itch against her skin without her chemise, but it would be warm. And all she could concentrate on at the moment was how to get warm.

Her fingers still shaking uncontrollably with every movement, she unfolded the dress only to find an impossibly long row of tiny black buttons lining the back of the dress. Buttons already secured in their matching loops.

Damn.

She started at the top button, fingers trembling uncontrollably with the cold. Tensing the muscles in her arms, she tried to still the tremors in her hands long enough to unbutton the top one.

The fabric slipped out of her fingers.

Damn.

She picked it up, another attempt.

Failure.

She picked it up again, setting her forefinger in place just before she lost control and it slipped out of her hands, the button popping free.

Success.

And only twenty-four more to go.

Her teeth gritting, she picked up the dress again and started on the second button.

A waft of cool air hit her cheeks.

"You're not dressed yet?"

She looked up. Lachlan had popped his head into the tent. His gaze dropped down to the dress in her lap, a frown setting on his face when he saw her trembling fingers.

"Your hands are out of control, Evalyn." He stepped into the tent and pulled the dress from her lap, then dropped it to the blanket that covered the ground. He grabbed her shaking hands and pulled her up and the pain of her weight on her toes sent scorching needles through her freezing feet.

She lost her balance, falling into him.

"Hell, Evalyn." His arm wrapped around her shoulder to catch her weight. "I'll deal with the wretched buttons. You need to warm by the fire."

Stepping slightly behind her, his arms wrapped around her to tighten the long blanket about her body so none of her skin was bared to the air. He set an arm along the back of her shoulders and his fingers clasped onto her upper arm as he steered her out past the front flap of his tent and to the main fire. Close to the blazes, he gently pushed down on her shoulders until she was sitting, able to warm herself by the fire.

The heat of the healthy flames stung, almost too much against her frozen skin.

"Sit, Evalyn, and warm yourself."

Exhausted by the short steps it took to get to the fire, she nodded, her lips too tired to move. Her fingers tightened along the edges of the blanket, securing it in front of her. A waft from the blanket lifted to her nose. It smelled of Lachlan. Campfire and spice and rosewood. She focused on the fire, not wanting to look around at the men's gaping stares she knew were pointed in her direction.

Lachlan deserted her, moving away from her for a moment. A quiver of panic fluttered in her stomach. Instinctively, she knew she was safer with him directly beside her and she didn't care for her nude body being one blanket away from baring her to all.

Her gaze refused to move from the fire. The silence in the air pounded, palpable, and she wasn't about to look up and open herself to the men jeering her.

Lachlan returned, dipping to sit on his heels in front of her. He held a metal cup to her lips and tilted it back.

Whisky warmed her tongue and sent fire along her throat as it chased down to her stomach.

"Good." He lifted the cup in his hand and filled it, then handed the bottle to Domnall on his right. Finding her left hand gripping the front edge of the fur-lined blanket at her chest, he slid his fingers under hers, popping free her fingertips one by one until he could wedge the cup into her hand. "Drink. This will warm you."

He stood and Evalyn looked up, her eyes finding enough steadiness to focus on Lachlan's face. The glow of the fire behind him made him look like a Greek god straight from an Ares's blaze-soaked battle.

She nodded, her eyes dipping back down to the fire as he walked back to his tent.

The first long swallow of the whisky settled deep into her belly, creating fire where there was none and encouraging her to take another sip from the cup. And another. And another.

Four more sips and the fifth time she lifted the cup to her lips, it was empty.

Movement next to her, grunting, and she watched with wariness out of the corner of her eye as Domnall moved closer to her. He was the oldest of the men aside from Rupe, or at least she thought as such from the graying of his dark hair along his temples. Good natured, he was also the nicest of the men, never once calling her a wench and his thick face usually held a jovial grin.

He sat with a whoosh of air as his thick form settled into place next to her. "Another spot, lass?" He lifted the bottle Lachlan had handed to him.

She nodded, lifting her cup.

With a mischievous tilt of his head, Domnall filled the metal cup in her hand. She took another sip and it was only moments before her head started to weave in a slow circle.

She just wanted to sleep. Lie down by the warmth of the fire and sleep. As long as she kept the blanket tucked together, covering her bare skin, this was the perfect spot to sleep. Much better than her cold hole under the wagon.

Her hair. Dammit. If she didn't get her fingers through it now while it was wet, it would be impossible to untangle once it was dry in the morning.

She took another sip of the whisky and then wiggled her hand out of the folds of the blanket to set the cup onto the ground by her covered knees. Extending her left arm up further, she began pulling free small strands of hair at her brow from the rat's nest that was now her hair.

Plucking methodically, she smoothed strand after strand with her one hand, her eyes glazing over as she stared at the fire. The chatter amongst the men had started again, a constant low buzz in her ears. She could only pick up rare snippets of the conversations for how slow her mind was processing the words.

She'd had too much whisky. Far too much. It was already muddling her thoughts.

Pluck, smooth. Pluck, smooth. Pluck, smooth.

"Lass, yer temple." Domnall blurted out from her right side. He sat up straight, his look intent on her face.

Her fingertips flew to her right temple. Hell. She'd thought it was still hidden.

She quickly shuffled her smoothed hair forward, draping it along her right temple.

"That be wicked, lass. How'd it happen?" Domnall asked.

Her face grew hot, near to steaming with the added warmth of the fire. "It is of no matter."

Domnall let loose a low whistle. "A wretched scar like that and it'd be a matter, lass. What happened?"

She glanced at Domnall and then drew a deep breath. Nothing but honest curiosity shone in his eyes. And where she always drew into herself when people asked her questions, the kindness Domnall had showed her demanded an answer.

Her look strayed to the sparks of the flames sizzling onto the dirt in front of her feet. The whisky loosening her tongue when she knew to keep her mouth shut. "I brought him the wrong slippers."

"Wrong slippers?"

She nodded. "My stepfather. I brought him the wrong slippers. And I thought I could escape his wrath. But escaping never worked—it was always worse that way. I relearned that lesson that night."

Domnall clucked his tongue, leaning back on his elbow as he downed a swig of ale from his tankard. "How old were ye?"

"Thirteen. I tried to run from the room before his anger could find me. I didn't make it but five steps into the main corridor that ran the length of the abbey."

"And he caught ye, lass?"

She glanced at him, her look quickly scurrying back down to the dirt. She'd never told this story before. She'd never needed to. Everyone in her stepfather's home knew what happened to her. And there were never any visitors that she was allowed to talk to.

Except for Mr. Molson. She had been presented to him like a roasted pig on a platter. He knew the story. Her stepfather had boasted about it to him.

She cleared her throat. "My stepfather caught me and slammed my head into the stone wall. I don't remember anything after that."

"The wall was where the scar came from?" Domnall asked.

"I don't know—the cut started there, I imagine. I went to blackness and when I woke up, the open wound on my temple had bled and the blood had dried to the stones of the floor. My skin was stuck to the stone. I cried out for help. Cried for hours. Begged. No one came."

Domnall's face cringed with a sharp intake of breath.

"I learned later that I was like that for two days. Dead to the world. Stuck to the floor. My stepfather had forbidden any of the servants to touch me. Said I would live or die by my own sorry will. He beat the chambermaid that had tried to press water to my lips to rouse me. She didn't deserve that." Her head shook and then she shrugged. "After that no one dared to come to me. Not even when I awoke."

Her eyes slipped shut. "I had to rip my head from that stone floor. That moment…" A shudder ripped through her body. "It tore my skin. Left me this." Her fingers pointed to her temple which she had already smoothed her hair over.

She cracked her eyes open, her downcast gaze shifting to Domnall and then settling on the flames of the fire. "I'm sorry you had to witness the scar. I know it is grotesque and

I am careful to keep it covered. I will take better care in the future."

Domnall nodded, his face solemn. Nodded for a long moment.

It took her several unsteady breaths to realize the entire camp had gone quiet. The constant buzz of the male voices, the Scottish burrs steadily streaming about the campfire had died.

She looked up.

Every man around the fire was looking at her.

Looking at her with the same solemn countenance of Domnall's face.

*Hell.* Why had she swallowed the whisky? So much of it.

Her cheeks flaming, she bowed her head, unable to take the pitying stares of the men about her.

Disdain she could take. Pity she could not.

What she wouldn't give in that moment for a graphic hand gesture aimed in her general direction.

Domnall cleared his throat. Her head stayed tilted downward, but her eyes lifted to him.

He was grinning, his eyes sparkling in the light of the fire. "Lass, ye dinnae ken grotesque until ye've seen Finley's back. Fire got the bastard after he ran from a widow's bed—a widow that wasn't a widow—and he tripped over a fire as he ran from her husband."

The men laughed, jeers and caterwauls flying at Finley.

"Go on, show her, Finley," Rory called out from the left.

Chuckling with a wild grin on his face, Finley stood up opposite the fire from Evalyn and yanked his shirt up, turning his back to her. Mottled flesh, bumpy and stretched tight to a fine white, cut a swath across the expanse of his skin. Smirking, he dropped his shirt, looking about his brethren. "Best lay ever from a widow, though, lads."

Bawdy chortles filled the night air.

"And, Rory, show the lass where that boar ripped yer leg through."

With a maniacal laugh, Rory jumped to his feet, dropping his trousers and turning his bare ass to her. Her hand flew to cover her eyes, her head turning away, but not before she saw the ragged scar that ran from the back of his knee up past his buttocks.

"And, Colin, the lass needs to see where ye ran at my sword when ye were a pup and I sliced yer side," Domnall said. "Festered for weeks."

"Ran at your sword, my ass." Colin hauled himself to his knees and unbuttoned his waistcoat, yanking up on his shirt.

She held her hand up, laughing. "Enough, enough, enough. You all are marred more grotesquely than me, I understand."

"But ye should really see what that ole bugger Domnall did to an innocent lad like me." Colin freed his shirt, spinning to the side so she could see the thick, ragged band of flesh that had been stitched closed. He tilted his skin to the light. "Miss Mable was soused when she stitched me up." His fingers pointed along the length of the scar. "Ye can still see the spots where she missed the wound completely, stitching closed skin that was already together."

Evalyn groaned. "Why didn't you stop her?"

"I was soused too."

She laughed.

In that moment, in the middle of laughter flying freely from her throat, it struck her. She had never felt this before.

Warmth.

Whether it was from the whisky, from the fire, from the moment of laughter where she didn't feel like a burden.

It was warm.

And it was wonderful.

Wonderful and fleeting.

# { CHAPTER 7 }

"Evalyn. I need you in the tent."

Lachlan's voice cut into the air from where he stood behind her. Hard. Clipped.

It cut the laughter still bubbling from her throat.

Cut the easy laughter from all corners of the camp.

He didn't mean it to sound so harsh, but he did mean to extract her from the men. In the span of twenty minutes she had just turned his men from adversaries to allies.

She jumped at his command, glancing downward and seeing how far down her bare shoulder the blanket had slipped.

She yanked it up, clasping the fur-lined wool tightly about her neck as she got to her feet.

Better.

Once upright, the blanket about her swayed—no, she swayed, near to stumbling.

Worse.

How many times had Domnall refilled her cup with whisky?

Holding her balance, she spun to Lachlan. Her cheeks had gone rosy, the liquor or the laughter sending warmth to her head. The back half of her auburn hair was still askew and knotted with snarls, the front was smoothed perfectly over her right temple. He'd watched as her fingers had threaded through the locks again and again as she spoke. He doubted she even knew she did it.

The remnant of the smile that was still on her lips faded when she found his face. For an instant, he wanted it back. Wanted to see her eyes glow with the merriment of the moment that the waning vestiges of the grin only hinted at.

He'd stood behind her for the last ten minutes. Silent, listening, but not moving into her sightline.

Now he wished he had.

He hadn't seen laughter breach her face, ever.

Fear, he'd seen. Her chin jutting out in stubbornness. Outrage. Sorrow. She'd even rolled her eyes once at Rupe.

But never a laughing smile.

Her mouth pulled to a tight, wary line as her eyes met his. "The tent?"

He nodded, his voice gruff. "The tent."

He turned and pulled aside the front flap of his tent and she shuffled past him into the confines.

Stepping in after her, his neck curved forward as he hunched to fit inside. He picked up the woolen dress he'd procured for her at Lord Jameson's estate, holding it out to her, the row of buttons now freed. "Your shift is still sopping so I'll set it by the fire while you pull the dress on. I'll be back in to button it."

Her look dipped down from the bland grey dress to the ground next to the front flap of the tent.

"Evalyn?"

She didn't respond. Had she managed to fall asleep standing up with her eyes open?

Her look crawled up to his face, the gold flecks in her green eyes sparking in the glow of the lantern. "Where's my gown, Lachlan?"

"Gone."

"Gone? What—where? No."

"Yes."

Jerking the blanket around her, she pushed past him and stalked out of the tent, searching the cold ground. Finding nothing, she walked around to the back of the tent, searching the shadows.

Lachlan followed her.

"You don't need the damned dress, Evalyn. It'll do you no good in Scotland."

She whipped to him, her palpable fury cutting through the dark. "You have no right—no right to dispose of it, Lachlan. No right to it at all."

He bristled, his arms clamping over his chest. "I do because you'll do as I say, Evalyn. You asked for this. You. You wanted to join our party—well, this is our party. And there isn't margin for the additional weight of that monstrosity."

"Monstrosity?" Her voice screeched into the night. "That is my mother's dress, Lachlan. The last—the only thing I have of her." Her voice cracked and it took her a long moment to steel her breath enough to continue. "Please—it's the only thing. I know it's not practical. I know it is of no use to anyone but me, but I couldn't leave it behind at Wolfbridge. That's why I wore it. And I cannot leave it now. I need it. Please, just tell me where it is. I will carry it. It won't be a burden. I swear."

She flung an arm out from the blanket wrapping her and ripped the wool dress from his hands, then spun away from him. "Here—see—I'll wear your damn dress and I will carry the gown." She bent, the blanket hanging over her back as she stepped into the serviceable wool dress. She straightened and the blanket slid off her bare back as she yanked the dress upward.

For half a second, her backside was bared to him. Even with his tent between them and the fire, he could see her clearly. Her creamy skin, the gentle slope that dipped in along her lower back then led to her smooth backside—curves that begged for his fingers to cup.

She tugged the dress upward, covering her bottom, but the fabric still gaped wide from her shoulder blades down to the small of her back.

Spinning around to him, her hand flattened on her chest to clasp the bodice of the dress to her breasts. Desperation laced her words. "See—I have it on. Just as you wanted. Now please, just tell me where my mother's dress is, Lachlan. Please."

Curse it all to bloody hell.

Had he known what it was, what it meant to her, he never would have been so casual in disposing of it. He knew about keepsakes. Knew about mothers that passed well before their time. He'd carried about his mother's favorite mother-of-pearl hair comb—the one she would always let his tiny fingers set into place in her fine russet hair—somewhere on his person every day for years after her death.

He exhaled an exasperated sigh. "The dress is at the wagon with Rupe. He was to rip it into strips and use it as kindling."

Her jaw dropped, air escaping, though words didn't leave her mouth.

She shoved by him.

"Evalyn—"

She didn't stop, charging away from the tent and running to the wagon.

He followed her, watching as she found the sopping wet pile of the white and gold gown on the ground next to the rear left wheel. Rupe was still busy at the cooking fire making bannocks for tomorrow's journey. It didn't look as though he'd gotten to it yet.

Small favor.

She gathered up her dress, clutching it to her chest and sending water dripping from the fabric.

"Damn…Evalyn, no." He reached out to snatch it from her, his fingers quick to grasp onto a piece of the dress. "Give me that."

"No, damn you, Lachlan." She yanked it backward with a step and the fabric tore. "Damn you."

His fingers flew wide, releasing the silk. Both of his hands lifted, palms open to her to calm. "No, I'm not going to ruin it. It's wet and you're going to be soaked again in another minute if you keep pressing it to your dress."

"What?" The word screeched through her teeth, clear disbelief in his statement.

He couldn't blame her.

Lachlan leveled his voice to what he hoped was a non-threatening timbre. "I don't have another dress for you, Evalyn. The one you wear is all we have and we can't afford to get it wet as well." He took a cautious step forward. "I'm not going to take your mother's gown from you. I didn't know what it meant. I'm just going to drape it along the wagon so it can dry. That is all."

The glare in her gold-green eyes waned, confusion setting in. "You're going to what?"

"Dry it."

"You're not going to have Rupe wreck it?"

"No."

She glanced back over her shoulder to look at Rupe. He'd stood as straight as the stoop in his back would allow and was now intently watching the scene by the wagon.

"You swear it, Lachlan?"

"Yes." His look stayed on her as he half turned his head to his cook. "You hear me, Rupe?"

"Yes, Lach," Rupe said as he sauntered over from the cooking fire, large wooden spoon in his hand as he watched the proceedings.

Lachlan motioned with his fingers for Evalyn to hand the dress to him. He wasn't about to try and wedge it from her grasp again and risk tearing more of the fabric.

It took her a long moment before she slowly lifted it away from her body, offering it to him.

Gently, so as to not startle her, Lachlan took the gown and moved to the front side of the wagon. He unrumpled the silk fabric, stretching it out and draping it along the front boards—acutely aware the entire time of Evalyn's disbelieving gaze pinning him.

The fabric was beyond dirty, probably beyond salvageable for ever being worn again. But he smoothed it out with as much care as he possibly could.

He worked along the edge of the skirt hanging off the end of the wagon, snapping the fabric tight to take out the deep-set wrinkles.

Rupe pointed at Evalyn with his spoon. "Ye need help with the buttons on yer back, lass?"

Lachlan dropped the skirt, moving back to Evalyn and stepping between her and Rupe. "I'll take care of the damn buttons, Rupe."

He grabbed Evalyn's shoulders, spinning her and guiding her back to the entrance of his tent. He ushered her in and then stood behind her, his head cocked to the side so it didn't hit the top of the tent. She had no problem with the tent height as the top of her head barely reached his mid-chest.

Standing with her bare back to him, she didn't turn, choosing to stay still and silent until he stepped forward and his fingers started on the first buttons.

Working upward, his knuckles brushed the back of her bare skin. It was enough to drive a man to madness, buttoning up the dress instead of dragging it down her sleek body.

But she was foxed and he was in no mood to make her his mistress yet. That would need to wait until they got to Vinehill. Wait until she was no longer shooting arrows at him with her gold-green eyes.

"Thank you."

"For?" Lachlan looked to the back of her head.

She lifted one hand from holding the front of her dress to her chest and twisted her long auburn hair around her hand. She pulled the mass of it forward over her shoulder so he would have clear access to the buttons moving up her spine. "For not destroying the dress."

"I made an assumption about it that I was mistaken on."

"What assumption?" Her head shifted slightly to the side and he could see her delicate profile, though she didn't look at him.

"That you were too harebrained to know enough to put on a sturdy dress for the journey."

"And you no longer think me harebrained?"

"I find that you are determined, not necessarily harebrained."

"I fear I must take that as a compliment."

Lachlan chuckled.

As he worked the buttons up her back, he realized that under the light of the lantern spots of her creamy skin were yellowed, some darker than the others. One that was almost black. Bruises that were in various states of healing.

"Evalyn—no one in camp has touched you since Colin slapped you? Have they?"

She glanced over her shoulder at him, her eyebrow lifted in curiosity. "No. Not a one. I thank you for that. I haven't mistakenly insinuated so, have I?"

He shook his head. Her face shifted forward, her hands tightening along her chest where she held the dress to her breasts.

Three more buttons up and he paused, his forefinger flicking out to trace the mottled edge of a blackened bruise just below her shoulder blade. "Yet this is recent." He looked up at the back of her neck and leaned forward, his voice low. "What exactly are you running from, Evalyn?"

She spun around, jumping away from him. "I shouldn't take your time such as this." She dodged to the right to move around him. "I'm sure Rupe will help with the rest of the buttons."

He grabbed her upper arm, stopping her motion. "I will finish them."

Panic instantly set into her eyes. Panic Lachlan recognized. She was trapped.

He released her arm, stepping behind her so she was the one closest to the entrance of the tent. "It is no trouble. Only a few more." He started fastening the remaining buttons before she could escape him.

To her credit, her feet stayed in place. Just being close to escape was enough to halt her instinct to flee.

Interesting.

"You heard what I said by the fire, didn't you?" Her words came out small, tired.

His fingers stilled, his pinky set on a bump of her spine. "I did."

"Then you already know the answer to the question."

"Your stepfather?"

She looked back to him. "Yes. Life was…difficult. And it was about to become more so."

"Why?"

"He had bartered me away to a man he partners with."

"Falsted sold you?" The words whispered from his mouth.

"Whereas I never knew what would set my stepfather to anger or when, the man he sold me to has had no quandary in telling me exactly what he plans to do to me. How he will rip me to shreds." She visibly shuddered. "This was my last chance to escape before I was forced to marry him."

Hell. That bloody blackguard. Of course Falsted would set a monster onto his stepdaughter. "You've tried to escape before?"

She nodded, a dark cloud shadowing her eyes before she turned forward, her look evading him. "Twice. Both times I was by myself, and I was quickly found."

Lachlan cleared his throat, his fingers quick on the last three buttons up the back of the dress. "Then I daresay it was with luck that we met in the Wolfbridge gardens."

Her shoulders lifted in a heavy sigh and she smoothed down the front of the dark wool dress against her stomach.

For a long moment she was silent, and then her lips pulled inward as she turned her face slightly toward him.

Yet her eyes avoided him.

"It wasn't luck, Lachlan. I must confess I planned my approach of you from the moment you stepped foot into the duke's castle."

# { CHAPTER 8 }

Several heartbeats passed before Evalyn found the nerve to fully turn to Lachlan and risk a glance at his face. She wholly expected to see wrath like she'd never known in his eyes.

Instead, she was met with curious hazel eyes. Almost a grin along the edges of his mouth.

His eyebrow arched. "You planned it?"

"I am sorry." She shook her head slightly, sloughing off his odd reaction to her confession. "I have been meaning to tell you since the first day, but there has not been an opportunity. I have quite despised my actions in how I had to trap you into taking me with you."

"You trapped me?"

"I did—splitting my dress, threatening a forced marriage. But there was no other way for it."

"Because of Falsted selling you?" His tongue curled around her stepfather's name, almost vicious.

"Yes. Again, I apologize, yet I must admit to the fact that I would have done the exact same thing given another chance." The edges of her eyes crinkled in a cringe. "I understand the brunt of the ill-will you must hold against me. I will happily work in another household once we get to your estate, if you would be so kind as to refer me to a suitable post."

His right cheek lifted in a half smile, but he said nothing.

"What?"

"If anything, my respect for you just increased tenfold, Evalyn."

She blinked hard at him. Then blinked again.

His hazel eyes almost twinkled in the light of the lantern hanging by the front of the tent. Hazel eyes that, for the first time ever, seemed to look on her without scorn lacing the edges.

She looked around the tent.

Was this a joke? A cruel joke set up by the men who were now surrounding the tent and hiding their laughter?

Her look centered on Lachlan. "I lied to you, and that purchases me respect?"

He shrugged. "In this instance, yes. You were desperate and you were willing to do whatever it took to change your circumstances. That is admirable. Far too many martyr themselves to their circumstances without attempting to change them."

"Even though I entangled you in my dire predicament?"

"Why did you entangle me?" He ran his fingers through his ruffled brown hair. "From the moment I stepped foot into Wolfbridge, you said."

"I was in the drawing room when you arrived with your men. I watched the lot of you trail down the main corridor. You were at the front, raging, searching for your sister."

"That should have evoked fear, not pinned me as a savior."

She chuckled. "I think it did—for most of the women in the drawing room. They shrieked and gasped at the clanging."

"But you are not most women?"

"No. I saw you pass by first and I slipped out into the corridor, hiding along the shadows of an alcove to watch. Then I went up to the gallery to observe you and your men once you entered the great hall." Her fingers twisted together. "That was where I heard you say you were there for your sister. You wanted to stop the wedding."

He stiffened. "I did."

"I thought you were to drag her out of there. But then you cleared the room and it was just the two of you."

"You eavesdropped?"

"I did. I knew I should not, but I was already hidden in place above in the gallery and I didn't want to draw any attention by moving away. But what I saw there—you, with your sister. You softened."

"I was yelling at her."

"Yes. But you were yelling with kindness. I could see that, even if she could not. You were trying to stop her from making the worst mistake in her life."

"Yet she still did it."

"And you supported her—or at least didn't stop the wedding." Evalyn drew a deep breath, a soft smile coming to her face. "That moment in the great hall, I expected you to strike her for all the anger palpitating from you. But you did not. You held. That was when I knew you could possibly be the key to my last chance."

"You made the determination of my worth from that moment? I'm surprised you didn't run as far and as fast as you could away from me."

"I did determine your worth—or at least what I hoped it was—in those minutes. But I would have chanced anything to escape out of there—including the puffed up ravings of a man that was only trying to protect his sister."

Lachlan ran his palm against the dark stubble of hair along his chin that had filled in during the past days. "So that night in the gardens was not happenstance."

"Not at all. I heard you talking to your men—you had gathered them in the billiards room during the festivities. I was against that wall—you didn't notice me—no one noticed me—and I heard you make plans to leave with your men. So I followed you when you moved out to the gardens."

He slowly nodded for a long moment, then his head stilled. His hazel eyes pinned her. "I noticed you, Evalyn."

He said the words with a rough rumble that almost turned to silk by the time it reached her ears. Heated, raw even.

She'd never had a man speak to her like that. Her stepfather only spoke to her with disdain. And Mr. Molson's words were always sneering, laced with lechery, threats—what he would do to her, do to her body.

But Lachlan's voice, the way he looked at her, was the exact opposite—as though he wanted her just the same, but only so he could worship her body.

She could feel herself slipping, getting caught in a current she had no way to control. Slipping away just as quickly as she had hours earlier in the stream.

She had no right to look at him like that. She was to work in his kitchens. Or as a maid. Whatever it took. She had to remember that.

Heat flushing her cheeks and threatening to tie her
tongue, she blurted out the first thing she could think of.
"This turned out nicely for you."

"How?" His left eyebrow lifted.

"You managed to get me into this blasted dress."

He chuckled, clearing his throat and taking a step back.
A rush of air separated them. "That I did. And it only took
an icy dunk in the river to do so." He pointed to her feet.
"You'll also need to take off your boots and let them dry by
the fire or your feet will blister raw tomorrow."

He reached down to grab the simple plaid woolen
blanket from the ground. "Take this, wrap yourself in it
and sleep next to the fire. The men will make room." He
bundled the blanket in his arms, then held it out to her.

She nodded, silent, and took the blanket from him.
Turning, she lifted the flap of the tent and shuffled to the
fire.

The spot she had sat in remained vacant and the
rumble of the voices of the men didn't stop this time when
she approached.

She sat, loosening the laces of her boots, then kicked
them off and set them close to the edge of the fire. Peeling
off the torn silk stockings that still managed to hold to
her calves, she draped them over the top of the boots. Not
that they would be worth even putting back on in the
morning—the silk so shredded, they had done nothing to
stop the painful blisters that had started to swell on the back
of her heels and on her toes.

Ignoring the pain of the throbbing blisters hitting air,
she wrapped herself in the blanket, and the scent of Lachlan

enveloped her. She curled into a ball on her side and tucked her bare toes deep into the folds of the blanket.

Warmth. Finally.

Her head hit the ground and she was asleep before she could even focus on the fire.

~ ~ ~

Lachlan twisted on his horse, looking back to the wagon that trailed the band of men.

Stubborn chit.

Evalyn had trudged along the entire day, the bundle of her dress—twice as heavy as normal for it was still wet—locked in her arms.

Stubborn.

No one had asked her to carry it. They could have wedged it into the wagon.

But upon waking, that was the first thing she'd done as the men were breaking camp. Go to her dress and fold it up with the utmost care.

Lachlan hadn't seen her farther than a foot away from it the whole day. Even with his word, she didn't trust him—trust the men—not to destroy it.

Not that she should. They'd done a fine job these last seven days in making sure she knew that every step she took—everything she did in the camp—was wrong.

All because he'd had the asinine idea she was a shallow chit running from her life of plenty because she had a bothersome hangnail. But even more grievous, that revenge upon her odious stepfather would be best served by ruining Evalyn.

He hadn't imagined she'd had anything to escape. But if the story she'd told at the campsite was any indication, she had everything to escape.

He hadn't given her that margin of possibility.

His horse cleared the crest of the hill they traveled upward on and Lachlan scanned the landscape. They'd journeyed from lands of green rolling hills to steeper, craggy outcroppings interspersed with moors and forests that harbored haunting shadows of ancient civilizations. They'd moved into countryside he knew. The land that was born in his bones.

He glanced back at Evalyn. She trudged up the hillside, her lips gritting into a tight line as her boots slipped on the loose rocks on the road.

The boots he'd procured for her were painful, that much was obvious. She hadn't complained once, but now he wished he'd taken better care in sizing them correctly. He'd just grabbed the first pair Baron Rogerton's housemaid had offered, not noting the size.

Domnall nudged his horse next to Lachlan's and coughed.

Lachlan looked at his old friend.

"We're more than halfway home, Lach." Domnall pointed straight ahead at the dark rolling clouds stretched long across the sky before them. "And while that rain ahead may not bother ye, these old bones would like a bed under them for a night."

Lachlan looked to him. "You going soft upon me, old man?"

"Possibly." Domnall shrugged with a smirk that lifted the grey grizzle on his cheeks. "But I can still scrape ye onto yer back, lad, and don't ye forget it."

Lachlan chuckled. Domnall hadn't flipped him onto his back since he was fourteen and they both knew it. "So you're thinking of Bellingham?" Lachlan's look scanned along the edge of the ominous clouds.

"It would favor us all." Domnall's thumb jabbed over his shoulder. "Plus it's the only coaching inn along the way that has space for the lot of us. Not to mention we're all tired of Rupe's stew."

"I never thought I'd hear you say you'd rather grace a bed than a rock under your head." Lachlan nodded. "We veer to Bellingham, then."

# { CHAPTER 9 }

Evalyn stood on the bottom step of the staircase, her fingers tapping the worn wood banister as she flattened herself into the shadows. She leaned forward slightly and peeked around the wall into the wide dining room of the coaching inn.

Dozens of round tables filled the room—mostly men surrounding each of them. The boisterous ale-fueled din filled her ears, making her question coming down the stairs. She was starving, but she hadn't any inclination as to how to order food at a coaching inn. Much less how she would pay for it.

When they had arrived, Lachlan set the landlady to showing her directly to her chamber above. A finely appointed room greeted her—truthfully, more luxurious than her stepfather would ever allow in his home—with sheets that didn't scratch her skin and splendid dark blue velvet curtains that weren't faded with years of use. She'd sat in the room for an hour before the insistent rumble of her stomach brought her to her aching feet.

Her eyes swept the dining room once more until she found him. Lachlan. She could only see his profile as he sat at the largest of the round tables with half of his men jabbering on around him. Whereas his men were laughing, gorging on fresh grouse, Lachlan leaned back in his chair, observing but not partaking in the eating and merriment surrounding him.

The men were all relaxed—as relaxed and jolly as she'd ever seen them.

But not Lachlan.

He stayed perched at the table with the same cool countenance she'd grown accustomed to seeing on the strong lines of his face.

Her eyes moved from him, searching amongst the serving women delivering ale and food for the landlady that had showed her to her room. If she could find the woman, she could inquire as to how she might procure some food.

No luck finding her in the dining room.

Evalyn leaned out further from her spot on the step, looking toward the back of the main room where a long, tall wooden counter denoted a bar. No landlady.

Shoes clunked on the treads of the stairs behind her until the sound ceased and a man cleared his throat. She glanced over her shoulder. A man and his female companion had stopped on the step above Evalyn. She rocked back onto her heels, pushing herself against the wall so they could pass.

The couple moved by her, not giving her a second glance. It was jarring—and oddly refreshing. She was accustomed to the stares of the staff at her stepfather's castle. The pitying glances. To have that couple pay her no more heed than a speck of dust was proof of how far she'd already traveled.

"Were you to just hover about the stairs all evening, Evalyn?"

Her chest jumped and her look whipped to Lachlan. He'd made it halfway across the room to her in the blink of an eye.

With a silver tankard of ale in his left hand, he stopped in front of her, his short brown hair mussed like he'd run his hand through it a hundred times, his jacket wrinkled and disheveled from the days on the road. Yet he stood with such inherent confidence that it was hard not to acknowledge him for the force he was.

She pushed herself from the wall. "I was not sure what to do in this situation. I have never been to a coaching inn before."

His brow furrowed. "Was your room not satisfactory?"

"Oh, yes—it's splendid. Very comfortable."

"So then?"

"I'm hungry." She hoped her voice didn't sound like the pathetic begging street urchin that she felt.

His lip pulled back on the right side, his cheek lifting. "Shall I have food sent up to your room?"

The landlady walked behind Lachlan in that instant, balancing a large tray of heaping dishes atop. Evalyn watched her over Lachlan's shoulder. The harried woman ran about the tables, juggling five plates on one arm. "I—I don't want to make a fuss. Can I not eat here in the dining room?"

"Women in establishments such as these are either married and they can eat in the main dining hall with their husbands; servants and they eat in the kitchens; or unmarried respectable travelers of the gentry or noble birth and they eat in their rooms unless they are looking to be ruined." Lachlan shrugged. "I placed you in the last category when I secured your room. Unmarried. Of noble family. So the correct answer is no."

Her fingers slipped along the railing, her palm gripping tight to the smooth wood. "But do those labels even apply to me any longer?"

He gave a slight nod. "The unmarried one still does. And just because you have plans to be a servant in my household, it does not negate the fact that you're still of noble birth."

"Yes, but does it matter?" Her lips drew inward for a moment and then she exhaled a long breath as she found his hazel eyes. "I know I'm ruined as far as society looks upon it, Lachlan. But that was the purpose of this. Escaping what I was. What I was going to be forced to be."

He glanced over his shoulder, his head twisting as he surveyed the room. He looked back to her. "Then join me at a table."

Lachlan walked across the dining room and Evalyn followed, weaving through the chairs until they reached a small table situated next to the wide fieldstone hearth that swallowed one wall of the large room. He pulled the chair closest to the roaring fire for her, she sat, and then he followed suit across from her, setting his tankard on the worn wood of the table.

A young barmaid was quick to their table, her pretty blue eyes hungry on Lachlan. "What ye be havin', sir?"

"The grouse is gone?"

She nodded.

"We'll both take the mutton pie and I'll need another fill." He lifted his near-to-empty silver tankard to the woman, then tilted his head toward Evalyn. "And the lady will have port."

The barmaid nodded, an indecent smile curling onto her lips as she looked Lachlan up and down. "Straight 'way, luv." She didn't bother with the slightest look toward Evalyn.

An exhale of relief escaped her. Not noticed again. She was actually starting to enjoy the anonymity. She watched the barmaid move away from the table, stopping, stooping over to flirt with men along the way, her fingers on their shoulders, a willing smile on her face as she angled her bare ample bosom to them. A brutal pang of jealousy sliced through Evalyn's chest.

That woman was free. Free to be a flirt. Free to eat wherever she chose to. Free to insinuate exactly what she wanted from her customers.

"You didn't need to carry the dress all day, Evalyn." Lachlan's deep voice snatched her attention forward.

Her brow furrowed. The backs of her upper arms still twinged with the weight of carrying the heavy wet dress all day. "But I did."

"There was room in the wagon for it."

She exhaled a quick sigh. "You said there was no room and I said I would carry it. So carry it I shall. It's no one's burden but my own."

Lachlan lifted his tankard and swallowed the last drops of his ale, his hazel eyes fixed on her. "You're a stubborn one. And you don't trust us—trust me not to leave it behind."

Her eyes grew wide. "I…I…I didn't say that."

He inclined his head to her, leaning back in his chair as he studied her. "But you thought it. It's a funny thing, that you trust us—me—enough to escape your stepfather.

But you don't trust me enough to not destroy the dress. I promised I would leave it be."

She met his scrutinizing gaze. "I've been promised things before, Lachlan."

"And?"

"And promises are made to be broken."

"I think you mistake the definition of a promise, Evalyn."

"I know exactly what a promise is, Lachlan. But I also know in practice a promise usually ends up as the exact opposite of the definition. Promises are cruelty. Promises are snares tossed to collect hope. To collect trust." Her fingernails curled into the rough wood of the table. "What I know is that it is one of the cruelest punishments to make one believe in a promise when it's never intended to be kept."

"You've never had someone keep a promise to you?"

"My stepfather was cruel with his promises, though not nearly as cruel as my mother was."

The barmaid arrived at the table, juggling two plates on one arm and the fresh tankard full of ale in her fingers along with the glass of port for Evalyn in her other. She set the drinks to the table and then unloaded her left arm quickly.

Evalyn stared at the thick crust of her pie, her stomach no longer rumbling, no longer the slightest bit hungry.

Lachlan waited until the barmaid took several steps away from the table before his hazel eyes pinned Evalyn. "What did your mother promise you?"

She looked up from her plate of food. "That she wouldn't die. She promised she wouldn't until her last breath."

He nodded, his hand moving to the fresh tankard. He tilted it back, taking a healthy swallow. It clunked as he set it back onto the table and his look didn't veer off of her. "How old were you?"

"Five."

"And you've been under your stepfather's care since then? Did she have no other family?"

Evalyn shook her head, her fingers going to her fork. She lifted it, jabbing the tines mindlessly into the crust of the pie.

Lachlan followed her lead, picking up his fork. He ate in silence, studying her with each bite he took, his gaze boring into her.

She didn't care for it. Didn't care for telling him anything of herself. The pity she was sure to see if she lifted her eyes to meet his.

But the silence of the table overshadowed the boisterous cacophony bouncing off the fieldstone walls of the dining room. So much silence it was hard to bear.

Evalyn forced what she hoped was a smile on her face and looked up as she lifted a bite of food to her mouth. Her gaze drifted to the window past Lachlan's head. Sheets of the angry rain that had started an hour ago assaulted the glass.

"How far are we from your estate?"

Lachlan took the second to last bite of his mutton pie, chewing slowly before answering. "Another three days if this rain doesn't muck up the roads too drastically. I had hoped to be home sooner."

"The horses looked like they needed a break." She took a bite of the pie, not able to taste it, though she forced the dry lump down her throat. "Why do you need to get to Vinehill so quickly?"

"There's a trial in Stirling I need to attend in five days." He set his fork down on his plate, leaving the last bite of pie. "I had hoped to be home well before it."

"A trial? Is it someone you know?" She looked down, attempting to cut a fatty piece of mutton with the side of her dull fork.

"It is someone I need to see swinging from the end of a rope." Lachlan pushed back from the table, standing as he grabbed his tankard of ale and moved away from the table.

Evalyn had barely blinked and he was gone.

Looking up from the mangled piece of stringy meat on her plate, she searched the room. He'd gone straight to the back of the large room, standing and leaning against the bar as he drank from the tankard in his hand, talking to the barmaid that had brought their food. The woman dipped forward, presumably to get something from behind the bar, but more likely to plump up the top swell of her chest. An offering to Lachlan if there ever was one.

She stared at his profile and she realized how handsome he was to not just her—to all members of the opposite sex. Until that moment, he was a key—the key to escaping her stepfather and Mr. Molson. A handsome key, yes, but most importantly, her deliverance.

But watching the barmaid offer herself up so willingly made Evalyn realize just how virile Lachlan was—his face, his body, the whole of him. How he held himself and talked to people, his hazel eyes intent on listening. Intent on understanding. Intent on learning every secret that people held dear.

He'd already pried from her more than enough secrets she held close to her heart.

Evalyn couldn't look away, waiting with held breath to see Lachlan's reaction to the creamy bared mounds angled enticingly toward him.

A shadow appeared in front of her.

Without asking, Domnall sat heavy into the chair Lachlan had vacated. "What did ye say to him, lass? Lachlan doesna storm away from women—they usually storm away from him."

Evalyn pulled her gaze away from the bar to eye Domnall. "Women walk away from him? I doubt that. I doubt women do anything but exactly what he asks of them."

Domnall chuckled, taking a swig of his ale. "'Tis usually the case, lass. But he doesna possess the charm like some of the men. Gets directly to the point with his propositions, that one." He pointed with a forefinger flicked out from his tankard toward Lachlan. "And it's earned him his fair share of goblets of fine sherry tossed in his face." His eyes twinkled as his look pinned her. "So did ye reverse the roles, lass? Did ye proposition him? Is that why he stormed away?"

She laughed. "No. Nothing of the sort, Domnall. I merely asked him why he has to get back to Vinehill so quickly."

"Ahh, the trial." Domnall nodded, leaning forward and setting his thick arms along the edge of the table as his voice lowered. "Aye. That would make him flee. The boy holds that one close to his chest."

"Boy? He's not more than ten years younger than you."

"And that makes him a boy." Domnall's mouth stretched wide in a grin. "I do it to rankle the lad. He hates that I'm older and wiser."

Evalyn chuckled and her look drifted to Lachlan. It looked like he had yet to take the bait of the breasts. Her gaze went back to Domnall. "Lachlan said the trial was for someone he wanted to see hung—what did the man do?"

She jabbed the piece of meat she'd cut away from the fat and plopped it into her mouth as she studied Domnall with hooded eyes. That he'd even come over to her table, offered up what appeared to be normal conversation was welcome, but suspicious.

Anything normal was suspicious. She knew that well.

Domnall picked up the fork on Lachlan's plate and ate the last bite of his pie. "He's one of the men that caused the fire that killed his older brother."

Her eyes went wide. "Lachlan has a brother—had a brother?"

"He did," Domnall said. "Jacob—he was a fine man, rest his soul."

"Was the fire at Vinehill?"

"No, not near it. Lachlan's sister, Sloane—ye met her at Wolfbridge Castle, I presume?"

Evalyn nodded.

"Her companion, Torrie—also a third cousin—had learned her family's home on Swallowford lands—a wee bit north of Vinehill lands—was being cleared. Sloane and Jacob went with her to stop it."

"Cleared? What does that mean?"

"It means atrocities in the wrong hands." Domnall's grip tightened around the fork and he jabbed it into the wood of the table. "It means all the farmers' cottages and lands are razed—the people forced out of their homes, their houses destroyed—so that some English bastards can set the land to pasture for their blasted sheep."

"The people are forced out? But why does no one stop them?"

"They can't. Not by any rights of the common man. Much of the land in Scotland was bought up after the glorious rebellion in forty-five. Clans were broken apart. Estates were sold. The tenant farmers had always rented the lands in a fair system. But now…" Domnall pushed back from the table and stretched against the back rung of his chair. His mouth had pulled back in a terse line, a growl in his words. "Now the English bastards that come to scavenge like vultures piss upon the fine, hardworking families. They find the sheep more valuable than the people."

Her brow furrowed, she nodded. "So Jacob, Sloane, and Torrie went to stop it?"

"Yes. Torrie's father was resisting, the family barred inside their cottage when Jacob, Sloane and Torrie arrived. Four brutes were outside of the cottage, some with torches already in hand. They'd already set flame to the rest of the buildings. Jacob convinced them to halt, at least until Torrie could go inside and convince her father to leave."

Evalyn's stomach dropped. "She got inside?"

"Torrie did. But then she took too long and one of the bastards tossed his torch on the roof. Sloane said he laughed when he did it. The other brutes were about to follow suit—but Jacob sent his sword through two of them." Domnall paused, his head shaking. "And Sloane ran into the cottage to get them out."

"What happened?"

Domnall shifted in his chair, looking across the room to Lachlan's back, then took a long swig of his ale before his gaze traveled back to Evalyn. "Part of the roof collapsed almost immediately, trapping the family and Sloane inside. Jacob went in after his sister. He and Sloane dragged Torrie out—her skirts were aflame and Sloane burned her arm putting out the fire. Jacob went back in for Torrie's mother, father and brother."

Evalyn drew a sharp intake of breath.

"Exactly." Domnall inclined his head back toward Lachlan. "Lachlan got to the cottage just as the rest of the roof caved in. He'd seen Jacob go into the building. He flew off his horse and killed one of the remaining brutes that was about to attack Sloane. The other blackguard there escaped, ran for a few days, but made the mistake of trying to travel through Vinehill lands. He was captured a few days after the fire. The magistrate captured him. If Lach had caught him, he'd have been dead three months ago."

"So he's the man on trial?"

"Aye. 'Tis an outrage. Torrie's kin were good folk." He shook his head. "And Jacob, he was heir. A leader from the day he was born. A loss that still stings." Domnall pointed to her plate. "Ye going to finish it, lass?"

"What?" Her head shook, and she followed the line of Domnall's outstretched finger to the half-eaten mutton pie on her plate. She pushed the platter across the table toward him. "No. It's yours, Domnall. I seem to have lost what little appetite I had."

# { CHAPTER 10 }

His horse's hooves sucking from the muck of the road with every step, Lachlan glanced over his shoulder to the wagon that trailed the line of men. If the infernal thing got stuck one more time today, he'd be of sound mind to ditch it and all the goods here on the roadside and stay at coaching inns the rest of the journey.

The wheels of the wagon were rolling fine, if slowly, and his gaze lifted up. Something was missing.

Someone was missing.

Evalyn had been a constant figure moving along behind the wagon since this journey north had started. But she was suddenly absent.

He'd asked her this morning if she'd prefer to ride on his horse with him, but she'd eyed him suspiciously and declined, clutching her mother's dress to her chest.

He looked to Domnall on his horse next to him in the front of the line. "Keep moving."

Domnall nodded and Lachlan tugged on his reins, turning his horse around and trotting back past his men to the wagon.

He stopped by Rupe walking and tugging on the reins of the draft horse that pulled the wagon. His eyes flickered to the back to the empty road. "Where is she?"

Rupe thumbed over his shoulder, not breaking his stride. He couldn't if he was going to keep the wheels from getting stuck in the mud. "Back over the crest of the last hill. She tripped and fell against the wagon—been doing that all morning."

A frown set upon Lachlan's face as he looked to the top of the last hill they'd just passed. He'd seen her do that hours ago, but thought she'd just slipped in the mud.

His gaze fell to Rupe. "It was more than once?"

"Aye."

"And you didn't stop to see what troubled her?"

"On the last tumble she called out that she was fine, she just needed to remove some rocks from her boots. Said she didn't want the wagon to get stuck again and that she'd catch up."

Lachlan nodded. "Keep moving."

"Don't plan on stopping," Rupe said, the sound of his boots sucking from the mud overriding the grumble in his voice.

Lachlan sent his horse back along the road. It was actually two rolling hills back before he found Evalyn.

She sat beneath an oak tree, her form crumpled forward, her attention on her feet. Her bare feet. Her boots were off, lying askew ten paces from her as though she had thrown them. To her left sat the damn dress in a crumpled mess on the ground.

Stubborn, stubborn woman.

She looked up to see him just before he pulled his horse to a halt.

As Lachlan dismounted, she ducked her head down and swiped at her cheeks with her left hand while her right set her skirts to hide her legs as she drew her feet inward, hiding them.

He tossed the reins of his horse over a low branch and walked to her, stopping in front of her with the toes of his boots touching her grey skirts.

She looked up at him.

Damn. Tears.

For as much as she managed to wipe away, tears shone bright in her eyes, drops on the verge of falling.

She forced a strained smile that barely lifted the corners of her mouth. "I told Rupe I would catch up. I was just about to start forth again. You didn't need to come back for me."

He bent over, lifting her skirt and grabbing her ankle.

"Stop." She kicked at him, trying to shove the edge of her skirt over her foot. "Lachlan, stop."

He didn't release her ankle, pulling it toward him.

She shoved his arm with both hands. Weak, at best.

"Stop, Lachlan, please stop."

He looked up, his iron gaze skewering her. She stilled.

Silently, he looked down and dragged her left foot free from the folds of the skirt.

She still put up resistance, her leg pulling against him, but not enough to stop him.

Her foot cleared the fabric.

*Bloody hell.*

He dropped to his knees. His right hand holding her left leg in place, he searched with his free hand under her skirt until he found her right ankle and pulled that foot into daylight as well.

"Dammit, Evalyn."

Her feet were chewed up. Bloody from festering blisters that surrounded the tender skin of her heels. Bloody from blisters that ran along the sides of her feet and gnarled the tips of her toes. So red and pus filled, he could barely make out where her skin had remained solid under the swelling.

"The devil take it. Why didn't you tell me this had happened? Why didn't you tell me they were too small?"

She tried to swat his hands away from her feet, still trying to pull them back into the confines of her skirts. "I didn't know this was happening except for the pain. You had been so kind in procuring the boots and it need not be your concern."

"Not my concern? How can you bloody well walk on these things?"

"I thought it would be fine today. I soaked them last night at the inn, but to no avail. It seems to have only made the sores worse. It was hard to get my feet into the boots this morning."

He stared at the bloody mess, twisting her feet back and forth, trying to convince himself it wasn't as bad as it looked. He'd had blisters like this once, riding along his heel, and he knew full well that it hurt like the devil scratching pins into one's skin.

He twisted her left foot and his finger slipped across her heel.

"Ouch." She yanked her foot away, his fingers tearing at the skin on the way.

Her face crumpled, her breath coming fast and hard and she fought the pain.

"Evalyn—"

Her hand flew up, pushing at him as she tried to yank her right foot away, a scream at her lips. "Stop. Don't touch me. Please just stop, Lachlan. Please stop."

His jaw dropping, he released her foot. The force with which she didn't want him to touch her was palpable.

He rocked back on his heels, staring at the auburn sweep of her hair atop of her downturned head. He steeled his voice to calm. "What do you propose to do, Evalyn?"

Her head tilted slightly up, her gold-green eyes shooting venom at him. "I propose you let me be, Lachlan."

"Let you be? Leave you in a quivering mess on the side of the road?"

"Yes." Her look shifted to her boots on the ground. "I will force my feet back into those torturous leather prisons and I will catch up with the party. I swear it." Her look centered on him. "Just leave me be."

*Stubborn woman.*

He met her gaze, his own look immovable for a long moment. She wasn't going to let him help. Not without some incentive.

Lachlan stood and went to her dress, picking it up and refolding it into a tight bundle that he tucked into his arm. He veered to pick up her boots, setting them atop the dress.

"Lachlan, what are you doing?"

Ignoring her, he went to his horse, setting the gown and boots behind the saddle and securing them with a leather strap.

"Lachlan, no." Her hands supporting her, walking up the trunk of the tree, she tried to get to her feet. "No, I said—" She gasped, wincing hard as her feet took the full weight of her body when she tried to step away from the tree.

She fell back against the trunk, starting to slip down the bark.

Three long steps and he was back to her, catching her along her waist before she sank to the ground.

"Is that enough for you?"

She looked up at him, squirming in his arms even as pain sent her brow into wretched folds. "Enough what?"

"Enough pain so you will accept my help?"

He loosened his hold, setting her back on her feet.

She winced, her eyes squeezing tight. She nodded.

He wanted more from her, more acknowledgment, but he didn't want to make her admit to it again—he didn't want to have to set her on her feet and cause her even more pain. Bending, he slipped an arm under the back of her legs and picked her up, carrying her to his horse.

He set her sideways atop the back of his horse in front of his saddle, then grabbed the reins and mounted it. "You can sit there, but it will be uncomfortable, or you can spread your legs and sit in front of me on the saddle. It'll be more comfortable and you've done it once with me, but that was out of necessity. This may be an affront to your sensibilities."

"I don't think I have many of my sensibilities left."

He shifted slightly back on the seat of the saddle. "Then swing your leg over and shift back here. You're so slight it won't be much of a squeeze."

Awkwardly, she lifted her leg to straddle the horse. She started to scoot back but ran into the pommel. He wrapped an arm around her and lifted her, setting her securely in front of him.

Her back went incredibly stiff against his chest, the tips of her shoulder blades digging into his lower chest. She didn't know what to do with her hands, they went to the curve of the leather pommel, then to her belly, then to clutch the cloak along her chest, then back to the pommel.

She found this awkward and not at all proper.

A smile found its way to his lips. Her reaction was oddly comforting.

Comforting until they started to move.

The sway of his horse, the extra effort it took his steed to suck each hoof out of the muck of the road, sent her backside rubbing against him in a way he wasn't prepared for.

His arms about her sides clenched.

She riled his body—and why shouldn't she? She was beautiful—he'd seen that since the first. Hell, his first instinct in that garden sent him to kissing her. Beautiful, but a mouse. A mouse trying to escape a teeth-gnashing terrier.

Except she wasn't a mouse.

He knew she wasn't. And every step she'd taken from Wolfbridge Castle had set her shoulders higher, her voice more confident.

Proud. Stubborn. Every step had taken her further from the mouse he'd agreed to take to Scotland and closer to the type of women he was accustomed to. Women that held no reserve. Women that spoke their minds. Women that carried their own weight.

He'd witnessed the transformation in Evalyn, even if she didn't realize what she'd become.

And if he couldn't get his thoughts under control, she was about to grow even more awkwardly uncomfortable when she realized what this rock in his trousers was that jutted into her delicious backside.

Lachlan looked around, searching for something, anything to take his mind off the maddening scent of her auburn hair just below his nose. It smelled of tangerines. How, after days traveling on the roads, her hair still smelled like citrus, he'd like to know.

His gaze studied the mostly empty oak trees that lined the west side of the road. A few leaves held to the branches, but not many. Cold was quick to the land this year.

He glanced down and caught sight of her left toes peeking out from under the hem of her skirt. He stifled a sigh. Now her feet would not only be bloody, but cold as well. He should have taken more care in what size those boots were.

His horse stumbled a step in the mud and his arms clasped tight around her. For one fleeting moment, he liked the feel of her secure in his arms, the length of her body pressing into his—oddly right.

Quite the opposite, Evalyn stiffened to steel-like consistency.

Her breath quickened and her head started to dart about.

It took him several seconds to realize what had happened. She was trapped.

He shifted the reins into his left hand and removed his right arm from her body, settling his hand on his knee. In position to catch her should his horse stumble again, but giving her a clear path of escape.

It only took a moment for her breathing to slow and for her shoulders to relax.

Lachlan stared down at the crown of her head. He didn't even think she was aware of how her body had just reacted.

They reached the trail of his men and Lachlan sent his horse to the front of the line, setting his stallion into step with Domnall.

Domnall gave one appraising glance at the two of them, his weathered eyes pausing for a long moment on Evalyn's bloody foot hanging past her skirt. He looked to Evalyn. "That can't be comfortable, lass. Why did ye not speak up?"

She shook her head. "I told Lachlan it was fine. I was just about to pull my boots back on when Lachlan arrived to gather me. And gather me he did."

"Those dinnae look fine, lass."

"Bearable, then. It was bearable," she said.

"Those dinnae look bearable, lass."

Lachlan cleared his throat. "You have a better saddle for two, Domnall. Would you mind taking her on your horse? She could ride behind you." He looked down at her head. "I think that is what she would prefer—yes, Evalyn?"

She glanced up at him, her eyes slightly squinting as she nodded.

Domnall's look lifted to Lachlan, his left eyebrow lifting and curiosity ablaze in his clear blue eyes. "Aye. There be ample room on my saddle." He moved forward and patted the leather behind him, a grin on his face. "Just as ye dinnae mind being downwind of the stench this travel has put on me ole bones."

Evalyn chuckled. "I fear it is nothing compared to the stench of my own body."

"Then hop over, lass."

They stopped their horses and Lachlan grabbed her about the waist, lifting her as she threaded her right leg behind Domnall.

Safely in place, her skirts arranged to hang over her legs the best they could and her fingers lightly clutching the sides of Domnall's overcoat, and Lachlan set his horse forth once more.

Not even four strides of his horse and he could breathe freely again. He hadn't been prepared for his body to react to her like it did.

Loss of control. Loss of his center.

For those few minutes that she was trapped against his body, he had been unmoored, the sensation of her muscles alongside his stirring not only his loins, but also something in his gut.

Something he'd been ignoring for days.

Mistress. He had to remember his original plan for her. She would work in his kitchens. Become his mistress, if she was amicable to the thought.

That would flush the feel of her from his blood. He could have her and then be done with her. And though he wished her no harm personally, taking her as his mistress would still carry the weight of revenge against her stepfather.

His tongue curled against the roof of his mouth. The thought didn't sit as well with him as it had days ago when it was the sole purpose for allowing her on this journey.

Lachlan could feel the curious stares from his men behind him. Curious stares that he'd have to answer to eventually. They all hated Lord Falsted the same as he did.

Five minutes passed with Domnall peppering Evalyn about her blisters—how many she'd counted, which ones had burst open, the ratio of pus to blood.

The man loved to talk about blood and pus.

He'd just tuned out Domnall's jabbering when the blasted man chuckled to himself.

"Lach tell ye 'bout his betrothed?" The note of mirth in Domnall's words cut through the rampant thoughts flying about in Lachlan's mind.

His gaze whipped to Domnall, his glare shooting arrows at his friend.

"Betrothed?" Evalyn looked to Lachlan, a smile frozen on her face.

"I'm to marry in a month." Lachlan's gaze didn't shift from Domnall. The ass was smirking.

"She's a beautiful one, that lass," Domnall said.

Lachlan exhaled a long sigh. "Yes, and as vapid as they come."

"Vapid?" Evalyn's eyebrows drew together.

"The girl can't hold two thoughts in her head at once."

Domnall scoffed. "Says the man that hasn't said more than four words to her."

Evalyn looked up to Domnall and then back to Lachlan. "Then why are you marrying her?"

"His grandfather, the marquess, deemed it so." Domnall spoke up before Lachlan could answer. "And don't listen to Lach on this one. Karta is a bonny lass from MacDougall lands. Fine Scottish bloodlines in her. And we need the union so we can expand our sheep stock."

An odd smile breached her lips. "So you are to marry for sheep?"

Lachlan sighed, rubbing his hand across his eyes. He flung one more death glare at Domnall before looking to Evalyn. "Much of the lands surrounding ours have been cleared away for grazing, and herders have been brought in from England to tend to the sheep flocks. It is where the funds to support the lands and the people currently are. Tenant farming is not enough to suffice any longer."

Her look shifted to Domnall. "These are the clearings you were telling me about?"

"You told her about the Swallowford lands?" Lachlan's words cut through the air.

Domnall met his look and then shrugged.

Lachlan's look shifted to Evalyn. "Yes. The clearings. Some lands, like the ones north of ours, have been bought up by Englishmen and the farmers have been removed from their homes—entire glens hacked to barren wastelands."

Her gold-green eyes softened. "Domnall said it has been harsh."

"Yes. Cruel in some instances." The muscles along his neck, across his jaw tightened into hard spasms. He had to take a breath to relax enough to continue. "But on Vinehill lands, we're bringing the sheep and retraining our farmers into the trade so they can stay in place. We're building factories for the processing of the wool. New roads for trade."

Evalyn nodded. "So you need her family's sheep?"

"We do. They have the finest sheep—Cheviot—in the land. If we can cross breed with their herds, improving our stock, the value of our flocks grows considerably. And the roads we are building lead to theirs and they can cut us off from the closest ports if they choose to. They also have investment funds for shared mills. A new one was to be built in the new year."

"I understand." A bright smile flashed across her face, though it didn't reach her eyes. "That does make proper sense. It sounds like it will be a fruitful partnership for both families."

"That is the thought behind it," Lachlan said, unable to stifle the sigh that had welled in his chest. "Believe me, I've heard my grandfather laud the many ways it will behoove us."

"But you are not happy with the match?"

He shrugged, looking ahead. "It was never supposed to be my responsibility to marry her."

"No?" Her head tilted to the side. "Who—oh, your brother."

His look snapped to her. "What do you know of my brother?"

"I...I..." Her eyes flickered to Domnall. Quick—so quick he almost missed it.

But he saw it.

"Bugger it, Domnall, can't you keep your yapping trap shut, for devil's sake?"

"It's no secret, Lach, what happened to yer brother." Domnall flicked his hand in the air. "The lass was due to find out soon enough."

Lachlan's lip sneered, his head shaking as he set his heels into his horse's flanks. It sent him several strides in front of Domnall and Evalyn.

Exactly where he wanted to be.

Exactly where he needed to be.

# { CHAPTER 11 }

"You didn't need to tell her every blasted last thing about me, Domnall."

Lachlan shifted the reins in his hands as his horse stepped in place, but he didn't bother to glance to his left where Domnall had sidled up to him, alone on his steed. He must have left Evalyn in camp.

The air clear and unusually cloudless, Lachlan kept his eyes forward, looking out from the ridge they were perched on to the rolling land unfurling before them for as far as the eye could see. Another day and they'd be past the Scottish border.

Domnall set his sights on the same vista, shifting his body on his saddle as he settled his left hand on his thigh. "We all lost Jacob, Lach. His death isn't yers to own the suffering."

That, Lachlan couldn't deny. His brother had been the beacon that was going to lead the people, the Vinehill estate into the future. Vibrations of Jacob's death still took the ground out from so many of the men and women of Vinehill lands.

"Aye." He glared at Domnall out the corner of his eye. "But to tell her? You know who Evalyn is—who her stepfather is. Her of all people?"

A low chuckle fell from Domnall's lips. "Ye still attempting to be hostile to the lass, Lach?"

"Shouldn't we all be?"

"Ye tell me." Domnall lifted his forefinger from his thigh and pointed it at Lachlan. "Ye were the one that picked her up when she trailed."

"I'm not an ogre, Domnall." Lachlan's hand gripping his reins curled into a fist. "You'd have done the same after seeing her feet."

"Aye. But I also would have owned the reason as to why I picked her up to help her."

Lachlan twisted in his saddle, turning fully to Domnall. "Exactly what are you insinuating?"

Domnall shrugged. "Why'd ye want her to ride with me, Lach?"

"You saw how uncomfortable she was, did you not? She felt trapped with me. Aside from Rupe, she's talked to you more than anyone in the camp so I thought her more comfortable with you."

"I see." Domnall nodded slowly, disbelief evident in the squint of his eyes. "Ye be concerned on her comfort now, do ye? And it widnae have anything to do with the fact that ye couldn't take her body next to yers?"

Lachlan scoffed. "No."

Domnall's eyebrow cocked. "Yer trousers told a different tale when she moved away from ye and onto my horse."

"I don't know what you saw, Domnall, but you'd be wise to keep your hallucinations to yourself, lest we think you've gone mad."

"Bugger it, Lach—ye think to talk out of an ass's arse to me?"

Lachlan's left hand flew up, palm to the sky. "What do you want me to say, Dom? Yes, her body was far too close to mine. Yes, I reacted in spite of myself. Do you know how long it's been since I've had a woman? Far, far too long. That is all that was. All you saw."

Domnall's wide frame lifted in a heavy sigh. "If ye say it's so, it's so." He nodded, looking out to the rolling hills.

For long seconds, neither man moved, their focus on the distant land.

"Ye ken she don't belong in either world, Lach?"

Lachlan's gaze lifted to the branches of the trees above, then dropped to Domnall.

His friend's focus stayed on the horizon. "She cannot go back to her kin. Yet she does not belong in the kitchens neither." He looked at Lachlan. "Mrs. Fitzsimmons widnae let the lass in her domain for more than a day. And I don't rightly ken if she'll take to being yer mistress."

Lachlan's hand that had momentarily relaxed clutched back onto his reins. "What do you know of it?"

"I seen how ye look at her, Lach. I saw what I saw today. Ye been planning on bedding her since we left Wolfbridge."

"So what of it?"

"A lass like that." Domnall's head shook. "T'would be sacrilege to let her fall for that course."

"What are you telling me, Dom?"

"I'm just speaking the facts. She's already ruined in the eyes of her kind. Leaving with us, the nights on the road did that."

"So?"

"So from here on, she'll be the one that suffers whatever happens next. Not her demon of a stepfather."

"And?"

Domnall's gaze shifted to his horse's brown mane, then out to the landscape. "I'm telling ye that the men are already lining up to marry the lass, Lach."

Lachlan's head jerked back. "What?"

Domnall pinned him with assessing eyes. "Ye heard me."

"Dom—"

"But her best chance is ye, Lach."

"What bones are rattling about in your skull now, old man?"

"Her bones, cracked and broken if she doesna marry soon. Ye think a man like her father is going to let her just disappear?" Domnall shifted in his saddle, turning more fully to Lachlan. "No. A man like that sees the lass as his property. And I can guarantee that demon's not the sort that lets his property be taken from him. It won't be long 'fore he puts together who she ran off with and he'll be coming after her. He could already be on his way."

Lachlan nodded, taking Domnall's assessment seriously. He'd had the exact same thought of Evalyn's safety too many times over the last week.

But to marry her off?

The notion of it struck him, slicing through his chest with the precision of a Spanish Toledan steel rapier.

He tamped down the clenching of his gut and cleared his throat. "Any of the men would make Evalyn a fine husband."

"Ye truly mean that?" Domnall leaned forward, setting himself in front of Lachlan's gaze. "Ye can stand by and watch another man bed the lass? That be the real question, Lach."

Lachlan's head instantly started shaking, the thought of her naked under one of his men stinging even deeper. "I...I..."

Lachlan's stuttered words of denial stopped, his head stilling.

How would it be to watch Evalyn walk off arm in arm with another man? To stand by as another man stripped off that impossibly long row of buttons along her spine?

Domnall snorted. "Yer lack of words tells volumes, Lach." He looked out to the hills before them. "It sounds to my ear like ye'd best decide sooner rather than later what ye mean to do with the lass."

"Your ear is made of tin, old man."

Domnall smirked. "Not so old she wouldn't make me a proper wife, as well."

"You?"

He shrugged. "I'd put my hand in line, were she partial to it. She's a bonny lass, strong for her thin bones, and the fire she gets in her eyes when we needle her would be particularly suited to the marital bed."

Lachlan's teeth clamped down, his molars grinding.

Damn that Domnall would make her a fine husband. Better than any other of the lot.

Better than him.

Domnall rubbed the long whiskers, some white, some brown, along his chin. "Above all that, yer grandfather won't take kindly to Baron Falsted's daughter on his land."

"Stepdaughter."

"Ye think that'll make a difference to the marquess?"

Lachlan's look drifted from his friend and he shook his head. It was what he'd had planned, to leave her to the mercy of Vinehill—the very little mercy his grandfather possessed.

A plan that now needed to change.

He glanced at Domnall's profile. His friend would make her a fine husband.

Hell. *Any* one of his men would make her a better husband than he would.

But he already knew he wasn't going to allow any of them the opportunity.

~ ~ ~

Her skirt lifted high, Evalyn bit into the edge of the fabric and then tore another strip off of the bottom of her chemise. The motion shifted her feet in the shallow pool at the edge of the brook she sat next to, sending sharp pangs of torture from her heels up her legs.

Her head bowed as she caught air into her lungs and her look steadied on the tiny smooth pebbles along the tips of her toes. She let the pain wash over her for a long breath. Letting it come and go was far easier than fighting it.

"Does it help—the cold water on your feet?"

Her head snapped up and she twisted on the boulder she sat upon to find Lachlan standing behind her.

She hadn't heard him approach. After helping her down to the brook, Domnall had said she would have privacy so her guard hadn't been up.

She turned back to the bubbling water and shoved the skirt of her dark wool dress down over her shift. "It does. At least the coolness of it does, though I thought that as well last night when I soaked them. If anything, at least the blood has been washed away."

"Don't stop what you're doing on my account." He flicked a finger at the bottom hem of her skirt and stepped forward, his black boots crunching along the pebbles that lined the water's edge. Stopping next to her, he settled his hands on the hilt of his sword as he looked down at her. "What were you doing?"

"I was ripping strips from my chemise." She picked up the pile of already torn linen and held it up to him. "They're to wrap around my feet. I'm hoping I can at least hobble along with these swaddling my skin."

"The roads will shred the fabric within fifty feet."

"No, Domnall cut out the toes and heels of my boots." She leaned over to pick up one of her mangled boots and lifted it to him. "And I can loosen the laces so there is space for the wrappings and my feet will still be protected at the top and bottom."

Lachlan took the boot from her, turning it around in his fingers as he studied Domnall's craftiness with his blade.

His mouth went to a terse line, his brow furrowing. "Most enterprising of him."

She blinked at the harsh cut of his voice. "I'm sorry, is there something I don't understand that is amiss? Should I not have accepted his help?"

"No—no." Lachlan shook his head slightly and the annoyance on his face disappeared. "It's good that he was helping you. These and the strips you are to wrap your feet with should work until we can procure new, properly fitting boots for you."

He handed the boot down to her. "But you do understand that no one is going to make you walk from here on?"

She shrugged. "I didn't know, so I wanted to be prepared. I would at least like to be able to hobble down to the water's edge and stand enough to help Rupe with the meals."

Lachlan pulled his dirk from his waist and dropped to balance on his heels. "Can I help?"

Her look fixed on the blade only inches from her and she had to force herself not react, not to scramble away from him. "Help?"

"With the strips." He motioned to her skirts and the chemise she hid away. "It looks like you'll need at least five or six more and it'll go faster with a blade."

"Oh." She had to override her instant alarm and ignore the sudden adrenaline coursing through her veins. "Then yes. Yes, that would be helpful."

She lifted the gray wool skirt and tugged out the now ragged bottom edge of her chemise. Her legs were bared to him, but there would be no helping that. Of course, he'd seen far too much of her bare skin when he'd stripped off her wet dress in the tent. Any propriety she attempted to feign had been lost days ago.

He set to work, quickly slicing the fabric into long even strips, much more even than what she was able to accomplish by tearing at the fabric. His work went further and further up her legs, over her knees to her thighs, but in a small kindness, he managed to keep his fingers from brushing her.

When the pile of the strips appeared sufficient, he set his dagger back in the sheath at his waist and moved to sit on a boulder next to the one she sat on.

He glanced down at her feet soaking in the water. "Your feet do look better without the blood smeared all about them. Are they already healing?"

Evalyn looked down at her toes, lifting her foot to inspect her heels. "I hope. The blisters that were still holding pus don't look quite as angry as they did earlier."

She glanced up to catch a half-smile lifting his left cheek. It brought a slight crinkle to his eyes, enough spark to catch her gaze on his irises as he looked at her feet. She'd noted them before, his hazel eyes, but she'd never really studied them, separated out the streaks of blue and brown, along with the random flecks of green that made a kaleidoscope of color. She stared at the variations, trying to trace them, transfixed.

Transfixed for far too long.

His gaze lifted from her feet and she started, caught in her stare. A flush traveled into her cheeks and she turned her head, searching for something—anything—to move her past the awkwardness.

The cloth.

Even though her feet felt so much better submerged in the coolness of the brook, she picked up a strip of the cloth and pulled her left foot from the water.

She crossed her left leg atop her right so she could hold her toes in midair, swirling them slowly to dry before she started wrapping.

He cleared his throat. "We are to cross into Scottish lands on the morrow."

"How much farther is Vinehill beyond that?"

"Another day."

She nodded, her look drifting away from her foot to settle on an eddy across the rippling surface of the water. She'd finally learned how to navigate this small crew of men and now it would be ripped away from her, a whole new life to navigate in Lachlan's household. If she'd been more successful in making herself useful with these men instead of a constant burden, perhaps she'd walk into Vinehill with a modicum of confidence.

As it was, she feared a lion's den where she was set to be the hunk of meat.

"That makes you nervous?" Lachlan asked.

She looked to him, her head bobbing in a slow nod. "How did you know that?"

He pointed to her hands.

She had just twisted the strip of cloth in her fingers into a mangled mess.

Her knuckles fell to her lap, her fingers loosening on the cloth. "Yes, I am nervous." She forced a strained smile. "But I was nervous leaving with your party as well. So I will work through it again, just as before. I asked for this, and I mean to see it through."

His eyes narrowed slightly at her and for a long breath, his hazel eyes bored into her, appraising her.

"Here." Lachlan motioned toward her foot. "It'll be easier if I wrap it."

"You?" Her eyebrows drew together. He wanted to help wrap her feet?

"Yes, me." He picked up several strips of cloth that sat on the ground between them and then motioned with his fingers to her leg. "Give me your foot."

Her mouth slightly agape, she stayed frozen in place.

He shook his head, a crooked smile curving his lips, and he leaned forward to grab her ankle. Pulling it toward him, he settled her heel gently into the cradle of his knees.

After snapping one of the strips in the air to straighten it, he set the end of it under her big toe and wrapped it slowly and evenly about her foot, each overlapping row moving downward toward her heel.

"I have a proposal for you, Evalyn." His focus stayed on her toes, his large fingers managing to be the softest whisper against her raw skin as they wrapped her foot. "Something that will ease the transition to Vinehill."

"Yes?" Relief filled her chest—she knew enough to accept any and all help he advised.

"Marry me."

"What?" She jerked her foot away from him.

Any help except that.

His fingers still clutched the strip of cloth and his grip on it made the cloth tighten around her skin, strangling her foot as she yanked her heel from his lap.

"Ouch."

He dropped the edge of the cloth and snatched her ankle in midair, pulling it back toward him.

Shaking his head, he glared at her. "I'll need to redo this one." His concentration went downward and his fingers were quick to unfurl the cloth from her foot and start the whole process again. "And you need to stay still."

Once he had her foot half wrapped again, he glanced up, his eyes searching her face for a long second. His left hand moved to wrap around her ankle, locking it into place. "I think you heard me correctly before, Evalyn. I am proposing marriage."

Her foot involuntarily attempted to jerk from him again, but his clamp on her ankle kept her foot securely on his lap. "M—marriage? To me? But—but no. No. You're betrothed to another. You need to marry that Karta woman."

Her hands went to her left leg and she gripped her thigh, trying to pull her leg free from his clasp. No success. His grip on her was unbreakable.

"I am betrothed, yes. But that can be broken."

"No, Lachlan, no. You need do no such thing on my account. You need to marry her for your lands. For your grandfather. For the future. Domnall made that very clear."

"Domnall likes to pontificate upon subjects he should generally avoid."

"He sounded quite certain of himself."

"Of course he did. But what Dom likes to speak of has little influence over what I actually choose to do."

"Oh."

His eyebrow lifted. "Does that mean the matter is settled?"

"Settled?" Her head snapped back. "As in I agree to marry you?"

He nodded.

"No—no, it means nothing of the sort. You don't want to marry me, Lachlan, I am very sure of the fact."

"Now you think to pontificate on matters you know nothing about?"

"I know I would make you a terrible wife."

"You do?" His bottom lip jutted up and his head tilted to the side, considering her words. "Interesting. Do tell me how."

"Well, for starters, I'm English. That will not sit well with your household, an English mistress."

"Not ideal, but my household will grow accustomed to you, English or not." He looked down to her foot, releasing his grip on her ankle and grabbing a new strip to continue the wrapping. "What else?" he asked without looking up.

"Well, I only speak one other language—French, my knowledge of running a household is quite limited, and I am only marginal at sewing."

He didn't give her so much as a glance. "All things I couldn't care less about. What else?"

She searched around her, her look frantic on the trees and brook for something—anything to dissuade him from the mad thought he'd latched onto. She caught her blurred reflection in the water.

Her gaze whipped to him. "You—you haven't seen the scar along my face. I am not what you think I am."

"Beautiful?"

"I—a—no." Her fingers twisted together, a heated flush invading her neck.

His fingers paused and he looked up at her, his hazel eyes serious. "Has no one ever told you that you are a beauty, Evalyn?"

She shook her head. "No. Save for my mother, but I was five. And she didn't know that this"—she pointed at the hair carefully covering her right temple—"would befall me. I will never be beautiful."

He straightened slightly, his gaze pinning her as his fingers rested lightly on top of her ankle. "Then let me see it."

"You want to see the scar?"

Her throat collapsed on her. No one—no one ever saw her scar. She made sure of it. That her hair had fallen away from it the other night at the campfire had been a gross oversight on her part. But at least that had been in the darkness with only the campfire—not in the brutal light of day.

She eyed him. Why would he want to see the hideous scar?

A trap.

This had to be a trap of some wild machination. Wanting to see her scar. The suggestion of marriage.

And he held her foot hostage, no matter how lightly his hand on her ankle sat. His fingers only needed to slip down and he'd have her locked in place.

But a trap to what end?

She glanced over her shoulder, looking for help, looking for escape.

"Evalyn?"

Her head swiveled back to him.

His eyebrows lifted.

Trapped.

And there was only one way to get her foot back and flee.

She sighed, then brought her fingers up to her hair and lifted away the smoothed locks from her right temple. She set her stare on the gnarled, bared roots of the tree behind him as she tilted her head slightly toward him, letting him have full view of the scar that marred her face.

It was hideous.

She knew it.

She'd studied the scar for far too long. Too many hours to count. How the flesh had twisted as it healed, not put back together by neat stitches, but by white, tough flesh building upon white, tough flesh until she was whole again.

"There is much pain that exists there." He moved, lifting a finger to reach out and touch the scar that curled around her temple into the spot where her hair no longer grew.

She snapped backward on the boulder, sending her heel scraping against his trousers. Instant pain she had to swallow. "Please, no." Her hand dropped from her head, her hair falling back into place.

Scooting forward on the rock, she tried to ease his pull on her foot. Her bottom lip jutted up even as she attempted a smile, her eyes meeting his. "So now you know how ruined I am, in more ways than one. I thank you for your offer, Lachlan. It was very kind of you."

"The offer still stands, Evalyn."

"I—it does? But I…but my—" Her hand swept up to press against her temple through her hair.

He didn't flinch. "You're no less beautiful now than you were a moment ago."

"But…but…" Her words trailed, her tongue tangling against the roof of her mouth.

This had to be a trick. It had to be. And Lachlan was not giving up his game.

His head slanted to the side as he stared at her. "Why are you truly refusing me?"

"I...I'm not refusing you."

"You're concocting reasons for me to change my mind, then. It is the same as a refusal from your lips."

He knew the answer. She could see it. But he was going to make her say it. Make her speak it.

She exhaled, long and hard. "You're trapping me and I don't know why—what pain is ahead."

His chin tilted downward in a single nod. Without lifting his head, his hazel eyes pinned her. "What if I swear to you that if you ever feel trapped—ever feel that you need to escape the life that I offer you—Domnall will take you to the Vinehill dower house on the Isle of Bute."

"A dower house?"

"Yes. No one lives there except for a few staff that maintain it. It would be a simple life and no one would bother you. Me included." His head tilted, his words pointed. "Far from everything. Hidden."

Her mind racing, she flipped the thought over and over again in her head.

Escape. An escape if she should ever need it.

Her eyes narrowed at him. "Can Domnall swear it to me as well?"

"I can bring him over here directly to swear to it, if it will ease your mind."

Evalyn half nodded, half shook her head. She wasn't sure which inclination was winning over the other, for promises held such little weight in her world.

Except she wasn't in her world anymore.

She was in Lachlan's.

"I don't think I can accept promises, Lachlan."

The edges of his lips pulled down as his look narrowed at her. "If I'm never afforded the chance to prove the value of my promises, how will you ever know for certain if I'm worthy of them?" He leaned forward, his fingers along her ankle slipping under her leg, pressing into her bare calf. "I just may be the one person that you need to trust, Eva."

"Or the one I never should."

A light sparked in his eye. A gleam of triumph, possibly. Or hope. Or lust.

"Aye. But how will you ever find out if you do not chance it?"

# { CHAPTER 12 }

Lachlan followed the coaching inn maid that had brought up a wide platter of food across their room to the door. She exited and he clicked the heavy wooden door closed.

He paused for a moment, staring at the long grain lines of the oak door. It was late and he needed to be moving this along. It had already taken far too long to cross the border and travel to Moffat that day, and they'd had to squeeze in the blacksmith wedding once on Scottish soil.

It had been perfunctory. Their hands joined over the anvil. Horace, the blacksmith, performing the ceremony with as few words as possible. Domnall was the only one to dismount and come in to witness the vows.

Not that Evalyn appeared to mind. If anything, her look kept twitching to him, almost as though she were expecting him to pull away at the last second. Bracing herself to be abandoned at the smithy. Set adrift on her own.

The dumbstruck look on her face when they left the heat of the blacksmith's fires and stepped into the waning light was laughable.

Laughable, if she hadn't been so positive that this whole affair was a cruel joke on her.

His gut tightened. That her blackguard of a stepfather had put such distrust in her eyes—in her every motion—set aflame a primal rage in his belly that took him aback.

It no longer mattered that she was related to the man, she'd suffered for years as the prime victim of the man's cruelty.

His look still centered on the back of the door, he debated for another moment. Food or maidenhead first?

Lachlan turned away from the door only to find his answer.

Her back toward him, Evalyn was already by the bed, the scraps of her boots absent, though the bandages still wrapped her feet. Her arms awkwardly bent to reach her upper spine, her fingers freeing the top buttons of her dress.

Sex it was, then.

He squinted in the low light that the fireplace afforded the room. Her fingers were shaking, slipping on the buttons as she popped them free. Straining, her elbow high, she could reach no more buttons.

She glanced over her shoulder at him, her look quickly scurrying to the corner by the fireplace. "If you would be so kind?"

He stepped across the room, stopping behind her. His hands lifted to the row of black buttons, popping them free, one by one, watching her profile, trying to figure her. Of all things, he hadn't guessed she would be so willing to beguile him into the marital bed.

"Are you not hungry, Evalyn?"

She looked to the table, then shook her head. "Not particularly—not at the moment."

"Are you tired?"

"No."

His mouth tugged to the side as he stared at the twisted knot pulling the brown-red strands of her hair into an upsweep. "Do your feet pain you?"

"No more so than an hour ago."

The last button popped free under his fingers and she immediately tugged the dress forward and off her arms, letting it drop to a puddle by her legs.

Her chin dropped slightly toward her chest. "My stays, if you would unknot them as well, it would be most helpful." Her voice even, it belied none of the shaking that had been in her fingers.

He made quick work of the laces and, without preamble, she let her stays and chemise slip to the floor.

Without glancing back at him, she crawled onto the tester bed sideways, flipping to lie down on the deep blue coverlet. Unpinned, her auburn hair fell haphazard about her shoulders and she settled her arms close and straight to her naked torso, then looked to him, a strained smile on her lips as she gave a slight nod. "I am ready." Her look left him, fixing on the carved mahogany panel above.

His head cocked to the side.

No kisses? No words of seduction? No tantalizing build?

Just her open nude body on the bed.

How very odd. And efficient.

His eyes settled on her breasts. Perfect mounds of sweet white skin, nipples already taut and pointed in the chill of the air. His cock jumped alive.

She was exquisite, the scars and bruises merely existing to make the goddess human.

Lachlan shrugged to himself. One more thing left to do and he may as well get to it with haste. They had to leave early in the morning if they were to make it to Vinehill before nightfall tomorrow.

He stripped his clothes off, then moved to her, setting his right knee on the bed.

She was a virgin, as expected. He could tell by the way her body tensed as he settled over her on the bed—the way her eyes stayed open, but locked onto some miniscule point in the wood above them, far, far away from his head.

His hand went down, sliding to her inner thigh and separating her legs. He moved into place, hovering over her. "You said you were ready for this, but are you, Evalyn?"

She nodded, no hesitation. "I am. Proceed."

If she wasn't lying naked under him, her body open to him, Lachlan would deem that no invitation. But what did he know of taking a virgin? He'd only bedded women who were well versed in the bedroom.

He set the head of his cock at her entrance, pausing. She didn't flinch. Didn't move.

He slid into her, her warm folds incredibly tight, wrapping him, and then he hit the barrier. A thrust, and he broke through, his shaft deep into her.

He stopped his motion, his look intent on her unmoving face. "Does it hurt, Evalyn? Do you need me to stop?"

"No. I am fine. Continue as you need to." The words were wooden, but quick. Her eyes still managed to stay averted from him, even though he was blocking much of her view.

Lachlan pulled out, sliding slowly into her once more.

No reaction.

Her body rigid, she didn't move. Just lay there, her arms clamped tight to her sides like a stiff fish.

He drove into her as gently as he could five more times. She didn't move.

He pulled himself out of her, shifting backward and moving to stand by the bed, his cock still rock hard but unable to come.

Blasted awkward.

For a long moment he stared down at her. At her wide eyes, now open to him, watching him. She wasn't resisting. Not at all. And hell, she was beautiful. Her breasts perfect creamy hills, the dip of the smooth skin between them that traveled down her belly, her hips that offered just the right amount of flesh to grab a hold of during an onslaught. But she was also as pliable as the plank of mahogany wood above them.

A brandy. He needed a brandy. He turned from her, walking over to the small round table laden with food and drink and poured himself a dram.

"We are done?"

"For now." He tipped back the glass and swallowed.

"That—that was not awful."

He turned to her. "You expected it to be awful? Is that why you wanted to get it done with so quickly?"

"No, I…" She sat up on the bed, her hands angled behind her to support her torso.

"Yes?"

"I have been waiting."

"Waiting for what?"

"For you to announce this was all a farce. A joke upon me you were playing with your men." She spotted the blood on her inner thighs and quickly scooted forward on the bed until her legs dangled off the side. Onto her feet, she leaned forward, grabbing her chemise from the pile of clothes. Her face disappeared for a moment as she set it about her body. It only went down to her knees now, but she was covered to him once more. She bent, shifting through the scraps of cloth that had wrapped her feet, finding one, and then wiped the blood from her thighs.

Her voice was small as she stood straight and adjusted the straps about her shoulders. "I wanted to get the business of this done with, to the point of not going back—either my humiliation or the consummation of the marriage. Either way it would be over. It is the waiting that is unbearable."

He nodded and set his glass down, then contemplated her for a long moment. He rapped his knuckles on the table. "Come, eat. You must be starving."

Evalyn gingerly hobbled to the basin of water atop a chest of drawers, rinsed her fingers, and then moved to the table. She began to sit before she reached the chair, swinging her backside into place just before she fell to the floor.

Lachlan set one of the plates in front of her and she dug into the food before he sat across from her.

He was accustomed to being in the nude when alone, so it took him a long moment to realize he'd just sat down across the table from her fully naked. He motioned toward his torso. "Do you mind if I don't have clothing on?"

Her fork full of asparagus spears paused halfway to her mouth and her eyes dipped down to his chest. For a second, she looked like she would protest, but then she shook her head. "If you are comfortable, then I will be so as well."

She was accommodating, at the least. Even though the tinge of red running up along the sides of her neck told him just how uncomfortable she was. Small favor that the table hid his still engorged member from view.

Her eyes averted to the fire in the hearth across the room and she swallowed several bites of potatoes before looking to him. "Why is it that we are at an inn tonight? There is no storm."

"You would rather be in my tent with the men naught but six steps away?"

A small smile lifted the corners of her lips. "No. It is just that I assumed we would be at an estate of an acquaintance of yours as you appear to know everyone of importance from Lincolnshire to here."

Lachlan cut a bite of roast beef and slid it into his mouth. "It is my grandfather's doing. The marquess has lived through too much unrest in his years. He was born during the Jacobite rising of forty-five and his father and a number of our kin died in the Battle of Culloden—on both sides of the sword. He's witnessed from birth onward the upheaval of the land. So he's spent his life forging alliances up and down this isle."

"To protect your lands?"

"Yes. For the fiend of a man that he is, he's managed to hold the Vinehill lands together. Kept our people from starving."

"He's a fiend?"

"He isn't a rosebud." Lachlan leaned back in his chair, tapping the tines of his fork on the edge of his plate. "My grandfather has always been a difficult man—at least since I can remember. I have heard tell amongst my aunts that he was once kind, but I've never witnessed it. He lost his wife and my father and mother in one horrible winter due to consumption. That us three bairns lived through it—my older brother, my sister and I—was a miracle."

"How old were you?"

"I was six. Sloane was a wee one. Jacob was eight. They said my grandfather was never the same after that winter. And he was left with three young bairns in his household to raise."

"He still interacted with you?" Evalyn asked.

He shrugged. "Enough to make us into what he wanted us to be."

She took a bite of an asparagus tip. "What did he want you to be?"

"Me, I was to be the soldier of the family. The one to bring honor to the name."

"And your brother was brought up to be the next marquess?"

"Yes."

"What of your sister?"

"Her, he wanted to make key alliances with, so she was to be docile and bonny and do as bade."

Evalyn chuckled. "I met your sister at Wolfbridge. He failed entirely on that score—except for her beauty."

Lachlan grinned. "That he did. As much as we fought it, Jacob and I fell into line with what he'd deemed for us. Sloane never did. And we helped her—Machiavellian so."

"But it sounds as though you had each other to depend upon?"

"We did." His smile spread. "Sloane used to love to climb the vines on the southern side of the castle. It used to drive our grandfather to madness, but we would always help her to do so."

"She would climb vines?"

"We all did. The vines of iron, as they are known. And they are actually iron."

A bemused smile set onto her full lips. "What?"

"There is lore about the time that the castle fell into Viking hands. To reclaim it, my ancestors scaled the vines that grew along the southern side of the castle in the dead of the night." Lachlan took a sip of his brandy. "The vines were so sturdy, enough men made it up onto the different levels to invade and win the castle back from the Vikings. Two hundred years later, when the southern wall was rebuilt, one of my ancestors decided to commemorate the victory by having vines of iron built into the stone, which are now hidden under the live vines that still grow there."

The smile widened on her face. "That is fantastical."

He nodded, jabbing a chunk of potato and popping it into his mouth. "It is, and especially irresistible to mischievous bairns. Our governesses couldn't keep us off that wall in the summertime. It was a game we played— Sloane, Jacob, our cousin Torrie and I—the Valor of Vinehill. We would storm the castle, climb as high as we dared and crawl in through the windows. It was always a competition."

"Who usually won?"

"Sloane. She was the lightest and most agile of us. Plus the most stubborn. She could hang off the tiniest slip of iron for what seemed like hours. Torrie was the most timid, but the smartest—she could pick the perfect line up the wall and follow it without fail. Jacob and I spent much of the time daring each other to leap from spot to spot in the stupidest show of virility that ever was."

"Did any of you ever fall?"

"Yes, all of us. Jacob did once from a too high spot and broke his arm. Grandfather threatened to tear the whole wall down. But by the next summer, we were back to our same antics."

She laughed.

"It behooved us in that particular instance that Grandfather bothered very little with us. But then Jacob was eventually off to Edinburgh. Two years later I joined him there and soon after I was focused on entering the crown's forces. We just stopped climbing at some point. I couldn't tell you when." He shook his head, the nostalgia of it making him pause.

"The soldier in you explains much." Her head bowed as she cut her roast beef.

"What does it explain?"

Her eyes lifted to him. "The inherent rigidness in how you've moved from place to place on the journey. What you expect of the men around you. It is disciplined and unrelenting. And you do not care for unexpected things."

He eyed her. "Such as?"

"A rogue woman tagging along with the party and causing mayhem with every step."

His right cheek lifted in a smile. "Aye. You, lass, I've had to get accustomed to."

"It also explains why you've been so abrupt with me."

"I've been abrupt?"

The impish glint in her gold-green eyes said he'd been much worse than abrupt, but she shrugged as she picked up a hunk of bread and began to tear a piece off. "Domnall said you lacked charm. And I would not disagree with him."

"I lack charm?"

"He…mmm…" She tapped her forefinger on the table next to her plate. "He said you're direct with women. Straight to the business of the matter." She motioned to the bed with her hand clutching a bite of the bread. "I had hoped that was the case. And it was. I didn't want you to have to cajole me into bed."

"So I *do* lack charm?"

"Oh, no." She looked at him, her eyebrows drawing together. "I did not mean to imply—what happened was not awful as I expected it to be, Lachlan, and I…" A burst of dark terror flashed across her gold-green eyes and her words stopped.

"Why did you think it was to be an awful act?"

She shook her head, then shoved the chunk of bread into her mouth, her eyes avoiding him.

"Does it have to do with the man your father was to sell you off to?"

Her look flew up to him, her eyes round.

Lachlan sighed. "What the hell did that monster tell you of the act, Evalyn?"

She chewed the bite of bread several more times and had to take a sip of wine to force it down her throat.

She opened her mouth, but no words came forth. She took another sip of wine.

With a slight nod to herself, her look dipped to the main platter of food between them, her eyes glazing over.

The tip of her head nodded to the bed. "I didn't know it could be as easy as that—very little pain."

Her lips drew inward for a long breath and Lachlan wasn't sure she would continue. But then she met his eyes, opening her mouth, her voice tiny, wispy. "He told me there would be a blade involved. That he would carve my flesh as he drove into me. That he would smear the blood on my body. On my nipples. That he would bathe his…his… member with it and force it down my throat. That the fear in my eyes was exactly what was necessary and right. That he would tear me in two with his thrusts. That he would—"

"Stop." Lachlan's fist slammed down onto the table, making the platters jump. His plate of food flew off the table, clattering onto the floor. "Stop, Evalyn. Just stop. And wipe everything that brute ever said to you from your mind." His words were a growl.

Her look skittered to the food on the floor and then jumped up to land on his fist, still clenched, still gripped in rage on the table. Her eyes fixated on his straining knuckles.

Fear gripped her face. She wanted to run. To escape.

With control he didn't think he had, he managed to unclench his fingers and set his palm flat on the table.

With that one tiny motion, her look flickered up to his face, the need to escape almost instantly dissipating.

It helped ease the growl from his voice. "Did no one ever tell you what is supposed to happen between a man and a woman, Eva?"

A flush curled along the line of her cheekbones. "I— my maid, she was a year younger than me—she described a scene, but it didn't make any sense. And what that troll said was so…so vicious in how he spoke of it. He knew what he was talking about, Lachlan. I never doubted it."

He heaved a sigh, his hand running through his hair as he leaned back in his chair, making the wood creak under his form. "Then we need to start this all over. All over. You knew enough to get naked and that was good. But from there, you need to strike from your mind anything and everything that was ever uttered to you on the act—from your maid—and especially from that bastard." He leaned forward, pinning her with his look. "Can you do that?"

For a long moment she hesitated and then offered him a skeptical nod. "I can try."

He reached out, his fingers sliding around her hand that still clutched a piece of bread, smothering it. Slowly, he pulled back each finger until he could pry the mangled bread from her grasp. "Now, we start again. With bellies full. Our minds clear. Yes?"

Her look lifted to him, the gold-green of her eyes shining—almost in wonderment. A look so overflowing of innocence and timid trust that he almost smiled.

For all she refused to trust, refused to hope—her innate nature was winning out. She had taken a leap of faith in latching onto him at Wolfbridge Castle and—damn—he didn't want to do anything to destroy that. He liked that look in her eyes. Liked that she looked at him as if he were the only man in the world.

And to her, maybe he was. She'd had one monstrosity of a man after another in her life. He wasn't about to be the third.

He wanted another go at her.

He should wait. She would be sore. But his shaft had jumped back to life with the look on her face, the blasted appendage insistent after its earlier disappointment.

Lachlan wavered, trying to read her gold-green eyes and the answer became suddenly clear. He wanted—needed—to fulfill every drop of cautious hope she was allowing herself to have in that moment. That life could be different. That life could bring pleasure instead of pain. That life could reward hope rather than vanquish it.

He squeezed her hand then stood. "Come with me to the bed?"

Her look dipped down his naked body, the flush in her cheeks deepening into a crimson hue as her gaze paused at his engorged member. Her eyes lifted to his face. "You wish to do it again?"

"I do. And this time, you are not to lie down on that bed until your knees are weak and can no longer support you."

"Why would my knees go weak?"

He smiled, wicked, and tugged her to her feet.

"If I perform my duties correctly, you're about to find out." He stepped into her space, his head dipping down to brush his lips along her jaw, light, gentle, the caress of a midsummer's breeze. His thumbs hooked under the straps of her chemise and he slowly dragged it downward off her body.

She didn't resist, not that he thought she would. His new wife was overly accommodating in the bedchamber.

Accommodating would not do.

He didn't want her accommodating—he wanted her writhing, his name a mewl on her tongue, begging him for release.

Her chemise landed in a pile about her feet and his hand slipped behind her to the small of her back. His lips parted, his tongue tracing a long line down her neck, tasting the salt of her. He instantly wanted more—a deep thirst for her taste he couldn't quite place.

A soft moan and her head tilted to the side, allowing him better access, and he shuffled her backward three steps toward the bed. Her body had gone pliant, easy to maneuver.

Shifting her long russet locks behind her shoulder, he smiled into her skin as a quivering breath lifted her chest and his mouth trailed a line of kisses along the fine line of her collarbone.

Lifting his head, he found her lips, his tongue parting them, raking against her teeth, and he was rewarded with the tang of sweet wine still on her tongue. The lightness of the kiss deepened to a brutal feast without conscious thought.

Just when he thought he'd gone too far, needing to pull away before scaring her, her body pressed forward, her skin touching his, her breasts on his chest, her hips pushing her belly onto his cock.

Heaven. Pure, sweet heaven.

There wasn't the slightest shyness in how her body molded into his—almost awkward without the suave movements of a seasoned lover. No—her body did what instinct demanded, her skin needing his.

The hardness of his member strained viciously, demanding to be sated.

It would have to wait.

He broke the kiss before it sent him too far down a path he could not veer from and he set his lips to her neck once more.

Her breathing sped, soft gasps every time his mouth swept over a sensitive nerve. He sank farther, his mouth finding her left nipple. It was already taut as he drew it into his mouth and he sucked it, teasing it with the tips of his teeth.

"Lachlan." His name tumbled from her lips, raw and breathless.

Just like he wanted it. Filling his ears again and again.

Her hands shifted to the back of his head, her fingers digging deep into his hair and clutching him to her breast.

As much as her left breast wanted him, he wasn't about to neglect her right. He shifted, ignoring the disappointed gasp escaping her as his lips left her. The gargled sound in her throat died out, satisfied as he clamped onto her right nipple.

It was only moments before her breaths started to heave, erotic moans bubbling from deep in her chest.

"Lachlan."

"Yes?"

"My knees are weak."

He chuckled into her skin, the salty sheen of it pressing to his lips.

His tongue still swirling about her nipple, not breaking contact, his hands slipped around the swell of her buttocks, lifting her and walking her the last two steps to the bed.

As much as it tortured him to pull his lips away from her, he did so, setting her down on the edge of the mattress. His eyes found her gaze. "Do you feel safe, Eva?"

She nodded. "Yes." Even through the passion-fueled haze in her gold-green eyes he saw the trust, the submission. She was counting on him to take her through this—to not disappoint.

He didn't intend to.

"Then your knees aren't the only thing that will be going weak."

Her eyes went wide and a shameless smile lifted the side of his mouth. He kissed her, long and hard, then drew away, his mouth finding its way down her body. One breast. Two. The valley between them that stretched down her belly. Her navel.

His lips consumed her skin, letting no morsel go untasted as he pressed her backward onto the bed. Fingers itching, he set his right hand under her leg, dragging it to bend upward as his thumb teased a line along her inner thigh. Her skin prickled under his touch and he set her calf around his waist as he drew further down her body with his lips.

His finger breached her, sliding into the slick folds. Folds that were ready for him with not the slightest flinch of pain from earlier. He found her nubbin, swirling it along the tips of his fingers.

The scent of her, the strain of her hips swiveling toward him with every swipe of his fingers nearly undid him. He forged a finger, then two deep into her, testing her tightness.

"Lachlan." The guttural cry had everything to do with pleasure and nothing with pain.

Tight. But ready for him.

He sent his tongue to swirl on her lower belly as his fingers mimicked the motion on her nubbin and she bucked, not understanding her own body.

"Lachlan." Wonderment flush with anxiety made her cries speed, her raspy voice cracking with the weight of what was happening to her body.

A loss of control.

He heard it in her voice, because he felt it in his own gut. He felt it deep within, a burning like no other. A burning that threatened to sear him from the inside out.

"Just hold it there, Eva. Hold it there." His fingers stayed in place, stroking her ever higher as he straightened above her.

Watching as her head arched backward, drawing her whole body into a beautiful arc, he held himself back until the first cry of her release hit.

He slid into her.

Hard. Harder than he wanted. Softer than his base instincts demanded.

It didn't pause her, didn't halt the throes her body writhed in. If anything, his cock, full and deep in her, sent her body into vibrations that overtook her limbs.

"Lachlan. Again."

The words, breathless and begging, hit him in the chest. He withdrew, slamming into her again.

Again. And again.

The rapture that surrounded his member with each stroke shook his body to the tips of his nerves.

Her legs wrapped around him, drawing him ever closer, her screams reaching to his gut and ripping it out.

Hell. It wasn't supposed to be like this.

Not flames so deep in his core.

Not ripping his insides to shreds.

But he was no force against it.

He lifted her hips, driving into her deeper than he thought possible. Immersed so far into the abyss, the hooks of it so ruthless he had no choice but to come, ferocious and hard, every fragment of him and parts unknown emptying into her in a raging explosion.

He collapsed, then rolled, dragging her still quaking body on top of his. He wasn't breaking contact with her. Ever. Time and space and natural laws be damned.

"I didn't know—" her breathless words into his chest paused and she curled her head onto him, taking a deep breath before setting her chin on his chest and looking up at him "I didn't know that existed."

*Neither did I.*

The words sat there on the tip of his tongue, unsaid.

He had never felt fire in his veins like this. Fire that consumed him. Fire that built to explosion, then refused to yield with relief, instead remaining in his blood, seeping into his bones.

He couldn't bring himself to say the words, but he knew it the same as she did.

This was nothing like anything he'd experienced before.

It consumed his loins, his gut. An all-encompassing need for her body. For the touch of her fingertips against his bare skin. An urgency for her so brutal it devoured him whole.

And it felt like betrayal.

Betrayal for his brother.

# { CHAPTER 13 }

"The marquess said to come directly, m'lady."

Evalyn looked around Lachlan's spacious chamber, her gaze landing on the willowy slip of the maid in front of her.

"But I am under strict orders by my husband to stay in his chambers until he returns from the trial."

"Oh, ye are English. I heard tell it down below but couldnae believe it." The maid shuffled from one foot to the other, the pace of her words picking up. "I understand what yer husband told ye, m'lady, but his lordship insisted ye accompany me to 'im this very moment, and 'e's not one for disobeyin' orders."

Evalyn sighed, tugging her bottom lip from under her front teeth. Lachlan had been very direct in that she was not to leave his chambers that day. They had arrived at Vinehill late in the darkness the previous night when most of the household was asleep. When he'd left early this morning before daybreak for the first day of the trial, he'd had that one request of her.

Don't leave his rooms.

She glanced over her shoulder at the healthy fire in the marble-lined hearth that had been tended to by the other maid, Janice, since dawn. Judging by the cringed responses by both of the maids to her accent, she could only imagine how Lachlan's grandfather would react to her without proper introduction.

"But my husband was most insistent I stay here."

"Aye, as is his grandfather to see ye. But his is an order, m'lady. And one dinnae disobey the marquess." Her cheeks pulled back in a wince, crinkling the edges of her eyes. Evalyn recognized the exact look in the girl's brown eyes— the awkward position she'd been put in to retrieve Lachlan's new bride for inspection.

Evalyn offered a slight nod. "Can you afford me one moment?" Without waiting for an answer, she walked across the room into the adjoining dressing chamber and stopped in front of the tall mirror.

Her hand ran downward across her belly, smoothing the wrinkled creases of the grey wool as she looked at her reflection in the mirror. Her only other choice for clothing was her mother's dress sitting crumpled on the bench by the window. Lachlan had kindly brought it up from the wagon last night, but then had set it in here to be taken to be cleaned and mended.

She didn't want to meet the marquess in the worn wool dress, but her mother's ball gown would be an even worse choice. Her fingers ran along her upsweep, smoothing it across her temple, and she leaned toward the mirror to inspect the dark circles under her eyes. Even after the stupor her body was in from the hard day of travel, Lachlan had kept her up far too long last night, making her body writhe under him. And it was only a few hours later that his lips on her neck were nudging her awake, his insistent shaft pressing hard into her thigh.

Not that she would trade those moments away for less tired-looking eyes.

"M'lady?" The maid's voice reached her from the main chamber.

One last swipe across the side of her head to smooth errant hairs, and she moved into Lachlan's room, bracing herself.

She nodded to the maid, who promptly spun about and moved out of the room.

The maid's steps were quick and Evalyn had to follow her closely through the narrow stone corridors.

A maze. She'd followed Lachlan blindly last night to his chambers, but now she realized how many twists and turns there were in the corridors—as though whoever had built the structure had set trap after trap for anyone trying to navigate the halls. Or they were foxed beyond compare.

Whereas she'd assumed Lachlan had wanted her hidden away in his rooms, maybe he'd asked that of her because he didn't want her to get forever lost in the bowels of the ancient keep.

The maid pushed forth a heavy oak door reinforced with heavy iron strap hinges, and it creaked open until there was enough space for her to move past.

Following her, Evalyn turned sideways and scooted through the narrow opening.

A library, or a museum of some fashion, greeted her on the other side. Heavy drapes covered the windows, blocking the daylight and leaving only the roaring flames in the fireplace to lend light to the room. Books lined the lower cabinets—not taller than her waist—that ringed the spacious room, and above them paintings of every shape and size filled the walls. Filled the walls from bookcases to ceiling. Naught but slivers of plaster showed between them, the frames of all manners—from elaborate gilded masterpieces, to deep mocha-colored carved mahogany ones, to simple raw wooden casings.

Evalyn spun slightly in the room, instantly uneasy.

She'd lived in her stepfather's home where mounted animals of all sorts filled the rooms, their glass eyes immortalizing them in ever awake states, so she knew what it was to have soulless eyes watching her.

But this room sent a shiver down her spine. In every painting that hung on the walls—most of them portraits—eyes followed her. Female eyes. Male eyes. Eyes of children. Eyes of the elderly. Blue eyes. Green eyes. Brown eyes.

Men on horseback. Women in full court dress, adorned with jewels. Families seated, wolfhounds at their feet. Medieval scenes. Tartan clad men. Every portrait that had ever been painted on these lands, plus a hundred more, had to have been hanging in this room.

The chamber of eyes watched her as she stepped into the room. Followed her as she came to a halt on the middle of the Axminster carpet that lined only half of the stone floor.

Glared at her movements.

Judged her.

Hundreds of piercing eagle eyes that stared at her from every direction.

The shiver that had run down her spine skittered back up to prickle the skin on her neck.

"That will be all, Maggie." A craggy voice cut into the stale air and made her jump. She spun to the sound, finding the profile of an elderly man sitting in a wingback chair turned toward the enormous curved stone fireplace.

Maggie backed out of the room, pulling the heavy door closed with her exit.

"Don't just stand there. Move over into the light, girl." The voice, cracking with age, yet so commanding, made Evalyn hop and cautiously approach the fireplace.

She stopped three steps away from the wingback chair and turned to Lachlan's grandfather, locking her arms straight along her sides. She'd done this too many times before, her gut churning. Present herself for inspection. Inspections that she inevitably failed.

But this was Lachlan's grandfather. Her future. A future she was starting to allow herself the smallest margin to believe in, even though she knew it was foolish to do so.

She braced herself, looking to him.

The man was older than his voice. Deepset lines on his face were almost swallowed by the number of smaller wrinkles cutting across his skin. Hazel eyes she recognized— the very same as Lachlan's—squinted at her through the folds of skin.

His wiry grey eyebrows arched, or at least she thought they did, as it was hard to discern what did and did not move on his face.

His right fingers on the plush arm of the chair lifted, his crooked forefinger extending out, though curled with creaky bones that wouldn't let his finger truly straighten to point at her. "Well, yer a bonny lass, if nothing else." He sent his forefinger in a circle. "Let's hear ye speak."

"Hear me speak, my lord?"

He cringed, his layered wrinkles collapsing onto one another as his head snapped back. "I'd hoped to the last it wasn't true—that whelp bringing home a blasted Englishwoman for a bride."

She bowed her head and her voice settled into the well-practiced docile tone that she always maintained with her stepfather. "I understand that an English-born woman is not what you wished for in a wife for your grandson."

He jabbed his finger in the air at her. "Ye think I care about yer birthplace, child?" His eyes narrowed at her, almost disappearing into the folds of his transparent skin. His palm slammed so hard onto the arm of the chair she was afraid it would shatter his bones. "Well, I do. But I care more about the damn betrothal that was the key to the Vinehill future—key to keeping our people on our lands. That union was to gain us the best flock in Scotland and stability for our lands."

Evalyn kept her head inclined. "I apologize for the disappointment, my lord. This union was not planned upon by either Lachlan or myself."

"Eh? Not planned upon?"

She shook her head. "No. I was merely to accompany Lachlan here to Vinehill, and then I was to become part of the household, possibly work in the kitchens."

"Then why—did ye lift yer skirts for him and the fool boy fell besotted?"

A flush wrapped around her neck. "Ah—no. That is not what happened at all."

"Good, good—then we can fix this, child. I can have papers for a divorce drawn up today."

"Oh." Her eyebrows drew together. "I did not know one could divorce so easily and I do not think—"

"I don't care what ye think, child. This not be England, lass. A divorce is easy enough to come by in Scotland with some extra grease and then ye can work in the kitchens as planned."

"But—"

"But nothing." He flipped his boney hand into the air. "Go. I am done with ye."

Her open mouth clamped shut. With a quick curtsey, she moved out of the room.

Closing the creaking door behind her with shaking hands, she looked both directions in the corridor. To her left, the corridor quickly ended at a perpendicular hallway. To her right, the corridor curved, disappearing. Dank and cold in both directions.

She could swear she came from the right. She hoped.

Her footsteps light on the ancient stones, she walked to her right, slowing as the hallway curved.

"Ye don't want to be going that direction, m'lady."

Evalyn jumped, spinning around. Juggling a stack of fabric, the maid stood in the hallway staring at her. "I don't?"

"No. That way will lead ye to the stairs to the undercrofts. Unless ye want to visit the old dungeon?"

Evalyn shook her head.

"Come. I'll take ye back then." Her head motioned backward. "It's this way, m'lady."

"Oh, thank you, I could not find my way back without help—Maggie is it?"

"Aye."

"Can I help carry your load?"

"Aye. I was going up to the bedding chambers with these." She lifted the pile of fabric—sheets—in her arms

and Evalyn took the top half. She looked to the door of the library. "The marquess be done with ye?"

"He is." Evalyn glanced back over her shoulder as they walked away. "For now, he is."

~ ~ ~

The bastard was going to go free.

His feet brutal against the stone floors, Lachlan stormed through the castle, not pausing once as the servants he passed tried to gain his attention.

His grandfather wanted to see him. He knew that.

But talking to his grandfather was the last thing he could do in the moment.

He was liable to choke the old buzzard to death, he was so consumed with fury.

The bastard was going to go *free*.

The trial wasn't over yet, there was still a chance, but from what he'd witnessed today in court, that bastard from London that killed his brother was going to be set free.

Not hanged. Not shot. Not beheaded.

He never should have let Domnall talk him out of killing the bastard when the monster was captured after the fire.

Lachlan stomped up the south circular staircase, his boots on every step a heavy blow echoing into the bowels of the castle. The two-hour ride back to the castle had done nothing to calm the rage pulsating in every fiber of his being. No. If anything, every step his horse had taken had only heightened the wrath swallowing him whole.

The only thing that could break through the fury ravaging his body was the sole thought of sinking himself into Evalyn. Of losing himself in her.

There was only one place he was going. To his room. To his wife.

Dragging off his coat, cravat and waistcoat, Lachlan charged through the door to his chambers, slamming it shut behind him.

Evalyn jumped up from the chair by the fireplace, the book in her hand dangling to her side. "Lachlan."

Her hair long, let down from the blasted pins that kept it tight to her scalp, the tips of the auburn locks curled down about her breasts, stark against the white of her chemise.

"Where are your clothes?" Words had to fight their way past the stranglehold of anger about his throat.

"Lachlan—"

"You've been waiting for me?" His voice a growl, he stalked across the room and grabbed her around the waist, yanking her body hard into his. It knocked the book from her hand, the pages rustling, crumpling as they hit the floor.

Her dark eyelashes fluttered, confused. "Yes, I—"

"Good. Because I'm ready for you."

Her head snapped back, her forehead furrowing. "Lachlan—the trial—what is wrong?"

"Nothing." His hands slid down her body, wrapping around her hips, and he pulled her tight to him, grinding his cock into her belly. "Isn't this what you were waiting for?"

"I was waiting for you, yes—"

"Good." The growl in his voice deepened and he spun her around, picking her up, his mouth ravaging her neck as he moved them to the foot of the bed.

Setting her to her feet, he lifted both of her arms and placed her hands onto the left bed post to grip and then he bent, dragging her shift upward. His fingers went to the back of her thigh and he lifted her leg, spreading her, and then draped her calf over the footboard.

Five buttons on his front fall and he was free. Engorged and raging for her. Without preamble, he harshly slid into her from behind.

She doubled forward at the invasion, but it didn't make him pause. The fury speeding his blood still pounded so brutally in his ears that he could barely hear the gurgled gasp from her throat. His left hand clamped over her fingers gripping the bed post while his right hand wrapped tight around her hip, bracing her against his onslaught.

His face buried deep into her hair, her neck, he slammed into her twice more and he was lost. Lost in her smell. Her body. The taste of her.

Lost.

Just as he needed.

Then he heard it. His name. His name from some far off island.

"Lachlan."

Urgent. Troubled.

"Lachlan."

He froze in mid drive, his face lifting from her hair.

"Lachlan—this—not like this—I want it, but not like this." Her breathless voice spun around his head, sinking through the wall of fury into his consciousness.

Dammit to Hades, he was hurting her.

He pulled his shaft from her. Stilling.

She didn't move.

Of course she wouldn't. She would stand there and take whatever he doled out to her. It was all she'd ever known.

He was a blasted ass.

But hell, he still needed his cock in her. Needed it against the rage threatening to swallow him whole. Needed it before he did something entirely stupid to the bastard that killed his brother.

He released her fingers clamped to the bed post and his left hand went to her hip, lifting and spinning her to face him.

But he couldn't look at her face. Meet her eyes.

So he sank. Sank to his knees in front of her. She was still parted to him, her right leg had remained high and draped over the footboard.

Before she could say a word, he dove forward, tasting the slickness of her, his tongue delving into her folds, swirling. His left hand moved up along her inner thigh, his fingers caressing the delicate skin.

A gasp, and she leaned back against the footboard.

His tongue sweeping across her nubbin, stirring it into hardness, Lachlan dragged his fingers inward, slipping one finger, then two into her. She was tight around him, even though his cock had just been in her. He teased her nubbin more, plying her nerves into a frenzy.

A gargled moan and her hands sank into his hair, clutching the short strands. Her body gave over to him and the leg she stood on began to quiver. He snaked his right arm around it, his hand supporting her backside as he continued the assault on her senses, licking, sucking harder, faster.

He could feel it under his tongue, the swelling, the explosion that vibrated outward from her core and rolled through her body, curling her forward to coil around his head.

"Are you ready for me, Eva?"

A gasp followed by guttural moan, and she forced out the one word. "Yes."

Lachlan stood, his lips moving his way up her body, his fingers trailing up her vibrating legs. Lifting her shift upward, he dragged it from her body and tossed it onto the bed. His hands dipped to her breasts, pausing to cup them, rolling her hard nipples in his fingers, and then he slipped his hands under her backside and lifted her, setting her to balance on the fat top rail of the footboard.

The need to harshly drive into her took a hold of him, but he forced it into submission, sliding into her slowly. Every clench of her body, every roll of sweet agony pulsating through her core he could feel on his shaft. Exquisite.

Two more gasps, and breathless words escaped her. "You don't need to slow, Lachlan. Go deep." She lifted her leg, wrapping her calf around his back and locking her hands around his neck.

The words awakened the demon he'd tried so hard to control, and he pulled from her for only a heartbeat before plunging back into her, driving the full force of his angst into her body.

Again and again.

And all she said was, "Yes."

Yes. Over and over.

His cock stretching, impossibly hard, he could take no more and he sank into her, the eruption tearing through his body and sending a violent shudder across the masses of his muscles.

He sank against her, burying his face in her hair, her neck.

Standing, her body clasped to his, all of the anger that had consumed him—savagely eating him raw all day—dissipated into a thousand wisps of nothingness.

He stood propped against her balanced on the footboard until he could breathe again, could move his muscles without dropping her and falling to the floor himself.

Long moments passed, and he lifted his head, moving to see her face as she tilted her chin upward to look at him. "Hell, Eva, I hurt you. I'm sorry." His eyes searching her face, he dragged his right hand up from the clamp he had on the small of her back to brush his fingers along her cheekbone. "I had…had control…then I didn't. I didn't. I lost center—hell, I lost all of me."

Her gold-green eyes widened at him. "It hurt and then it didn't." Her fingers went upward, diving into the hair at the base of his neck. "After you slowed—I could take all of you after that. But I'm more concerned about why—what happened to put you in such a state?"

A long breath seethed from him. "The trial—it is a farce. And the anger built into such a raging mess that I was blinded, could barely get my horse turned back to Vinehill. And sinking into you was all I could think about—the only thing that kept me sane on the way home."

He paused, swallowing hard as he shook his head. "The thought of disappearing so deeply into you I could lose myself—it was the only defense I had against the rage. And then I came in and you were already in your chemise ready for me—but that was inexcusable—I hurt you and I swore I would never do so. I can only beg your forgiveness."

Her eyes squinted slightly as she looked up at him. "I'm not sure what to say. I don't know what to do with an apology."

His eyebrow cocked. "You've never received an apology?"

She shook her head, but the abashed tilt of her chin told him she hadn't said it for pity—she truly didn't know what to make of an apology.

"Hell, Eva." Fresh anger of an entirely different sort surged through his veins, but he stilled himself against it. He kissed her brow. "You accept an apology and know it'll never happen again."

"And if it does?"

"Then it wasn't much of an apology."

She nodded, her eyes dipping down to his chest.

She didn't believe him.

# { CHAPTER 14 }

For all that he'd given her no reason to distrust him, he was beginning to realize how very long it would be before his wife managed to trust his words. She was still waiting for the explosion, for her world to shatter.

Her hand lifted, her fingers settling on the crook of skin showing above his lawn shirt. "I did not know I could speak and it would actually matter."

His fingers curled along the side of her face, his thumb slipping under her chin to lift her eyes to him. "Your words always matter to me, Eva. You need never curb your tongue with me."

The corners of her eyes crinkled.

Another thing she couldn't quite believe.

He slid his hands down under her backside and lifted her off the footboard. Her legs wrapped around him, he carried her around the foot of the bed. Setting his knees on the bed, he laid her down beneath him on the sapphire hued damask coverlet. Her legs slipped from around his waist and her auburn hair spread onto the silk, shiny in the light of the fire. No longer matted with droplets of Rupe's stew. At some point today a bath must have been brought up to her.

He liked her in his bed. Her naked body still flush from sex. The white of her skin a beacon of softness against the dark colors of his room. So inviting, he tugged off his shirt and trousers and then rolled over to lie down next to her. He shifted her head to nuzzle on the crook of his shoulder.

He liked this even more—her bare skin draped over him. Every heartbeat he could feel pumping through her body. The scent of lavender wafting up at him.

She traced lazy circles on his chest. "What did you mean when you said you lost your center, Lachlan?"

"My center?" He sighed and moved his free arm to tuck under his head as he stared at the matching silk damask canopy above. "My brother, Jacob—he was always centered. He always knew exactly what his goals were with the estate—with life. What he needed to do to achieve them. He charged forth without doubt in everything he did. He was never angry, always just moving forth."

"He sounds exactly like what the eldest brother would be."

"He was. He took care of Sloane and me after our parents died. And he was heir to the Vinehill title and lands and he knew it his whole life. It was what drove him every day. This land. These people."

"Yet now it will be yours."

"Exactly. And my life had been free from all of this. The army gave me freedom that Jacob could never have. Whereas he was never angry, I have always been quick to it. The army gave me an outlet—a way to control my anger. But now everything is in disarray."

"How?"

"I'm not him, yet I've inherited everything Jacob stood for. So I strive for that—his center—but I lose it. Lose it sometimes in the anger. Like I did earlier. I never should have approached you in that state."

Her fingers stilled on his chest and she angled her head to look at his face. "Why were you so angry—the trial is a farce?"

His look met her gold-green eyes and instead of the anger at the trial surging through his veins and taking over, his heartbeat slowed. "It is. The man on trial for murdering my brother, Robert E. Lipinstein, is about to be set free."

"What? How could that be?" She jerked upright, sitting and spinning to him.

"The overseer of the clearings that are taking place on Swallowford lands is coming to testify tomorrow that the murderous bastard is not part of his crew."

The absence of her body long against his vexed him and he reached up to tug her into place against him once more. She resisted, her eyes still wide with injustice. "How is that possible? He was there, you saw him."

"The man's defense is that he's a smuggler and he had nothing to do with the fire. He was just in the wrong place and time."

"Why would a smuggler have been there?"

"He claims he had stored over-proof gin in the barns of Torrie's family, and once he heard word the family was to be evicted, he came to move the barrels. According to the defense, it was happenstance that he arrived there just when the brutes who came to evict them did."

Lachlan's hand tugging her downward finally succeeded, and she sank down next to him, settling her head along his shoulder once more.

"Did the family truly partake in smuggling?"

He shrugged his shoulders. "I don't know. But it is prevalent in the land these days. People have been squeezed out of their homes, their farming land, so they make rent any way they can. A smuggler coming by asking for space to store goods can be hope for some families—can get them by for another year, maybe more. But there's no way to prove or disprove the barrels were there, as the fire burned hot and fast—everything in all of the buildings." He took a deep breath as the fury threatened to overtake him again and exhaled it in a long sigh. "And I was too damn late."

"Late for what?"

"Too late to help. To save Jacob. To save Sloane and Torrie from the scars of the fire. To save anyone. I got there just as the house collapsed on Jacob. Too late."

"Lachlan—"

"No—there is no other truth than that. I was too late to save my brother. Just as I was too late to save my parents."

Her head shifted on his shoulder, her look intent on him. "Save your parents? But I thought they died of consumption."

Lachlan shrugged and it jostled her head. "I was six and the doctor had sent me out with a maid to collect herbs to make a concoction to help them. I had already been sick and was healing. We were out searching for hours in the cold. When we got back, they were both dead. I was too late."

Evalyn gasped. "Then there was no way that herbs could have helped them."

"No. But I was six. I thought I failed them. I thought I killed them for a long time. Jacob tried to convince me it wasn't my fault, but I didn't believe him for years."

Her hand lifted to curl about his neck as tears swelled in her eyes.

"I know now, looking back upon it, the doctor thought he was being kind. He just wanted me out of the castle, not witnessing their last breaths. But he took that away from me. I didn't get to say goodbye. That haunted me more than anything and it was the day anger took seed in me."

He shook his head, sucking in a heavy inhale. "I felt the same when I rode toward the fire. That I would be too late. And I was."

Evalyn nodded, her bottom lip jutting up against a quiver. "I understand now the anger you walked into the room with—or at least I think I do. This is a horrible injustice."

His arm tightened around the gentle curve of her back. He'd braced himself against the anger that he should be feeling in that very moment, talking about Jacob's murder, but it didn't manifest. Didn't overwhelm like it did every time he thought of his brother's end.

Her fingers started swirling slow rings along his chest again. Minutes passed in silence before her soft voice cut into the bedroom air. "I didn't know that about your parents, about your brother. This—who you are around your men—being the leader of the Vinehill estate appears so natural for you."

"Something Domnall didn't tell you about me?"

She chuckled. "Domnall kept me well entertained when no one else would dare to even glance my direction, much less speak to me."

"He has a mouth, that one. And no—it's not natural to me. None of this is natural. I should be out on a field loading a rifle or swinging a sword at this moment. That is what I know. Not this. Not the running of an estate."

She nodded, her cheek brushing along his shoulder. "It is hard to live up to what others want of you—I've been chasing my mother's ghost for more than fifteen years."

"Why?"

"I have always been terribly shy. The one thing my mother used to tell me before she died was that I needed to find my voice—the voice I have in the heart of my soul. It made sense to her—she was an adult. But to me, it never did."

"And now?" His fingers entwined in her hair, curling a lock between his fore and middle finger.

"I think I'm finding it. What she wanted for me. She wanted me to escape my stepfather. She knew what was ahead for me with him. And the only way I could escape was to find my voice." She shifted her face upward, seeking out his eyes as a smile danced about her lips. "And to find someone who would listen to it."

"You were rather convincing in the gardens at Wolfbridge."

"I needed to be. And for once, I was right with my gamble."

"I was a gamble?"

"Or a last hope." Her head bowed, her lips going to his chest to kiss his skin. "Thank you for listening to me."

"I am beginning to see the merits in bringing home extra luggage."

She laughed, nipping at his skin with the tips of her teeth, and then she settled her fist onto his chest to support her chin as she looked at him. "Why did you lock me away in this room today?"

He glanced to the door, his eyebrows drawing together. "I didn't lock you in here."

"No, but you requested I leave the room for nothing or no one. And this is odd—for a husband and wife to share a chamber. Is this the custom in Scotland?"

Lachlan stifled a sigh, his finger lifting to sweep an errant strand of hair across her brow. His fingertip grazed the edge of the scar on her temple and—small miracle—she didn't flinch away. Progress.

Progress he wasn't about to lose by telling her that their sleeping arrangements were a silent command for the staff and all the inhabitants in Vinehill—she was his wife, and he would tolerate no disrespect from them. She'd get enough hostility from his grandfather.

"It is common and uncommon. It depends on the marriage, I suppose." His fingers in her hair stilled. "And did you?"

"Did I what?"

"Leave the room?"

The edges of her lips pulled back in a grimace. "I met your grandfather."

He jerked upright, sending her rolling off his chest. "Hell and damnation—how—what?"

She flopped onto her back, propping herself up by her elbows. "The marquess sent a maid to retrieve me. I tried to resist the request, but she said it wasn't a request. It was an order. I thought it best to comply or be tossed out on my ear."

"Damn the buzzard." His fist slammed into the bed, his head shaking as he stared at the fire. "I wanted to be the one to introduce you, but there wasn't time before the trial started." He looked to her. "What did he say to you?"

"He knows."

"Knows you're my wife?"

"Knows I'm English."

"And?"

"And he's having a divorce petition drawn up."

His look narrowed at her. "He is?"

She nodded.

"Ornery ass." He chuckled, his head shaking at the foolery of his grandfather. Leave it to the man to try and snake a way out of a marriage for him. Be damned whether Lachlan wanted it or not.

Evalyn sat up, moving away from him on the bed.

"Wait. Why are you looking like you were just sentenced to an execution, Eva?"

She reached for her shift at the foot of the bed, her fingers pulling it inside out to right it. "I didn't realize it was what you wanted."

From behind her he reached out to grab her wrist, stilling her movements. "I didn't say a thing about wanting a divorce." He settled his chin on her shoulder, his lips next to her ear. "I laughed because it is exactly my grandfather's way, his way until his last breath is out of him. The old coot loves to have papers drawn up to shove in front of me—I swear he spends half his time concocting ways he's going to control me from the grave."

Her hand clutching her shift fell to her lap. "So you don't want a divorce?"

He pulled her arm up to his face, his lips brushing across the fleshy mound on the inside of her wrist. "The thought never occurred to me. It is the last thing I want in this moment."

"What do you want in this moment?"

He dropped her wrist, lifting his head from her shoulder. "First, I want to measure your foot."

"My foot?"

"Aye." He started to move around her on the bed but stilled when he saw her back in the light of the fire. His fingers rose, tracing a long ragged white scar that ran along the backside of her ribcage. Two smaller lines of scar tissue crossed the main line near the top. He'd seen enough scars to know a blade had cut her skin.

Bile stained his tongue. "Hell, Eva, what's this scar from?"

She stilled, her back tensing, going impossibly straight. "Evalyn?"

Her head tilted to the side, but she didn't look back to him. "It's from the time I asked my stepfather who my real father was."

He rounded her on the bed so he could see her face. Her cheeks had gone ashen. "You don't know who your father was?"

"No." She met his look. "My mother never told me, at least not that I can remember. From the whispers of the servants, I gathered it was forbidden to talk about him."

"So you asked?"

Her lips pulled back in a tight line, almost as though she was going to refuse to talk. She swallowed hard, her gaze averting from him and landing on the fire. "I did. Once. I asked my stepfather what my father's name was, and he didn't explode, didn't yell. Not like I was bracing myself for. He just silently went to the fireplace where a row of daggers hung over the mantel, took one down and then dipped the end of it in the fire.

She paused, her eyes closing for a long moment. "I thought he was contemplating because he was so calm—trying to figure out how much he was going to tell me. Instead, he turned around, paced behind me for a moment, then flattened me to the table—his arm across my shoulders holding me captive and he swiped that into my skin." Her hand lifted to point down over her shoulder. "His initial. He carved his initial into my skin—telling me there was only one name I ever needed know."

"A bloody 'F.'" Rage like he never knew swirled in his gut. His eyes flew across her back, each white scar he found singeing into his mind. His finger jabbed at the left side of her back. "And this one?"

She spun on the bed, grabbing his hand out of the air. "Lachlan, if we had to go through the story of every single scar on my body, you would burst into a flaming ball of fury."

"I would burst into a flaming ball of hatred."

Her head shook, her fingers tightening on his wrist. "We can't do that. They're not worth it. They're not worth the memories."

"They are a part of you, Eva, and I need to know all of you. Everything that made you."

"Lachlan—"

"Not all at once, then." He attempted to lessen the angry rumble in his voice. "We go through them, one by one. Every time I have your body naked, I get one story."

"And then we never speak of them again?"

He nodded. "Deal?"

She sighed, her lips pulling to the side in a decided frown. "Deal."

He leaned forward, capturing her frown under his mouth, kissing her until it softened, pliable to him. The stiffness of her body eased and she leaned into him.

Not quite yet.

He pulled away. "Wait. Onto your foot before you drive me to all distraction."

He turned from her and scooted along the bed to her feet. Picking up her heel, he held the length of his hand to the sole of her bare foot. The raw skin of blisters and the scabs were healing faster than he thought they could. Though he'd made sure she'd pointedly stayed off her feet as much as possible in the last days.

His fingers stretched over the tips of her toes and he nodded to himself. "I still need to find you proper fitting boots. My sister or mother's may match your size." His fingers left her foot and he snatched her hand, pulling it to his lips and trailing a lascivious circle with his tongue on the inside of her wrist.

A flash of raw desire cut across her gold-green eyes. "And next?"

"Next I want you to toss that shift far, far from the bed and let my hands wander all over your naked body. Give me a respite—make me forget about the blasted trial and my blasted grandfather and your blasted stepfather for just a few minutes."

A smile, so wantonly shy it made his heart thunder, crossed her lips and she moved to her knees, her eyes pinning him. "That, I can attempt to do—on one condition."

"What?"

"That you let me accompany you to the trial tomorrow."

"You don't want that, Eva." He shook his head. "You don't want to have to hear the horror of what happened. I don't want you to have to hear it."

"If I'm there, then I won't have to attempt to drag what happened out of you. I'll already know—know why you're angry. Please, Lachlan. It will help me to understand."

She grabbed his free hand and wrapped her fingers around the back of it, bringing it to her breast, cupping it. "This is yours to do with anything you'd like—just let me come with you."

Her nipple hardened under his palm and he groaned. "Not fair, you little minx."

Her wanton smile grew into unabashed indecency. She shrugged.

"Fine. Yes, you can come." He grabbed her around the waist, dragging her naked skin onto his. "But I expect to be rewarded."

Her smile went wider, the tip of her tongue licking her lips. "You will be."

# { CHAPTER 15 }

He was livid.

Livid to the point he was shaking. His foot bouncing up and down—energy with no place to escape.

She could hardly sit next to her husband without her own skin prickling, innate shots of panic skittering across her muscles.

*He is not my stepfather.*

Evalyn repeated the mantra in her mind for the thousandth time that week. Lachlan was not her stepfather. His anger would not find a target on her. He wouldn't let it.

How very much she wanted to believe that.

Aside from those few seconds when he'd first entered his bedchamber the previous night, he'd given her no reason to doubt him. To doubt his control—for once he heard her, listened to her voice, the curbing of his anger had been infallible.

Yet the raging whirlwind of angst swirling in the air about him on the bench next to her was almost too much to bear.

She glanced to her right. They sat in the second row of benches in the courtroom, the row in front of them effectively trapping her. Lachlan to her left. The high back of the bench in front. To her right she would have to push past one man at the end of the row to reach a door she assumed led out of the courthouse.

But no.

She couldn't do that to Lachlan. She couldn't abandon him to witness the atrocity of this trial by himself.

*He is not my stepfather.*

Her eyes swung forward and she concentrated on the young ruffian stepping away from the witness table. His brown hair had been combed over and slicked down with thick pomade to lend an air of respectability, but the holes in his coat belied how desperate the lad was.

Paid to take the stand, or so his mostly incoherent, rambling testimony gave evidence to.

But another one testifying to the fact that Mr. Lipinstein was a smuggler. Not a murderer.

A title her husband would soon have to add to his name if the fury consuming him didn't abate.

Whispered murmurs pitched to a rumbled commotion in the courtroom as the lad stepped to the back of the building and the main white-wigged judge addressed the crowd, asking for quiet. His voice was drowned out by the catcalls and whistles as he announced the next witness.

Lachlan shifted, his bouncing foot tapping harder on the floorboards, making the wood vibrate under her toes. His knuckles were clasped so tightly together, they had gone beyond white, the tip of each knuckle pulsating red.

She didn't need to glance at Lachlan's face to know he was ready to explode.

Her gut flipped, hardening into a rock as the urgency to escape shot through her limbs.

Now. She needed to excuse herself now.

Instinct told her to run. Run before the explosion. Run before misplaced anger found her as the target. Her legs clenched, ready to gain her feet and move to the right toward the door when her left hand did the oddest thing.

It wandered away from her body with a mind of its own.

Wandered away and set itself on Lachlan's arm, sliding down to wedge itself between his clenched hands.

It wiggled, forcing the brutal clamp he held onto apart, until her fingers could entwine with his. The blood pumping in his veins pulsated, angry against her hand.

Shocked at her own actions, she stared at their tangled hands. Her white kidskin-gloved fingers stark against his skin.

She stared until his right arm twitched and he brought their clasped hands closer to his torso, holding the back of her hand to his belly.

Evalyn braved a glance up at Lachlan's face. The fury that etched such deep lines into his forehead relaxed ever so slightly. Through his fingers, she could feel his frantic heartbeat slowing—just a touch—enough.

He looked down at her, the blue streaks in his hazel eyes glowing bright. At her, he wasn't angry.

Her head cocked to the side. Gratitude? Was that what she saw in his eyes?

He held her look for a moment that stretched into infinity. He was losing himself in her again. Losing his anger.

Astonishing.

Her hand against his and he could calm—which calmed her.

His stare only broke when the crowd around them erupted in jeers and they both looked forward.

The next witness was making his way to the front of the court. A short man, slightly rotund, with a thick mop of dull brown hair dipped forward, bowing before the row of judges. He turned to the side.

Heaven to hell.

Mr. Molson.

Her breath stopped, her heart freezing in place.

No. Not here. Not in the room with her.

She ducked her head to the right, hiding behind the man sitting in front of her. She edged one eye to the left, searching Mr. Molson's profile, unable to believe it was him.

What in the hell was he doing here? Doing here as a witness?

She saw the man wrong. It couldn't be him. It couldn't.

She leaned slightly to her left, her eyes frantic. Hawk nose that curled down into a point. Eyebrows that were as bushy as his hair, running in one long line across his forehead. Thin lips that always snaked over the crudest words when he cornered her.

There was no mistaking him.

"Mr. Molson, you are the person in direct charge of the men that were evicting the Wilson family, is that correct?" the head judge asked.

"It is." Mr. Molson looked out to the throngs of people in the assembly room, a sneer on his face.

Evalyn jerked, ducking her head down, shrinking, hiding the best she could manage in the second row. Blast it. Why had they sat so close? She should have insisted on the back of the room. She should have never come to the trial. What had she been thinking?

Her husband glanced down at her, his eyebrow cocking at her jerky movements.

Words. Words from the judge and Lachlan's attention turned back to the front of the room. Words she couldn't hear, couldn't understand for the terror seizing her body. Terror that cut all breath from her lungs.

Out. She needed out.

The crowd erupted around her, jeering, and she jumped.

Escape.

Now was the time.

She ripped her fingers from Lachlan's hand and tucked her head, struggling to her right along the bench, her hands clawing the wooden seat until she reached the man at the end. She stumbled past him—over him—pushing at the man's shoulders as she lurched to the door.

Her fingers slipping on the brass knob, it took far too long—seconds she didn't have—to open the door.

She staggered out into the daylight, slamming the door behind her, and then wobbled her way to the rear of the building, her gloved hand scraping along the rough red stone of the exterior.

Barely around the back corner of the building and she doubled over, vomiting and only narrowly missing the skirt of the mauve dress Janice had procured for her.

Her stomach twisted and she retched again and again, gasping for air in between heaves, trying to send breath into her lungs.

Tears burning her eyes, the clenching in her gut eased and her look lifted, frantic, not even sure where she had stumbled to. She needed to hide. Hide until Mr. Molson was gone. Hide until there was no way he could find her. For if he did…

Her belly coiled, sending a tremor of bile up her throat. Her eyes closed tight against the retch threatening to take her over again and she had to clutch the side of the building so the dizziness setting into her skull didn't send her to the ground.

No. She had to stop. She had to hide. Hide before he found her. How long would he be in there?

She forced her eyelids open and searched around her. Stables sat behind the building. But what if his horse was in the stables? She could go down the main road winding through the village and find a shop to hide in, but most of the townsfolk were inside at the trial. Jacob had been beloved by the people in these lands, so many of them were itching for justice.

The stables. It was her best chance. If she could find a horse and a saddle she could make it away from the town. Make it away from Mr. Molson. He couldn't know where she was. Couldn't find her.

A horse. That was what she needed to do. It didn't matter whose it was. Now. Now before he was done testifying. Before he could find her.

Evalyn pushed off from the brick of the building and made it two steps before the dizziness spun her world and she stumbled to the side.

Hands caught her from behind before she fell and she shrieked, sinking to her knees before she could scramble away.

"Evalyn—stop."

She craned her neck to look behind her as she gained her feet, her boots slipping through the dirt.

Lachlan.

He reached out and gripped her forearm, steadying her on her feet. "Why did you run out of there? You forgot your pelisse." His fingers left her arm and he draped her cape across her shoulders.

She'd forgotten how cold it was outside. Forgotten everything of what was happening around her—the need to escape had so harshly taken a hold of her.

Lachlan rounded her, both of his hands clamping onto her shoulders as he studied her face. "What are you doing out here? You look like you saw the devil himself—you still look it." He glanced back at the building, his look dipping to the vomit on the ground. Worry settled into his hazel eyes before he looked back to her.

She lifted the back of her hand to her mouth, her kidskin glove dragging across her lips. "You didn't need to leave the trial—I know how important it is to you."

His eyes narrowed at her. "You were running, Eva. Escaping. I've seen this look on your face before. Tell me."

As much as she tried to keep her eyes on his face, her look slipped to the red brick of the courthouse.

Hell. She couldn't tell him. He was ready to kill someone as it was. She couldn't give him a target.

His gaze followed her look, then snapped back to her. "Evalyn. You need to tell me right now what is happening."

"I will tell you back at the castle."

"You'll tell me now." His fingers dug into her shoulders.

"No."

"Eva—"

"What happened in there?" She lifted her hand, pointing at the building. "What did that man testifying say?"

Lachlan exhaled a seething breath, his head shaking. The worry in his eyes was instantly replaced with rage. "He said that Lipinstein isn't one of his men. That he had nothing to do with the fire. That he was now short three men because my brother and I killed them."

She gasped, her hand going to her throat. The callousness. Of course, that was exactly the person Mr. Molson was. "The blackguard."

Lachlan dropped his hands from her shoulders, turning from her as he pulled free a silver flask from inside his overcoat. He pulled the stopper and drank a long swallow.

"Exactly." Shaking his head, he looked to her, holding the flask out to her.

Her last foray with Scottish whisky did not go well for keeping her wits about her. But she needed the sting of whatever was in that bottle to wipe the bile from her mouth. To embolden her for what she was going to have to tell Lachlan.

She took the flask from his hand and set it to her lips.

One sip, and it burned a slow trail down her throat. Brandy. She took another drink, filling her mouth. Too much, but she choked the vile liquid down.

Her eyes lifted to see him watching her intently. As much as she guessed she needed a third swallow, she handed the flask back to him. "So what is going to happen to Mr. Lipinstein?"

Lachlan shrugged, taking one last drink before setting the stopper in place and tucking the flask back into his coat.

"Domnall talked to one of judges at the end of yesterday—he said they would send the bastard to Newgate in London to await trial on smuggling charges. The judges all knew and respected Jacob, so he said that they would ensure Lipinstein will rot there for some time before his trial—they were to make sure on it."

Her bottom lip jutted up in a frown. "A small consolation."

"Miniscule." Lachlan's face contorted in rage for a short second, and then he exhaled, looking at her. "But that's not my worry at this moment."

"What is?" Her look darted about, a rabbit in a snare.

"You. We're going back to Vinehill and then you're going to tell me exactly what has happened to light the terror in your eyes."

"Lachlan—"

"Or would you prefer to tell me here?" His eyebrow arched.

She glanced at the courtroom building. Mr. Molson would be exiting soon. Possibly coming back to the stables. Panic started to tighten her throat, but she forced what she hoped was a smile on her face.

She nodded. "Vinehill. As long as we leave directly."

~ ~ ~

Lachlan stared at his wife as she stepped away from the carriage. A rogue breeze, almost balmy, cut through the chilly air and a tendril of auburn hair that had escaped from under her small black bonnet lifted from her temple.

"You are positive your feet are recovered enough for this?"

"I believe so. You said the trail was not too long?" She lifted her foot out past the dress and military-inspired pelisse that a maid had procured from his sister's wardrobe this morning. "The boots you found for me have just enough room that they are not rubbing my skin raw again. When did you have time to retrieve them?"

"After you fell asleep last night."

"You got out of bed?"

"Yes—why?"

"It—" Her brow furrowed, perplexed. "It is odd that I did not feel you move—hear you leave."

Lachlan turned to the carriage driver and waved him onward up the long drive to Vinehill. He needed to talk to his wife alone and he didn't want to have a conversation with her in his chambers where he was driven to distraction with thoughts of stripping her bare. It had only taken a day with her ensconced in his rooms and he already realized he was helpless against it—could think of little else other than getting lost in her.

Last night he had thought it peculiar, how his anger over his brother's death didn't manifest when she was in his arms. Once—in his bed—it was an anomaly. But twice?

Twice was much more than that.

When she had grabbed his hand at the trial, it was as though a thousand sparks of light had descended upon him and doused away the searing hatred burning him from the inside out.

Her hand clasping his in the courtroom had been the second time her touch had quelled the demons that refused to set him free. He'd only been given that respite for a few minutes in the courtroom before she'd torn her hand from his and escaped from the room.

Now he intended to find out the exact reason she'd run so fast from the trial.

He turned to Evalyn and offered his elbow to her. She slipped her gloved hand into the crook of his arm and he was already regretting not bringing her to his room forthwith. If he had satiated himself, they could speak without the anger from the trial still coursing through his veins.

They started walking, leaves crunching under their feet as they moved onto the trail that branched into the woods from the main drive.

"It is odd that I left the bed or odd that you didn't hear me leave?" he asked.

She glanced up at him, her gold-green eyes intent on him for a long moment. Curious, even. "That I didn't hear you. I hear everything and don't usually sleep well. I wake up at the slightest creak."

He patted her hand on his arm. "Then I admirably performed my husbandly duties and sufficiently wore you out."

"Admirable, was it?" She chuckled. "Does that mean I failed my wifely duties since you didn't fall into a dead man's sleep?"

His look ran down her torso and back up again, his eyes hungry. "You performed splendidly. But you also possess a unique ability to compel me to want more—more of you, more of your body. That is what keeps me awake."

"Why didn't you rouse me?" A wicked smile lifted her right cheek. "And why in the heavens did you have us let out here for a walk back to the castle?"

Lachlan inclined his head. "For that exact reason. I didn't want to be driven to distraction. Not when I have answers to extract from you."

The mirth disappeared from her face. Easiness he instantly regretted scourging from her eyes.

There was nothing for it now. His look pinned her. "Why did you run from the courtroom?"

Her eyes scurried away from him, concentrating on the low, barren branches passing by above her head. "We cannot just leave this day behind us? Leave the trial to be buried as a distant memory?"

"We can if I know what sent you running—sent you trying to escape."

"I wasn't trying to escape you."

"I didn't say you were trying to escape me, Eva. But you were trying to escape something and I want to know what it is."

Her feet slowed, her look venturing to him. "That man I told you about—the one my stepfather sold me off to?"

His feet stopped and he turned to her. "You mean the bastard that threatened to make you bleed?"

She nodded, her lips pulling into a tight line. Her hand slid from his arm. "It was Mr. Molson."

"Bloody hell, Evalyn. The Mr.—the Mr. Molson that took the stand today? The one that clears the Swallowford lands?"

She nodded.

His words slowed, his voice dipping to a growl. "That same bastard that walked into the courtroom today—the very same?"

She cringed, nodding.

Rage like he'd never known swept through him. However it manifested on his face, it sent fear spiking through Evalyn's eyes and she took a step backward.

He spun from her, a visceral snarl churning from his belly and escaping into the crisp air as he stalked to the closest tree and slammed his fist into it. And again.

The pain of the shock vibrating up his arm only fed the fury. This wasn't his brother's fiery death. This wasn't his parents slipping away in their sleep. Those things had always been out of his control.

This was the devil himself threatening the one thing he'd sworn to protect in this life.

His wife.

A wife he was quickly realizing he would do anything to keep safe.

His fist slammed into the tree a third time, his glove ripping, blood splattering through the leather.

"Lachlan, stop." Evalyn's hands clamped onto his upper arm, halting his next swing.

He tried to shrug her off, but her grip was rock solid.

"Stop, please, just stop."

He looked down at her. The fear that had manifested in her eyes had been replaced with anxious worry.

Hell. He was scaring her. Scaring her and she was still trying to stop him—stop his anger from taking a hold of him.

But he needed that anger. Needed to carve it into a fine, deadly point that would be unleashed once he traveled back to Stirling and found Mr. Molson.

The main drive. The main drive would be faster than the trail.

He spun away from her, trying to shake her from his arm as he stalked toward the drive. "I'm going back to Stirling."

"No, you cannot, Lachlan." Her heels dug into the fallen leaves, the dirt, and she wouldn't let him go even as he dragged her along with him. "Just stop—you can't go back."

Her toe tangled with a root that tripped her feet. She fell forward, her hold slipping down his arm.

Shake her off and she'd fall to the ground—and he'd be free of her. Free to go kill the bastard.

Or help her to her feet.

He glanced back at her dangling from his arm.

Blasted stubborn woman.

*Hell.*

He spun, grabbing her arm and yanking her upward until her feet were solid under her. For a long moment their stares locked only inches away from each other, her breath heavy against his.

"Dammit to Hades, Eva." Lachlan let her arm go and ripped off his right glove. He shook his hand, staring down at his bloody knuckles. "This is why you didn't tell me back at the courtroom, isn't it?"

Her hands slipped from his upper arm even though she still looked ready to strike—to reach out and tackle him once more if needed. "Yes. I didn't want you to approach

Mr. Molson in your current state. He is well connected through my stepfather—through the Duke of Wolfbridge."

"You think I give a damn about his connections? You think that the man doesn't need to have my knuckles implanted into his nauseating face?"

"I think I don't want to see you hanged for murder." Her arms folded across her chest. "And I especially don't want him to see me."

"You think I cannot protect you?" His words seethed through gritted teeth.

"You need to stop telling me what I'm thinking, Lachlan."

"Then tell me what the hell you are thinking, Evalyn." His hands curled into fists. She noticed the motion immediately, her gold-green eyes flickering down to his hands before they lifted to study his face.

She didn't take a step back. Didn't cower. "What I'm thinking is that Mr. Molson doesn't know I'm here in Scotland—doesn't know I escaped Wolfbridge with you. He would have already come for me at Vinehill if he knew. He and my stepfather. He thinks he owns me, Lachlan, and he was done waiting for my stepfather to give me to him. They played a game of their own perverse battle of wills—and I was the ultimate prize. I knew that. And I knew it was soon to be over, that my stepfather was handing me over to him." Her right hand lifted from her chest and she rubbed her forehead. "Mr. Molson is not about to give one of his possessions up—and that's exactly what I am—a trinket to pull out and abuse whenever the mood strikes him."

Her voice cracked on her last few words and he realized how very terrorized she was at the possibility that Mr.

Molson saw her. Her fear didn't have anything to do with his ability to protect her. Didn't have anything to do with the fact that she was now his wife. It had everything to do with the years of living in fear of her stepfather and Mr. Molson.

His fists unclenched.

"Please, Lachlan." Her hand dropped from her forehead. "It is easier for everyone if he doesn't even know I'm here with you. That we married. I could be on a ship to America for all he is aware."

"He's going to find out eventually, Eva. Both he and your stepfather have too many dealings in the area not to find out. It's no secret at Vinehill that I took a wife."

"Yes, but the longer it takes…" Her chest lifted in a deep sigh. "It's just better this way—time—time will help." Her right cheek lifted in a wry smile. "Forever would help."

Lachlan exhaled a deep breath, his rage dissipating.

She was right.

What she didn't need was her husband stalking off fully cocked and ready to destroy a man. If he removed Mr. Molson permanently from her life the cost would be his own life and that would leave her to the mercy of her stepfather again.

That was the last thing he would let happen.

He'd have to talk to Domnall when they got back to the castle. Secure his oath to marry Evalyn should anything ever happen to him. He'd been thinking on it for days and he needed to secure the promise from his friend.

Blood still seeped from his knuckles and he wiped his glove against the raw skin, then looked at her. "I won't go into Stirling to find Mr. Molson."

"You swear it?"

His head cocked to the side. "All I can promise you is not today. Today he escapes my wrath."

For a long second she looked to protest, then she nodded.

"Shall we continue up to the castle?" He held out his elbow to her.

Evalyn took it and they started forth on the trail again. The leaves crisp under their boots, the sharp smell of decaying summer held in the air. Frost and snow would be blanketing the land before he blinked.

Halfway to the castle with Evalyn worrying her bottom lip the entire time, her steps slowed and she looked up at him. "Why did you marry me, Lachlan?"

He glanced down at her, his eyebrow lifting. He knew a trap when he heard one. "What do you need to know?"

"Why you decided to marry me, for a start."

Lachlan shrugged. "I married you because you needed marrying."

"That was all?"

Evade. Evade at all costs. He nodded. "I needed a wife. One of my choosing. And I like your spirit, Eva. Not to mention you are a beautiful woman."

Her lips drew inward and she took several more steps in silence, her fingers along his arm tensing.

"Need there be more to it than that?"

"No." She shook her head.

Ten more steps and her feet stopped on the trail, her hand dropping from the crook of his elbow.

Dammit.

A step past her he halted, closing his eyes for a long breath. He turned back to her.

"Evalyn?"

"If Mr. Molson is the one that has been clearing the Swallowford lands, then he is doing so on my stepfather and the Duke of Wolfbridge's behalf." She met his look, her gold-green eyes skewering him. "You know exactly who my stepfather is and you blame him for Jacob's death don't you, Lachlan?"

There was no denying it. Not if he was ever to gain the trust in her eyes.

"Yes."

Her lips drew in for a long moment, pulling so hard against her teeth her skin turned a bright white. She exhaled a puff of breath. "So tell me marrying me had nothing to do with the fact that you've always known exactly who I am. Who my stepfather is and what he's done to these lands. Tell me marrying me had nothing to do with your hatred for him."

Bloody hell.

He looked up at the grey sky through the barren branches above, hoping for intervention.

None came.

His look dropped to her and he met her piercing gaze. "Yes. It had everything to do with that, Evalyn. Everything."

# { CHAPTER 16 }

Revenge.

He'd married her for revenge.

Lachlan's face, his form went blurry before her as the fact rolled through her body like a ship being launched, slamming into her gut and sending waves of devastation into every nerve.

It hadn't been pity as she had suspected. It hadn't been because he'd actually taken a liking to her.

No. Revenge pure and simple.

She'd always been her stepfather's pawn to do with whatever he desired.

Now she was Lachlan's pawn.

She'd figured it out as she retched behind the courtroom, the disparate pieces of the last weeks finally fitting snugly together.

She'd known her stepfather owned lands in Scotland. But she'd never imagined this—that he was the one that owned the lands Lachlan's brother died on. Mr. Molson had her stepfather's full authority to do whatever was necessary to handle the clearings of her stepfather's lands. But it was her stepfather. His express order to clear the lands that had sent Jacob and an innocent family to their graves.

Revenge.

The word pulsated in her mind and with each breath her insides shriveled deeper into a dark abyss.

She'd thought Lachlan was an honorable man. She'd thought she'd been miraculously delivered to the one man that could see her. That could listen to her.

She'd been so stupid.

Lachlan only wanted her for revenge.

Revenge, and then what? He'd send her off to that dower house? Divorce her? When was he to do it? Maybe he'd just abandon her at Vinehill with its twisty corridors and people that spit on the ground as she walked past.

Or maybe he'd always planned to ruin her beyond the pale and then send her back to her stepfather.

Her stomach churned, threatening to upend itself.

She'd save him the blasted trouble.

Her sight out of focus for the blood that pounded in her head, she sent her feet flying, spinning and running as fast as she could along the path. The impact of every step ripped at the scabs on her feet, the leather of the boots scraping along her heels. Pain. But pain she couldn't even feel, couldn't place past the staggering crushing of her chest.

She didn't even make it around the upcoming bend before Lachlan's arm clamped around her middle and her feet swung out in front of her.

"Stop, Eva. For heaven's sake, stop."

She twisted in his arm, her hands curled into claws, pushing, shoving at him with all her strength.

It was nothing against his iron clamp on her.

It was never enough, her strength.

The searing fury of that fact sent her screeching, her hands swinging at him with every last drop of power she possessed.

It wasn't enough.

It was never enough.

He withstood the onslaught, second after second, drawing her closer and closer to his body. Closer until the length of her was pressed against him, her arms wedged into submission between them.

"Stop." The word was barked down at her, a growl so terrifying that she stilled, bracing herself.

Lachlan lifted his left hand, his thumb and forefinger gripping her chin and forcing her face upward.

"Look at me, Eva."

He could force her face up, but he couldn't force her to look at him.

The hand under her jaw tightened. "Evalyn, look at me."

She closed her eyes.

"Fine." The word hissed out. "Don't look at me. But you bloody well will hear what I'm to tell you."

Double the cad. She couldn't free her arms. Couldn't cover her ears.

"Your stepfather—yes, it was the reason. The reason for everything. The reason I allowed you to come north with us. The revenge of it was all I considered—we would take you from him—ruin you—all in the name of retribution. He's done so much harm to so many innocent people here—Jacob's death was a result of what he ordered—but just the last in the long line of devastation he's unfurled across the land. So taking you…"

He paused, a long exhale breaching his lips. "It was perfect and brilliant—the vengeance upon him. It wouldn't bring Jacob back—but it was something. Something to twist a knife into your stepfather's gut."

His hand dropped from her face, his voice sinking into a low rumble. "But all that was before."

Silence.

His arm around her waist fell away, releasing her, and he stepped backward, cool air rushing between them.

She cracked her eyes open.

He stood three steps away, his shoulders lifting and descending in heavy heaves. The blue streaks in his hazel eyes burned hot—seared—almost as though he couldn't stand the thought of touching her for another moment.

Her lips parted, breathless words escaping. "Before what?"

"Before you ran from the camp when Colin hit you—and a strike of fear cut into me so harshly all I could think of was dragging you back to it. Before you saved Rupe with that stupid dead rabbit in your hand. Before you fell in the river and my heart stopped. I was always meant to protect you, Eva, even though I fought it every step of the way."

"You fought it?"

"Until you let me strip you. You were freezing. But you let me. You let me touch you when you could have resisted. But you didn't. And my need for revenge vanished in that instant my fingers touched your skin." His words stopped and he swallowed hard as his hazel eyes lifted to the sky for a long moment. His gaze dropped to her. "In that moment, revenge was replaced with nothing but a visceral need to keep you safe. Even then, I didn't know what I was going to do with you. But I admitted to myself that I wanted you. Wanted you like no other."

For all the fervor behind his words, for all she wanted to believe it was more, Evalyn couldn't ignore the fact that she was still an object. For revenge or for lust, she was still nothing but a pawn. "And lust is better than revenge?"

His eyebrow cocked at her. "You need to understand, Eva, it became much more than lust without me even realizing it." His gravelly voice dipped even lower. "You were mine from that moment my fingertips slid down your spine. Domnall knew it. Rupe knew it. Hell, the whole camp knew it. I was just late to the realization."

He took two long strides to her, closing the distance between them. His hands lifted, settling onto her shoulders as his hazel eyes pierced her. "The revenge was everything, until it was nothing. You ask me why I married you? Here is my answer—I didn't marry you because of who your stepfather is. I married you in spite of who your stepfather is. I married you for you."

She exhaled breath she didn't know she held and her gaze dropped to his chest. For as much as she could reconcile it, he was telling her the truth.

Telling her she needed to start trusting him.

She nodded, unable to move sound past the lump wedged in her throat.

"So you need to stop running, Eva. Stop running from me. You're making my life increasingly more complicated every time you do."

Her gaze lifted. The edges of his eyes crinkled, shifting the serious countenance of his face into a wry tease. She had no defense against it—the irresistible magic when humor lifted his eyes like that.

A small smile curved onto her lips. "The last thing I want to do is complicate your life, Lachlan."

His lips descended onto hers, soft with resolute undercurrents of bridled promise. He pulled slightly away, his lips brushing against hers with his murmured words. "Then no more running. If you're mad at me. Scared of me. Want to throttle me. You stay. You plant your feet and fight, come what may."

"Is that permission to throttle you for using me as a vessel for your revenge?"

He chuckled, his head diving down, his lips trailing down her neck. "I'll take it, as it's what I deserve. Call it a temporary stretch of madness on my part."

Her head fell back, his tongue on her skin sending delicious fire sparking through her veins. "Then the throttling will commence once we get back to your chambers."

Lachlan's hands slipped down her backside, yanking her body into his, his member pressing hard into her belly. "I don't know if I can make it to the room without being properly throttled."

She leaned back against his hold, pulling her neck away from his lips. "And maybe that's part of your punishment. A tortuous walk up to the castle."

The growl expelling from deep in his lungs sent birds squawking, flying away overhead.

But she wouldn't be swayed. The man needed to be punished, and if a stiff-legged stroll was what she could muster, it would have to be his due comeuppance.

~ ~ ~

They didn't make it to his chambers.

Lachlan looked down at his wife's pink cheeks, her upsweep askew with wild tendrils as they walked through the labyrinth of corridors in the castle. He should have just ripped out all the pins and let her long hair fall to the wind, but that would have interfered with his tongue drinking in her skin when he sank into her.

A grin that hid nothing of what they'd just done in the forest danced across her lips. He should find out if she played whist—she'd be horrible at it. Strip whist.

Her smile widened as her gold-green eyes lifted to him and it sent a jolt through his cock. He needed to get her up to his chambers, as he didn't think he'd been duly punished quite yet. Only rewarded.

She dragged a lock of hair across her right temple, securing it in place. Her scar wasn't visible—even so, it bothered him that she felt the need to constantly make sure the ragged skin was hidden.

They'd lost her bonnet at some point on the trail. He wasn't exactly sure where, only that he'd stripped it from her head and dropped it as she led him on a merry chase.

The ancient oak tree that sat along the eastern moor would never be the same. Not with her back wedged against it, her fingernails digging into the bark as he lifted her skirts and drove into her, rutting against a tree like common animals.

He was waiting with trepidation for the moment he would be satiated of her body. For the moment when he didn't come in her and instantly want to be hard again, sending her through the very same paces. But it refused to be tamed—his appetite for his wife.

If anything, he wanted her more today than he did the previous day. It'd been that way since the night he'd married her and he was no force against it.

To his gratification, he thought he was finally starting to chip away at the massive walls she'd ensconced herself in. Yet even after what he told her on the forest trail—confessing all of why he took her from Wolfbridge—he knew she didn't fully trust him.

Not that he deserved it.

It vexed him—the portion of her that she still held away from him, wary to his words. Still waiting for her world to collapse—for him to make her world collapse.

Maybe it would always be so, his wife's lack of trust. Or maybe it would merely take time. Time where she was given no reason to doubt him.

It may very well take until he was on his deathbed for the moment that she finally trusted him with everything she was. A sobering thought. But if he made it that far without giving her reason to doubt him, he would venture their lives together a success.

They rounded one of the five bends in the corridor on the third level of the castle en route to his chambers, and the mass of Domnall almost barreled into them.

Domnall stepped back, his look going from Lachlan to Evalyn. His gaze returned to Lachlan, a suppressed smile playing at the edges of his mouth. "Lach—I was just looking for you. Your grandfather has been demanding your presence."

Lachlan's back stiffened, his thoughts sobering as his hand that had been wrapped along Evalyn's shoulder dropped to his side. "He knows the outcome of the trial? It ended as predicted?"

"It did." Disgust curled Domnall's lip. "Mr. Lipinstein is on his way to Newgate as we speak. A smuggler, but not a murderer."

A brutal wave of outrage swept through his gut. It was expected. But to actually hear it—that the bastard was escaping justice for his murderous ways—it cut deeply into his soul and tore at the raw, bloody wound that had festered deep in his soul since Jacob had died.

Done. It was done.

"And my grandfather?"

"Reacted as expected. Anything within his cane's reach was broken."

Lachlan nodded. "You were outside his reach?"

"My shin caught the first blow." Domnall shrugged. "Not but a scratch." His look went to Evalyn. "Shall I escort ye back to your chambers, lass?"

She looked up at Lachlan. "Do you wish me to accompany you?"

Lachlan studied her face. She looked almost hopeful at the prospect. Sweet, but now was not the time to set her in front of his grandfather, not with the fury that would be filling the room. "No, this I best tackle alone."

She nodded, a frozen smile on her face. "I understand." Her look swung to Domnall. "Thank you, Domnall, but I recognize where I am—I can make it to the rooms without a problem."

Domnall inclined his head to her and Evalyn stepped around him to move down the hall.

Lachlan motioned to his friend as he turned. "Dom, I wanted to speak with you anyway. Walk with me?"

Five minutes later, Domnall left him at the heavy oak door with its straps of ancient black hinges that led to the Vinehill library—effectively, his grandfather's living chambers, since he could no longer move up and down the stairs to his rooms.

He stared at the weathered rough grain of the door, ordering his thoughts. With a deep breath to steel himself, he shoved the heavy door open. "Boy, that you? Where have ye been?" His grandfather twisted his body in his wingback chair, craning his neck to see the doorway. "Ye should've been here, boy, what with the news—sending Dom to tell me."

Lachlan closed the door behind him. "I was taking care of a matter on the way back from the trial, Grandfather."

"A matter like that English chit ye dragged home? And why in the hell haven't I seen ye since ye've been back?"

"I stopped in the last two nights, Grandfather." Lachlan moved to the center of the room, settling his hands in a clasp behind his back. "You were asleep both times. I've been at the trial during the day."

"Asleep—phew—ye know I don't sleep, not when I'm this close to death. Yet Dom managed to find his way in here to tell me the news."

"We took the carriage, Grandfather. Dom rode to and from the trial."

"Ye think I don't know the carriage has been back for two hours, boy?"

Of course he knew. Even at seventy-one he knew everything that happened at Vinehill.

Lachlan inclined his head. "We walked back to the castle on the woodland trail. I needed to order my thoughts after the trial."

His cane slammed against the ottoman in front of him. "Ye don't need to think, boy, ye need to do. Thinking is weakness—ye should know what ye stand for the second it comes into yer head."

Lachlan stifled the instant argument bubbling in his throat. If he'd done that he'd be on his way to murdering Mr. Molson at this very moment. And he would have already sent Mr. Lipinstein to hell. Instead, he nodded. "Yes, Grandfather."

His grandfather's wiry eyebrows slanted together, the stiff white hairs an umbrella above his hawk eyes. "This better not be about that wretched Englishwoman you brought into Vinehill."

"She's not some random wretched girl. She's my wife."

His cane swung, striking the ottoman. A puff of dust flew from the top of the dark mossy green velvet. "She's the daughter of the man that killed your brother, Lach. Have ye lost all yer loyalty?"

"I haven't lost a damn thing." Lachlan's right hand curled into a fist, the fresh scabs over his knuckles popping free. "You think I don't dwell on that fact every day? Dwell on that fact in the moments I'm with her? The betrayal that I'm committing?"

"Ahhh, boy." His grandfather cackled, leaning back into the wingback chair. His madcap eyebrows arched. "Ahhh, well done. Well done. Ye married her for revenge, didn't ye, boy? What's the game afoot—why didn't ye tell me? Is the plan to drop her—ruined—on the doorstep of that devil father of hers? Hold her for ransom?"

Lachlan's head dipped forward, his glare piercing his grandfather. "Hold her for ransom?"

"Of course, boy, it's one of the best ways to exact revenge—hold the key to the future, to his standing in society, just out of reach. Better yet, hold her for ransom and then once ye get it, still ruin the girl. Divorce her and sell her. She's a bonny lass—would fetch a pretty coin."

Lachlan's look lifted to the upper right corner of the room where the dark portrait of his largest ancestor held up a severed head. Brutality immortalized forever. He stifled a sigh. Ransoms? Selling his wife? How had his grandfather become so warped? Had he always been so and Lachlan had just never noticed, or had his grandfather's grip on reality slipped, creeping along so quietly, so sneakily, he didn't notice it until this very moment?

His gaze dropped, centering on his grandfather. "Holding a woman for ransom may have been done in your time, Grandfather, but it is a very long time past that."

"Piddle that." His hand flung out, his skeletal fingers flashing an eerie white in the glow of the fire. "We still sell wives. Don't tell me we don't, boy. Wiggin in the village just put his up for sale not but three weeks ago."

Lachlan shook his head. Maybe his grandfather wasn't as mad as he thought. Wiggin *had* just put his wife up for sale. Of course, her lover had bought her and the whole affair was a gentlemanly transaction.

But still. Selling *his wife?*

"Evalyn will not be put up for sale, Grandfather.

"A divorce then? Simmons is working on the papers as we speak."

"He can put down his quill." Lachlan took a step toward his grandfather, his voice a harsh granite rock. "A divorce won't be necessary, as I have no intention of ending this marriage—no intention of abandoning my wife."

"What do ye intend to do with her then, Lach?"

"Quite simply, grandfather, I intend to keep her."

"Ye don't know what yer doing, boy." His cane crashed onto the ottoman again. "What about yer brother?"

"On the contrary, I know exactly what I'm doing. And I beg you to respect that." Lachlan spun, exiting his grandfather's room in six long strides.

The old buzzard was never going to understand.

And Lachlan couldn't explain.

# { CHAPTER 17 }

Just before the bend in the stone corridor, Evalyn's steps slowed as she heard approaching footsteps echoing against the stone. During the last week since the trial she'd tumbled into more than one person around the crooked bends in these halls and knew enough now to slow her gait.

At least she could find her way to and from the dining hall now. And she'd only gotten lost once when leaving the south side conservatory two days ago.

Progress.

She'd managed to map out a good portion of the castle in her mind and no longer needed to wait for Lachlan or a passing servant to escort her about.

The approaching footsteps didn't slow so Evalyn stopped and waited, avoiding the oncoming collision.

A woman in a crisp garnet day dress rounded the corner and drew up, her hand on her chest when she saw Evalyn. Slightly taller than Evalyn, the woman had the most gorgeous dark hair draped over her left shoulder, its glossiness sparkling in the light from the window at the end of the hall.

"You." The woman sputtered. "You. I have been waiting to see you."

Evalyn blinked hard, not only at the woman's beauty—at her flawless porcelain skin and her dark lashes setting off intelligent brown eyes—but at the thought of being stalked by this exquisite creature. "Me?"

"You are Lachlan's wife, no?" Her hand fell away from her chest.

"Yes." Evalyn's stomach tensed. "Forgive me, have we met?"

"Nae." The woman shook her head, her lips pulling back in a tense line. "Nae, I don't think introducing me to you was on the top of Lachlan's list."

The woman's words stopped and awkward silence filled the air as the woman studied her.

Evalyn cleared her throat. "Then I am at the disadvantage, as I do not know who you are."

"I am Lady Karta." Her head tilted to the side. "Lachlan's betrothed."

"His—"

"Well, no longer his betrothed, as you have seen fit to fulfill the job."

"You are the one?" Evalyn had to draw up her dropped jaw. "Then I do owe you an apology. I did not set out to marry Lachlan. I did not intend to interfere with his promise to your family."

The woman nodded, her canny brown eyes still taking measure of Evalyn from head to toe. "You are aware he married you as revenge against your stepfather?"

Evalyn's head snapped backward. What did this woman know of it? She offered a slight nod. "I do know."

Karta's pretty brown eyes widened for a long second, then narrowed at Evalyn. "You do? I would have thought Lachlan would keep that information to himself. Heaven knows he was never one to speak the slightest word to me."

Evalyn set an apologetic smile on her face. "He has not discussed the matter with me, but I can only imagine he has made recompense to your family for the broken betrothal?"

Karta flipped her hand in the air. "He has, or so my father mentioned. It's why we are here at Vinehill."

Evalyn searched her face. The woman obviously didn't like her, but she also didn't seem overly distraught at the thought of losing Lachlan. "Forgive me, Lady Inverton, but you do not seem overly distressed that Lachlan has broken the engagement."

"No?"

Evalyn shook her head.

"I suppose I'm not." Karta sighed. "I have been shuffled from one betrothal to another, and now I get the slightest hope that maybe—for once—I can have some say as to who I marry, and you, an uppity Englishwoman of all things, steal it from me, just as you stole Lachlan."

"Wait." Evalyn's hand lifted, palm to her. "You didn't want to marry Lachlan?"

"No." Her eyes lifted upward. "Nor his brother. That was my first betrothal that I was duty bound to. Something you would not understand." Her gaze dropped to Evalyn, the side of her mouth pulling back. "What I am distressed at is the fact that you seem to think you can lay claim on all the finest men here at Vinehill. It is poor form."

"I—what?"

Karta's arms crossed over the line of gold buttons lining her crisp garnet-hued jacket. "Domnall."

"Domnall? What about Domnall?"

"You can't take all the men—and having Domnall swear to marry you should anything befall Lachlan goes too far."

Picking up her skirts, Karta tried to step around her, but Evalyn threw out her arm, stopping Karta before she could pass. "Wait, please. What do you mean, Domnall is to marry me?"

She shrugged. "Lachlan asked him for the oath on it and now Domnall is duty-bound to it."

"But—but I have no intention of marrying Domnall."

Karta's left eyebrow lifted. "Yes, and you had no intention of marrying Lachlan, either. I understand exactly how you work, Lady Dunhaven." Her hand forceful, she pushed down on Evalyn's outstretched arm, then passed, moving quickly along the corridor and disappearing at the split at the end of the hallway.

Her footsteps drifted to silence as Evalyn stayed rooted to the spot, working through what Karta had just told her.

Lachlan. The bloody fool.

How dare he?

She spun, retracing her steps down to the conservatory, then veered to the left, searching for the study that she knew was on the main level of the castle, but couldn't quite remember the exact location of.

She flung open the doors of four rooms before the fifth door revealed the study.

Lachlan was sitting behind a wide walnut desk, papers and ledgers strewn across it. Mr. Simmons, the solicitor of the estate she'd been introduced to two days ago, sat perched opposite him. The man had oddly white hair, for how young his face looked, and she hadn't been able to decide if the man was older with a young face or younger with old hair.

Both looked up as the door she flung open slammed into the wall.

"Evalyn?"

She stepped into the room, stomped halfway to the desk and then stopped, her feet rooted in place, her arms lifting to clasp just below her breasts. "Lachlan."

His name seethed from her chest—from the pit of indignation that simmered into a boil the moment she stepped into the room.

His brow crinkled, his bottom lip jutting up for a moment before his look shifted to Mr. Simmons. "Would you excuse us?"

"Of course, my lord." Mr. Simmons quickly gathered up the three ledgers in front of him, stacking them on top of one another, and he stood, turning to the door.

With a kind smile that held not a hint of judgement, Mr. Simmons made his way past Evalyn.

"Close the door on your way." Lachlan's gruff voice instantly spiked her ire and drew her attention back to him.

The door gently clicked closed.

"How could you?" Before he could utter a sound, she pounced, stalking over to the desk, slamming her hands on the edge of the smooth walnut.

He looked up at her through hooded eyes. "I do a lot of things, Evalyn. You're going to have to be more specific."

"Domnall." The name dripped from her lips, full of spite.

"What about Domnall?"

"You pawned me off to him."

"I did what?"

"You made him promise to marry me if anything should happen to you. Do you have some sort of death wish that I don't know about, Lachlan? Something you should have told me? I know you're drowning in a cauldron of hate, but to pass me off to Domnall? What about what he wants? What about what I want?"

For a moment, Lachlan visibly held his breath, his head shaking. He slowly got to his feet. "I'm protecting you, Evalyn."

"Protecting me? You think you can just swap out one husband for another?" Her right hand lifted and slammed onto the desk.

His look dipped down to her hand, then slowly traveled up her body until he met her eyes. "Well, yes. I guess I did think I could do that." His voice was painfully even, devoid of any emotion. "I thought I was ensuring you were to be protected under any circumstance. I thought—"

"I don't want another husband, Lachlan." Her voice screeching, she cut him off. "I want you. I want you not doing something so entirely idiotic in the name of protecting me that I lose you. I want you."

His head snapped back, the vehemence in her words a blow. "How did you even find out about this, Evalyn?"

"Lady Inverton. I met her in a corridor on the way to our room."

His right brow arched. "You met Karta? I haven't even met with her and her father yet."

"Apparently, your grandfather has already taken care of that trifling detail."

Lachlan's fist clunked onto the desk, loose papers crunching under the force. "Damn him."

"Damn him?" Her eyes pinned him. "How about damn you, Lachlan? Did it ever occur to you to ask Domnall what he wants for himself? Did you know Lady Inverton wants him—apparently she has for some time?"

"No, I didn't know that." He shook his head. "But that's of no consequence now. Let me do this, leave things with Domnall as they are."

"No."

He drew in a deep breath and rounded the desk, setting himself next to her left side. Close, but their bodies not touching.

Space she imagined he was giving her for her anger.

It didn't matter. He overwhelmed her whether he was ten feet or ten inches away.

His fingers twitched as though he wanted to grab her, shake her to see his reason. "Let this be, Eva. I need this assurance for you in my mind."

She sucked in a deep breath, her lips drawing inward for several heartbeats. How to make him understand when she didn't truly understand her own anger setting her nerves on fire?

Clarity hit her with the fifth heartbeat—why this action of his shook her to her core.

"No. I'll not let it be." Her hands pushed off the desk and she turned to face him. "I'm so damn tired of being afraid, Lachlan. And if I let you do this—let you shuffle me off to Domnall—then I'm not in this with you—in our marriage. It makes me still afraid—afraid of the thousand possibilities that could happen—the ways you could leave me alone. It makes me build more moats around my heart for fear of the unknown."

Her right knuckles rapped onto the desk. "And I am done with it. Done with the constant fear. I am in this with you, Lachlan. For good or for bad. Not until tragedy happens. Not until I need to escape again. I'm in it with you. You alone."

For a moment, his eyes narrowed, his breath seething.

In the next instant, he rammed into her, his arms wrapping her, his mouth ravenous on her lips.

Instant, like it always was, how quickly he overtook her. How quickly she melted into the boulder of his body, needing her limbs entwined with his. The heat of him pounding deep within her. The whole of it terrifying in how much he made her want him—made her need him.

But no.

She had to stop this—had to make him understand.

Wedging her arms between them, she pushed against his chest.

No movement.

She shoved.

He broke away, the hunger in his eyes near to eating her up in just one blink.

"You'll rescind the promise from Domnall?"

"Eva—"

Her voice set hard, her palms pounded onto his chest. "Swear it."

He stared at her, the blue streaks in his hazel eyes on fire. He exhaled a breath, his head shaking against his words. "Yes—yes, I'll relieve him of his promise."

"It's only you, Lachlan. Only you."

"I'm beginning to understand that very thing, Eva."

"Good." She captured his face in her hands, drawing him closer, her already bruised lips finding his once more.

The frenzy of her core had already pitched high, demanding release, and her hands dropped from his face to attack his clothes. Dragging off his jacket, her fingers moved forward to make quick work of the buttons on the front falls of his trousers. The fabric fell and his shaft lifted high, demanding, into the open air.

He didn't need any cajoling, his hands running along her sides to her breasts, teasing her nipples through the wool of the fabric. Insistent, he tugged the bodice of her dress downward, freeing her right nipple.

His mouth left hers, diving to her breast, to tug the delicate skin with his teeth.

A guttural gasp flew from her mouth. Just like she liked it. Just like he liked it.

His hands went to the sides of her skirts, bunching the fabric up on either side of her. She twisted them so his rear was to his desk and she pushed him backward.

He dropped, sitting on the edge of the smooth walnut, scattered papers half under him.

Before he could say a word, she crawled on top of his lap, straddling him on the desk.

The rumble of a low laugh shook into the room. "Wanton minx."

"Debaucher of innocent maidens." She leaned forward, catching his lower lip in her teeth and tugging it. She nipped at it until he growled, lifting her hips and positioning her over his straining member.

She'd known nothing of the possibilities of the pleasures of the flesh weeks ago, but she'd been a quick study. And she knew her husband liked a little pain with his pleasure.

He also wanted to slow the pace. But she wasn't about to allow it.

Locking her knees on the desk in place, she settled herself downward in a rush, his shaft sliding up into her in one long motion. In quick succession, she lifted herself and drew him back into her—fast—the initial stokes brutal in her need.

She paused when he filled her to the hilt, their bodies fused. Paused to capture his mouth again, to kiss him so soundly he was panting for breath, gasping for release.

"Hell, Eva." Her name trailed off as his hands along her back clenched, his fingers digging into the muscles.

"Yes, my husband?" A lascivious grin caught her lips in between her labored breaths. Her thighs straining, she lifted herself up along his shaft. Slowly. Painful in the torture for him. For her.

At the rib of his tip, she stopped, hovering above him, her eyes locked on his.

"Only you, Lachlan."

"Yes." The one word lifted brutal from his lips, a plea and a promise.

She let herself drop, sliding down him and it was all he needed, his shaft expanding within her, filling her core to the brim. His growl vibrated into the air, into her chest and she lifted. Three more quick strokes against the power of his throbbing member and it sent her over the precipice.

Her body clamped down hard onto itself, the force of it shocking her so fiercely she thought it was death—death there to steal her away. Like every time with Lachlan deep inside of her, her body reacted in savage ways to his touch—and not only her body—her soul.

Terrifying and addicting, all in one.

He yanked her hard into his chest, clutching her so tight to his body their breaths were one. Gasp after gasp, and it still took long moments for the air dragging into their lungs to return to normalcy.

Lachlan shifted backward slightly, bringing his hands up to capture her face and cup her cheeks. "Know it was one of the hardest things I've ever had to do—extracting the promise from Dom, insuring you were taken care of." He paused, swallowing hard. "Having to imagine you with another man."

"I'll say it again, since you don't seem to be hearing it—I don't want anyone but you, Lachlan." Her look expectantly pinned him.

"Yes?" His brow furrowed, confused.

She chuckled. "This is where you tell me you don't want anyone but me."

A smile lifted his cheeks and he shook his head. "I don't." He tugged her face close to his, his breath caressing her cheek as his fingers ran along the sides of her jaw. A deep sigh and his voice escaped low, guttural. "I'm finding, against all my intentions…I need this, Eva. I need you."

# { CHAPTER 18 }

*Blast it all to hell.*

He knew this would happen. He just didn't think it would be so soon.

Lachlan's heavy steps echoed along the stone corridor, even as he tried to lighten the thunking of his heels on the ancient worn limestone.

He stepped through the open door onto the gravel path leading into the conservatory.

Evalyn wasn't on the bench in the far right nook of the room, though the book she was currently reading sat open on the adjoining side table. Secluded by the lemon-scented gum trees and with the sunlight streaming in, it had become her favorite spot at Vinehill.

He searched along the greenery of herbs, the rows of vegetables, and along the orange trees looking for her head. A brush of skirts rustled in the far left corner and he walked three-quarters of the way into the conservatory, stopping when he had full view of his wife.

Bent over, Evalyn twisted her body, her arm outstretched to pluck a tiny sprout of a weed from the plant bed where basil grew.

"Haagert is now letting you weed unsupervised?"

She jumped, a small gasp fluttering from her lips as she stood straight and found him. A smile, beaming with pride cut across her lips. "He is, can you believe it? And it only took eight days of pestering him straight for him to give me leave to do so." Her head swiveling, she glanced around her as she dropped the weed into a pile by her feet. "Though I would not be surprised if Haagert's hiding in here somewhere, watching my every move and ready to pounce and slap my hand should my fingers stray near a desirable plant."

Lachlan chuckled, though the sound echoed hollow to his ears. Blast it, he didn't want to have to pull her away from here. Away from the one room aside from their bedroom that she'd found solace in.

Evalyn wiped her fingers on the apron that wrapped her blue wool dress. A few alterations to the hems and his sister's wardrobe had served Evalyn well. "I'd never had time to think much on the growing of anything at my stepfather's estate, as I'd always been too busy being at his beck and call. But this is so much"—her head pulled back, her lips pulling to the side as she searched for the word— "fun, I guess is what I would call it. The little miracles of plants growing out of dirt."

"I doubt Haagert would classify this as fun—more akin to his life's work, I would think, for how possessive he is of this room. I'm impressed you managed to make him into a friend."

"I don't know if one could say friend just yet." She shrugged. "Thorn in his side, a buzzing bee that will not let him free—that is more the looks he gives me. But I am determined to learn all I can from him."

"You realize the likelihood of you ever having to pick berries for Rupe in the wild again are slim?"

She stepped toward him, her chin tilting up as she smiled at him. "Maybe, but one never knows and I am free to learn useful things here. I don't intend to ever mistake my berries again. Learning to identify edible berries was the first topic I tackled during this last week. What if we were on a picnic next summer and I wanted to pick berries?"

"You're already planning a picnic for next summer?"

"Of course. Picnics, day long rides." Her eyes widened. "Oh and I want to visit every inch of your family's lands. Meet the people, whether they want to meet me or not. I'm determined to put an end to the horrified suspicion in their eyes once they hear me talk and know I'm English."

The optimistic glow in her gold-green eyes was so hopeful for the future that a pang ran across Lachlan's chest. He knew he was about to destroy the spark of it.

At least for the time being.

Evalyn's hand lifted, drifting out to the surrounding plant beds. "And all these crops Haagert grows for the kitchens in the winter are a wonder. Did you know he has a crop of blackberries that will be ready at yuletide? Planted and timed just for the festivities. A marvel. He won't let me touch that plant bed just yet."

Lachlan looked at the plant bed she was marveling over. The green leaves looked the same to him as every other plant in the conservatory. For what little he knew of plants, he was nonetheless happy to find his wife so enamored of the room.

She glanced back to him. "But you are probably not in here to hear about blackberry bushes, are you?"

"Not exactly." His voice went grave, even though he tried to keep his tone even. "I actually need to pull you away for a few minutes to come with me."

Her eyebrows drew together, the glow in her eyes abating. "Is something amiss?"

"Yes." Lachlan sighed. He'd debated on the walk to the conservatory how much he should tell her before they got to his grandfather's room. The less the better. She would come willingly if he kept his mouth closed. He forced a weak smile. "But it just needs to be put to right, and then all will be well. But I need you with me to do so."

"Of course." She lifted her apron, wiping the dirt off each of her fingers individually. "Is he not well?"

"He is fine, at least for now."

*Until I kill the old buzzard.*

Lachlan stretched the weak smile on his face.

Evalyn hurried to the bench and removed her apron, hanging it on a nearby hook.

He held out his arm to her and she joined him without word, even as hesitation settled into her gold-green eyes.

They walked in silence through the twisting corridors. Pausing for a moment at the threshold to his grandfather's room, Lachlan took a deep breath, steeling his spine.

A smile—meant to reassure—twisted oddly on his mouth as he looked down at Evalyn.

Her eyes widened in alarm, but he gave her no time to react and pushed open the heavy oak door to his grandfather's room.

His hand on the small of her back, he nudged Evalyn into the room, his footsteps behind her only pausing to close the door behind them.

With the heavy curtains drawn against the daylight, only the fire and the four sconces spaced on the opposite wall lit the room. His grandfather sat in his wingback chair by the fireplace, laughing at something the man sitting across from him had just said. The visitor sat with his back to Evalyn and Lachlan, only the corner of his elbow perched wide on the wingback chair he sat in visible.

Evalyn looked back over her shoulder at Lachlan, her eyes crinkling in confusion as he propelled her forward.

"Grandfather, we are here." Lachlan stopped in the middle of the room, his hand on the small of Evalyn's back sliding around to wrap her waist and tug her tight to his body.

His grandfather's look swung to Lachlan and he lifted his cane, jabbing it in the air at his grandson. "Took ye long enough."

Lachlan instantly bristled. "It took an appropriate amount of time."

The visitor stood, stepping around the chair.

A gasp flew from Evalyn, her knees buckling.

Lachlan's grip around her back tightened, holding her upright as he assessed the devil.

A shorter man, only just as tall as Evalyn, he was stocky with a protruding belly. What was once perhaps a distinguished face was now wrinkled with time, his hair half grey and standing in odd tufts from his head. Grey eyes that weren't beady, weren't pinched as Lachlan had imagined they would be.

Far too ordinary.

Not the slightest visible inkling of monster about him.

The worst kind of monster.

"Daughter, it is good to see you in fine health." Evalyn's stepfather strode across the room, his hands outstretched to her. He stopped in front of her, his hands clasping both sides of her face, patting her cheeks with far too much force. "We were terribly worried on your well-being."

Evalyn jerked away from his touch, shrinking into Lachlan's side. Her head bowed but her voice managed to stay steady. "Stepfather."

A tremble ran through her, a tremble Lachlan could feel quite plainly against the side of his body.

"I apologize again for any fracas my grandson caused with yer daughter, Lord Falsted." Still sitting in his chair, his grandfather's words came clipped with spite. "Hot-headed one, he is. Always been so. Does not like to think on the consequences of his actions."

Lachlan ignored his grandfather's words, his gaze slicing into Evalyn's stepfather. "As you can clearly see, Evalyn is well and here of her own free will."

His eyes fixed on Evalyn, Baron Falsted's hand jutted out, grabbing her chin and twisting it upward. "This is true daughter?"

Evalyn nodded, her look not rising to him. Even with her chin captured by Falsted, her body pressed into Lachlan as though she were trying to crawl inside of him.

He knew she'd be scared at seeing her stepfather—but this—the complete and instant crumbling of her body and spirit he hadn't anticipated.

He resisted the urge to send his fist through the man's jaw—it wasn't the time. Not yet. Lachlan cleared his throat, taking a decided step backward and bringing Evalyn with him. It broke Falsted's hold on her chin.

Instant ire flashed in Baron Falsted's dull grey eyes. "Speak it, child."

Her voice came out tiny, a squeak barely heard above the crackling of the wood in the fire. "I—I do wish to be here." Her body tensed, defense against a sure blow to her person.

Lachlan took another step backward with her, moving her out of striking distance. "You heard her. Your stepdaughter left of her own accord and this is where she chooses to be."

"Except the choice wasn't hers to leave Wolfbridge." Falsted's look lifted from Evalyn to Lachlan. "You stole her away and I intend to take her back and bring charges against you, sir."

A cold smile pulled Lachlan's lips back. "You can try. But I have eight men that traveled with us that will attest to that same fact—she came with us of her own free will. Married me of her own free will."

"She had no choice but to marry you after you stole her away—the girl's not an idiot—she knew she'd been ruined." Falsted dared a step forward, his right hand flexing, the fat sapphire ring he wore on his index finger flashing in the light of the sconce behind Lachlan.

The trembles running through Evalyn exploded, turning into a full shake that took over her body. It twisted into a full fire the anger that had been coursing hot through Lachlan's blood since they stepped foot into the room.

Two minutes alone with the monster and he'd have his head smashed into the marble of the fireplace and Evalyn would never have reason to crumble like this again.

His grip around her waist went into an iron hold— now *he* wanted her to crawl inside him.

Lachlan swallowed, reining in his fury. "Whether you want to believe it or not, everything Evalyn has done since departing Wolfbridge she has chosen willingly."

"Ha." Falsted's caustic chortle boomed into the room. "You think you can hide the fact that she tried to escape you twice to no success? You wouldn't let her leave your traveling party. Does that sound willing? I don't think the courts will look lightly upon that."

Lachlan angled Evalyn behind him as he took a step forward, his glare skewering Falsted. "Where did you hear that?"

A demon smile curled the left side of Falsted's face. "It doesn't matter how I know, it matters that I do. It matters that your grandfather knows it as well."

The fire raging through his blood pounded into Lachlan's brain, turning his vision red. Who the blasted hell had been talking to these two?

"There will be some sort of retribution for stealing my only daughter away." Falsted's look went pointedly to Evalyn half hidden behind Lachlan. "Or I take her back."

"What—no." Evalyn turned her body into Lachlan's side, her hands going to his coat, clutching the dark fabric as her look went frantic to his face.

"Leave the room, girl," Falsted said. "This conversation isn't for a dim-witted chit like you."

She jumped and what little fire was left in her eyes went out, her gaze panicking, looking for escape.

"You'd be wise not to speak to my wife like that, Baron." Lachlan's voice had dipped so low, the rumble in his own chest took him aback.

The sneer on Falsted's face deepened. "Your wife? I was told she'd be no such thing for long."

"Who the hell told you that?" Lachlan's look shifted to his grandfather.

Of course the old bastard had told Falsted. He wanted Evalyn gone just as much as Falsted wanted her back.

"Get out of here, girl." His words barking, Falsted lifted an arm, pointing to the door. "You've caused enough trouble."

Lachlan took another step forward—ready to pounce, to pummel Falsted—when Evalyn ripped herself from his side. Her head bowing, she scampered to the door, her feet shuffling as though she would tumble if she picked up her heels.

Lachlan froze in place, his eyes trained on her back as she yanked the enormous door open and slipped out. How had she crumbled so quickly? How did this demon of a man have such a hold over her that she would run, even with Lachlan standing between them?

The door closed, blocking Evalyn from view.

"At least the marquess understands the severity of the situation," Falsted said. "We have already agreed to a divorce settlement of your so-called marriage."

Lachlan tore his look from the ancient door and pinned his grandfather. "What? Bloody hell, Grandfather."

His grandfather slammed his cane down on the ottoman. "I'll not have yer opinion on it, Lach."

Lachlan looked to the door.

Stay and fight his grandfather now or see to his bloody terrified wife?

The image of her gold-green eyes flashed through the red haze in his mind—her beaten look of panic, of escape.

It wasn't a choice.

His feet aimed for the door.

~~~

She hadn't made it far.

The rage pounding in his veins and clouding his vision hadn't subsided, but he didn't have time for it to quell. Evalyn was far more important.

Two and a half corridors to the left and he found her. Her shaking fingers trailed on the stone wall, holding her upright as she stumbled along.

At the sound of his clomping boots, she jumped, spinning around.

"Evalyn." He closed in the last seven steps to her.

"How could you do that to me—ambush me with him like that? I was safe." Her hand flew up to thump on her chest. "I was safe, secure, and now…" A gargled gasp cut off her words with a tremble that swept through her body.

The crack of her words and her crumpled face sent a spear through his chest. His hands lifted, settling gently on her shoulders.

She jumped backward, his hands searing her.

"I'm sorry, Eva, but I didn't think I could get you in that room any other way. I was told your stepfather was demanding to see you—see with his own eyes that you were unharmed. I had to prove that you are well and here on your own accord."

"Not that it worked—not that anything defying my stepfather is but a flickering fly of nuisance until he gets what he wants." Her words came out in stuttered gasps.

Lachlan stepped to her, stealing away the space she had gained between them. "He'll not get you." His hands lifted once more, his fingers capturing the sides of her cheeks.

She flinched, her eyes closing and her head shaking. But she didn't jerk away.

"You have to trust me, Eva. He'll not take you from me. No matter what." His words shook with vehemence. He glanced back over his shoulder, then bent his head so his eyes were directly in front of hers. "But for that to happen I have to go back and talk to my grandfather before he does something so dire there is no coming back from it. Before this turns brutal."

Her eyes widened, the gold sparks in them alarmed. "Lachlan—"

"Trust me, Eva. Just say you trust me."

Her eyes closed for a long moment. One breath. Two. Her eyelashes fluttered and she met his gaze. "I do."

He kissed her forehead. "Go to our rooms. Stay there. I will be up as soon as I have settled the matter."

# { CHAPTER 19 }

The ancient door creaking starkly against its hinges, Lachlan stormed into his grandfather's room.

"Where's Falsted?"

Staring at the fire, his cane propped under his chin, the marquess didn't lift his gaze to his grandson. "He is being shown to the north tower." His aged eyes, still far too canny, lifted from the fire to Lachlan.

"How could you do that, Grandfather? Letting that monster into our home?"

"How could I do that? How could ye do that, Lach? Bringing that girl into our home? With one fell swoop of yer fool cock ye lost half of the funds that were to build the factory in order to compensate Inverton for the broken betrothal. And then ye continue to lay with the daughter of the devil. Yer the one that betrayed yer brother."

"And you're the one that just invited the devil himself into our home." Lachlan sighed, his fingers running across his eyes. "Taking Evalyn as my wife is no betrayal to Jacob—she is an innocent in this."

"Ha. If ye believed that yer voice would be ringing with conviction, boy. Ye be the one that betrayed yer kin, and now I'm bound to make good on yer mistakes. Make the bastard pay."

Lachlan froze, ice filling his veins. "He's paying you for her?"

"Aye. The land between our western border and Fulton's Ridge. It's ours if we give him the girl back, marriage divorced."

"Bloody fucking hell." Lachlan exploded, the boom of his voice echoing into the tall dark corners of the room.

"It's what little we can salvage, Lach." The marquess leaned back in his chair, settling his cane across his lap, the matter settled.

Lachlan strode to his grandfather, planting himself inches away, leaning over him. "Evalyn is not yours to sell, you foolish old buzzard. She's my damn wife and if you don't stop interfering this instant I will leave these lands and never return."

The marquess's wiry white eyebrows lifted, slanting inward. "Ye would never."

Lachlan scoffed. "No, you have the wrong grandson—that was Jacob that would never abandon Vinehill. But I'm not Jacob, Grandfather."

"Ha, ye don't possess the audacity, boy."

"You don't know me at all, do you?" Lachlan stood straight, his head shaking. "I don't need these lands. These coffers. I own enough investments that Evalyn and I will do quite well on our own—with or without Vinehill."

"Ye ungrateful whelp."

"Not ungrateful—practical, Grandfather. I wasn't going to serve the crown forever. I knew that. I was ready for a life—my own life away from Vinehill before Jacob died. And as much as you like to think you can—you can't control me like you did Jacob. Not by far."

"So what, ye little wretch? Yer going to walk away from here for what? For that wisp of a girl ye'll tire of in six months' time? Walk away to prove yer a man? Yer no man, boy—not yet. Ye still haven't learned to control yerself, for if ye did ye never would have married that whore of a girl."

Lachlan stilled.

Too far.

He'd gone too far.

Insult him, Lachlan was used to it.

But to call his wife a whore?

Lachlan leaned over his grandfather, his movements lethal as his fingers went down to grip the arms of the wingback chair. "My hands are staying off your neck for that insult, Grandfather—that alone proves what control I possess." He exhaled a seething breath. "You're engulfed in a frenzy of spite, old man—you have been since my parents and your wife died. And when Jacob died it swallowed you whole and now you can spew nothing but hatred into the world. Hatred for me, for Sloane—for your own blood. Hatred that has nothing to do with Evalyn."

"Ye don't ken what I've done for ye, boy." The marquess's lip sneered. "And now I'm to be vilified because I'm trying to keep this estate alive for ye—for the next in line, for the legacy?"

Lachlan's brow furrowed. "A legacy? This is how you think to leave a legacy? You don't know—"

A sharp knock on the door cut into Lachlan's words and the door opened.

Dammit, whoever was daring to come in was going to get knocked on their ass. Everyone in the castle knew not to interrupt one of their brutal rows.

Lachlan pushed away from his grandfather's chair, spinning to the doorway.

Their solicitor scurried into the room, his head nodding to both men. "Edward, Lachlan."

"Now is not the time, Simmons," Lachlan's grandfather spat out, waving his cane in the air.

Simmons turned to Lachlan. "Lach, you said very specifically to find you and interrupt whatever you were doing instantly and immediately once there was word."

Lachlan froze. "You have word?"

"We do." Simmons nodded. "Verified. It is as you suspected."

"It is? You are positive?"

Simmons continued his nod, his eyes grave.

Lachlan's fist pummeled into his thigh. "Blast it all to Hades."

"What? What is verified?" Lachlan's grandfather jerked forward in his chair, working to gain his feet. "Simmons, you tell me this instant what Lach is about."

"Not a word to him on this." Lachlan pinned Simmons with a look threatening the man's future here at Vinehill.

Simmons inclined his head.

Lachlan turned back to his grandfather. "You can sit. For all the damn mess you just made, you can sit, Grandfather."

Without another word, Lachlan spun from the two men and stormed out of the room.

He had to find Evalyn.

~ ~ ~

She had to make this easy on Lachlan. Stop this before it escalated into the unimaginable. Stop this before she was turned back over to her stepfather.

*Before this turned brutal.*

Words from his own mouth.

Evalyn's fingers wrapped along the top rail of the half-wall of the stall, holding her balance steady as she watched the stable boy strapping the sidesaddle to the gentle horse he'd chosen for her.

She hadn't even made it to their bedroom before she turned left instead of right, her feet bringing her outside and down to the stables without even a plan in place.

Not that even now, minutes later, she had the slightest inkling of a plan. She knew she was panicking. Knew that the terror in her gut at seeing her stepfather had set her feet in this direction. Set her onto a path of escape.

But she couldn't turn her toes back toward the castle. Couldn't believe that there could be any future for her at Vinehill. And if she wasn't safe at Vinehill, then she needed to disappear. Disappear into the obscurity of a remote village far from most people, never to be thought of again.

Disappear, just as she had originally intended.

The saddle secure, the stable boy stroked the white speckled mare's nose and then looked to her. "Roseheart has been lookin' fer a ride fer days now. Shall I help ye mount 'er, m'lady?"

"No, it is fine. I will use the block. Please go back to the hay you were moving, I didn't mean to interrupt your work."

"Ain't no interruption, m'lady. It be my job." He strapped the horse's reins to the hook on the half-wall and tilted his head to Evalyn as he moved past her.

Her look didn't leave the mare as she listened to the boy walk down the main aisle of the stable, his boots rustling in the dirt as he exited out the front to the hay pile where he'd left his pitchfork.

This stable was now empty, except for her, thank goodness.

As much as the shaking in her limbs and the churning in her gut hadn't subsided, Evalyn couldn't step toward the horse.

She knew it was time to escape. Escape before her stepfather took possession of her again. Lachlan had said he would stop that and for as much as she wanted to believe him, he'd never faced her stepfather.

He didn't know the depth of cruelty in the man. She did.

It was time to leave. The only thing keeping her here was what she felt for Lachlan. And that, she'd always known would end. Knew it the moment Lachlan had filled her heart. Nothing good ever came of her happiness.

Once his grandfather and her stepfather had their way, what she felt for Lachlan wouldn't matter. Not in the slightest.

She had to set her feet forward. Had to face the reality of what was about to happen.

They were never destined to be together. Lachlan had wanted her for revenge and then he'd felt sorry for her. That was the extent of his feelings.

It *had* to be the extent of his feelings.

This was her one chance to leave before her stepfather got his tentacles back about her.

Yet her feet couldn't shuffle forward. Her fingers couldn't crawl to the reins.

Damn him.

Damn Lachlan.

Damn her feelings for him.

He was the whole bloody reason she wasn't miles away from Vinehill already.

Her head bowed and she concentrated on the blood pounding in her ears, her chest lifting and falling in short rapid breaths.

Trapped.

Trapped like she'd never been before. Damned if she stayed. Damned if she left.

"I'll not give you up, Eva." Lachlan's panting growl filled the air behind her. Breathless as though he'd just run a hundred miles. "Not ever. You're not going to run."

She jumped at his words—at the air about him swallowing her whole—but she couldn't lift her head, couldn't look at him.

If she did she would break. She would stay when she knew she shouldn't—when she couldn't trust what the future held for her.

But what if she could be sure? Sure of her trust in Lachlan?

The thought bubbled up from her roiling gut, taking a hold of her mind. There was a way to be sure. Sure that leaving was the right thing to do.

Determination skittered down her spine and bled to her fingers and toes, stopping the tremble that had taken a hold of her ever since her stepfather had appeared.

She had to risk this—risk it if she was ever to truly trust Lachlan. A broken nose. A broken arm. Painful, yes. But wounds would heal and then she would know. Know if she truly needed to escape.

If she stayed, she would have to trust Lachlan. Trust him implicitly.

Trust him through anything.

Trust him when he was angry. When he was truly, brutally, furious. Raging at her.

Her look lifted and she turned her head slightly, facing the already brewing storm in Lachlan's eyes.

"I'm leaving, Lachlan." The lie left her lips easily, her words far more controlled than she could've imagined them.

"What?" His head shook slightly, her words not making sense in his mind.

"I'm leaving. I have to."

"You're not, Evalyn. Your mind is not right at the moment—how you reacted when you saw your stepfather…" He shook his head. "There is no place that is safer for you than here—here by my side."

"Except it's safer for me to leave." She swallowed hard. "I needed safety, but you cannot offer me that, Lachlan. He walked right in here. Welcomed." She forced her look to hold his, unwavering even though all she wanted to do was collapse into him, hide in his chest with his arms wrapping her.

"You think I'm weak?" The deadly growl in his voice resurfaced, his hands itching at his sides, his fingers curling into fists.

He was so close. So close to exploding.

She just had to push him past the edge.

A deep breath and then the lie tore up her throat. "I think you cannot protect me, Lachlan. I am sure of it. My stepfather and Mr. Molson are too much for you."

The air between them stilled, died.

One heartbeat. Two. Three.

Lachlan spun from her, his foot and his fist connecting with a thick wooden post that separated stalls. Horses around them whinnied, startled, and the force of it shook the walls, dirt and dust floating down from the open rafters above.

He hit the post again, an agonized growl filling the cavernous space.

The third time he rammed into the post with his shoulder, threatening to take the whole structure down.

Just as brutally as his fury exploded, his body stilled, his hands wrapping around the rough-hewn wood. Gripping it, blood ran down his knuckles.

He leaned forward, clunking his head onto the wood, his eyes closed.

Her heart shattered, scattering into a thousand fragments that cut through her body. Pain in every nerve. That she could do this to him. Make him react so violently with just her words.

His forehead tilted to the side against the wood, his hazel eyes opening to her.

For a torturously long moment, he stared at her, his chest heaving.

Her breath nothing but a heavy stone lodged in her chest, she couldn't move, couldn't flex a muscle.

Lachlan shoved himself from the wood, stalking over to her.

He didn't slow when he reached her and she stumbled a step backward. Another. Another.

Her back hit wood and she was trapped in a corner, Lachlan hovering over her, every seethed breath of his a spike to her chest.

"Tell me you don't believe that, Eva." The growl gone, his voice had dipped raw, ragged.

"I—"

"Are you trying to leave me? You want to go back to your stepfather?"

Her eyes flew wide. "No—I—"

"Or the dower house—you want to hide away from life and all that it can offer you—all I can offer you." His hand lifted and went along her neck, cupping the base of her head as he leaned in, his breath hot on her skin, his mouth almost touching hers. "My hand running up your thigh, dipping inward to make you gasp. My lips caressing your neck, hungry. My cock sliding into you, thick and pulsating. Do you want to hide from that?"

"No—I—"

He jerked away from her, his hand ripping from her neck, a sneer twisting his lips "For if you believe your own words, Evalyn, then there is no room for you in my bed and you should go. Go to your stepfather. Go to the dower house. Get on that damn horse and ride off to wherever you thought you could escape to."

He spun from her and stormed toward the front entrance of the stables.

He was halfway to the barn door before Evalyn found her breath, found her courage. She shoved herself from the corner. "Lachlan—wait."

His stride didn't slow. If anything it sped.

Sped away from her.

Sped away from her hateful words.

He stomped through the wide opening and into the daylight, turning the corner, disappearing.

Her feet shuffled to a stop and she stood, silence pounding in her ears.

Stunned.

Stunned he didn't strike her. Hadn't even made a motion to do so. And she had pushed him so far. Too far.

He'd proved himself to be the man she knew he was.

He wouldn't hurt her, no matter what she did or what she said.

She loved him.

Completely and wholly and without doubt.

A breath seeped from her lips. Long and slow and painful. The reality of how her world had just truly crumbled around her came into brutal focus.

She had delved too deep into a lie that went beyond the pale. Told him he was unworthy. Told him he was weak.

A tear slipped down her cheek. She hadn't considered this, coming back from her words. How they would wound him.

How horrible, horrible, horrible she'd just acted.

She had to find him.

Her feet flying, she started down the main aisle of the stable, the only thing pulsating in her mind the need to catch Lachlan, to fall at his feet and beg for forgiveness for her monstrous lies.

She ran six steps when an arm flew out of nowhere, cutting her at the waist, knocking the wind out of her. She fell flat onto her back, sprawling into the dirt and hay.

Shock clouding her mind, she rolled in the dirt, trying to force air into her hemorrhaging gut.

Her eyes cracked open and shiny brown boots, the tips of them lined with steel, appeared in front of her eyes.

"He abandoned you, didn't he? Abandoned you like the coward he is."

Her eyes lifted, the face hazy above her.

But she knew the voice. Knew it all too well.

Mr. Molson.

# { CHAPTER 20 }

"Y—you?" She gasped, still trying to force air into her lungs. "Wh—what are you doing here?" Ice seeped into Evalyn's veins, shriveling her from the inside out.

"Who do you think brought your stepfather here, Evalyn? You think I didn't see you in that courtroom in Stirling?"

She blinked, his face coming into hideous, undeniable focus. Same wide nose that took up half his face. Same meaty neck that fell straight from his chin. Same soulless brown eyes that pinched at the edges. Same greasy brown hair tied back with a snatch of leather.

Mr. Molson leaned down and grabbed her arm, ripping her from the ground to her feet. "And now I get a nice surprise as my reward. The little mousey ready to leave."

Evalyn twisted her arm, trying to free herself. "What? No—"

"Oh, I heard you, Evalyn. And you're right about that fool you married. He's no match for me, so better he not even try." Mr. Molson started to drag her deep into the stables. "Come with me, mousey, I have something to show you."

She hit at his arm, digging her heels into the dirt, dragging them. "No. I'm not going anywhere with you."

He jerked her so viciously it made her head snap back.

"No?" His hand was quick and in the next instant the silver of a dagger flashed in front of her face. Polished to a shine, with a pattern of flames engraved along the high ridge of the blade. Evalyn had seen this knife before. The very one he'd promised to cut her with in that corridor at Wolfbridge.

"No, I think you'll ride with me." He pressed the length of the blade to her cheek, the tip of it digging into the flesh at the corner of her eye. "You recognize this? This is the blade that is going to carve your flesh, Evalyn. It can be deep, or it can be shallow. It's up to you. You'll ride with me or this blade will find your flesh the second you try to escape me." He leaned in, his putrid breath invading her pores. "But I won't kill you. Of that, you can be assured." He pulled away from her, his head shaking. "Your father was always too easy on you. Things will be different, now."

"Stepfather." The word mumbled past her lips. For all that she was in desperate danger, she needed to speak it. To correct that blasphemous slip.

Snorting a laugh, he slid the dagger back into the sheath at his waist. His dull brown eyes lifted to her and without warning the back of his hand flew, slamming against her cheek. "Did I ask you to speak?"

Everything inside her shriveled. Not again. She couldn't be at the mercy of this soulless beast.

Her look flew frantically around as he dragged her toward the back of the stable. She had to get out of here. Had to yell. Where was that stable boy? Or Lachlan—he hadn't truly meant to leave her—had he?

For the things she'd said to him, for the speed with which he stalked away from her, he was surely back up at the main castle by now.

A scream was her only chance. She tripped over her feet and Mr. Molson yanked her upright.

Her look landed at him. If she screamed and the stable boy came, Mr. Molson would gut the boy without blinking. There was no doubt. She'd overheard him laud his own kills with her stepfather—it was clear what little respect he had for the lives of those beneath him.

Mr. Molson spun her into the last stall in the stable, stopping for a stretch of raw rope. He wrapped it around her wrists, then lifted her onto the already saddled horse.

He heaved himself up behind her and the tip of the dagger pressed into her side just above her hip bone. "You only get one warning, mousey—make a word and this blade will be deep into your side and I will shove you from this horse. It's a slow way to die, bleeding out, your back broken—painful—so be a dove and keep your trap shut."

He sent the horse through the narrow back entrance of the stable and pushed the mare quickly into the adjoining woods. They disappeared into the thick of trees until they hit a trail that snaked away from Vinehill.

Her head craned, desperate, she kept the castle in view, praying for someone—anyone to see her—to see her being hauled away by this madman.

The last breath of hope exhaled from her lungs as the final glimpse of the top grey stones of the east turret vanished.

She was on her own.

~ ~ ~

They rode for six hours straight, almost to dusk.

Lachlan would think she'd stupidly run. Think she'd left him. That fact alone crushed her soul more than anything. More than the stench of Mr. Molson behind her. More than what he planned to do with her.

Lachlan would believe she didn't trust him. Didn't believe in him.

Didn't love him.

The first three hours on the horse she sat, collapsing upon herself while inner pieces of her broke off shard by shard, dying, leaving in their wake only a barren cavern of emptiness.

The last three hours she was left with nothing but numbness.

Happiness wasn't for her.

She never should have longed for more. Never should have hoped for more. Never should have tried to escape her life.

With her eyes downcast, moored deep in the cold stupor that had overtaken her body, it wasn't until Mr. Molson pulled the reins of the horse to a stop that she realized they approached a set of four small cottages set along a grassy hillside.

Mr. Molson poked her back and her eyes lifted slowly.

A group of three families. Two husbands standing in front of their wives and children. Two elderly ladies, both leaning heavily on canes. One lone mother with two children clinging to her skirts.

The group stood in the center of the four cottages, huddled into one spot, fear striking their features.

Six men, burly and dirty, stood around them. Two of the brutes held pistols, one a club, and the other three held swords.

She'd thought her insides were dead, but her heart burst alive, pounding, while her stomach found way to plummet further. Her gaze flew across the families. Nine children. None more than ten years old.

Mr. Molson's voice filled her ear. "I wanted you to see what I've been doing for you—the wealth I've been creating."

Her forehead scrunched and her head turned to him, though she couldn't take her eyes off the children in the middle of the circle. "W—wealth? What do you mean?"

"These lands, they're mine, or they will be. I've been making them profitable."

"Profitable?" Instant understanding made her chest tighten. "You're forcing these people from their homes?"

"No, Evalyn—I force them away and they just come back. They're nothing but a pestilence upon the land. So I burn them out."

"No." The word flew from her mouth, determined, not at all cowed.

"The people will only burn if they get in my way, lass." He chuckled. "But they have a chance."

"A chance to stay?"

"Yes."

A chill snaked about her spine. "How?"

"I'm not a stupid man, Evalyn, no matter how you like to look at me. Like I'm not fine enough to be the dung under your boot. That's about to change. I never thought you were to do as I bid without some encouragement and you've always had a soft spot for the weak. So I have a proposal for you."

Her shoulders started to tingle, the loss of feeling running down her arms. She was losing her body. Swaying. "What is it?"

Mr. Molson pointed to the group. "Simple. I can leave them where they be. Or I can tell my men to light a torch."

"And what do you want of me?" Her voice cut into the air, brittle, wooden, not her own.

"You ran away once, Evalyn. Now you run away with me. You don't fight it."

"No." Bile ran up her throat. "I can't. I can't leave Lachlan."

"You can't or you won't?"

"He's my husband."

"And your father has already petitioned for an annulment, claiming you were taken against your will. Between that and the divorce the marquess has put forth, your marriage should be dissolved within a fortnight. You made the mistake of marrying across the border."

"No…no." Her head shook, dizziness setting in. "No, he…they cannot."

"They did. And I'm giving you a chance." He grabbed her face between his meaty thumb and forefinger and forced it to the left in the direction of the tenants. "Look at them, look at the faces of those children. So scared. So very, very scared." A chortle escaped his throat, almost gleeful at their fear. "The choice is simple. The village burns, and whoever is in it with it. Or you leave with me and marry me."

"No—no you cannot kill them."

His words hissed in her ear, his fingers digging into her face. "I can do whatever I damn well please. This land is mine. And they're not leaving, so I have every right in the world."

"What kind of a monster are you?" She spit the words out through her cheeks mangled by his grip.

He leaned down to her ear, his voice low. "A monster with plans for you." His hand dropped from her face and he motioned to one of his men holding a sword. "The paper, Lewey."

The man stuck his sword into the ground and walked to Molson's horse, pulling free paper on a small board and a pencil from his coat pocket. He held it up in the air to Evalyn.

"Write a note, Evalyn. Write to your husband, tell him you want the divorce. Tell him you arrived at a pleasant village where you can work as a seamstress and that you want to disappear. That you never want to see him again."

"You heard that?"

"I heard everything, mousey. And I couldn't have planned it better. You accommodated me quite well in stealing you away from Vinehill, just as I planned it with your stepfather."

"But, no—no."

Shifting behind her, Mr. Molson pulled out his dagger. "No?" He pointed the tip of it at one of the little girls. Three at the most, her huge brown eyes, terrified, peeked past her mother's thick woolen skirts. "Are ye thinkin' of the children, Evalyn? Consider well what you do next. Save yourself or save the children. It's your choice."

She stared at the girl for a long moment, the girl's fear absorbing into her own.

Her hand shaking, Evalyn took the paper and pencil from the brute's hand. "I'll go."

With a snort, Mr. Molson grabbed her arm, the blade flipping and slicing through the rope binding her hands together.

She set pencil to paper.

# { CHAPTER 21 }

He tied her wrists back up.

She'd said she would go with him, but it was clear he wasn't going to trust her more than three steps away from him. That, or the lecherous monster just liked to see her wrists bound.

Maybe he wasn't as stupid as she'd always thought him.

But he was definitely more evil than she'd ever given him credit for.

He'd sent one man with the note back to Vinehill and left two of his men in the area of the tenants. A constant threat, ready to burn out the families—kill them if she decided she wanted to run.

He knew she wouldn't set destruction upon them. And no matter how she worked it in her mind, he was right. She wouldn't choose herself. Wouldn't try and escape as long as those families were in very real danger from Molson.

She would suffer anything if it meant those children were safe.

She knew it. Molson knew it.

She was trapped.

For as often as his hands paused at her breasts whenever possible as they traveled on the horse, he'd kept his paws off her the past two nights. He'd said if he couldn't enjoy her exactly as he wanted to—then he wouldn't at all. They'd stopped at a coaching inn both nights with his three men that accompanied them—with one of them always on guard at the door of the windowless rooms he stuck her in.

The landscape changed as they moved south—less stark hills and rocky terrain, but Evalyn had no idea as to their destination. Molson offered no information, and she refused to ask.

On the second day, she realized Lachlan would have already received her hastily scribbled note. The thought of the rage that would rip through him sent tears stinging her eyes and tore out her already shattered heart.

Or maybe he was already done with her. Maybe she'd pushed him too far in the stable and that was it. He was done with her. Maybe her note was a welcome reprieve for him.

Either way, the divorce would be finalized soon and Molson would force her to marry him.

She had to come to terms with that.

She also had to figure out a way to survive what was next. A way to remove herself so fully from her body, from physical pain, that what little was left of her wouldn't break.

She'd been good at that once. She could be again.

It would have to start with forgetting all she'd seen and done and experienced with Lachlan. Forgetting that she'd once had hope. Hope that wasn't misguided. Hope that was rewarded.

And she had to stop thinking about escaping. Escape would mean death to those children. Molson had sworn it.

It was on the third day when they were on the empty road alongside a river that the hairs on the back of her neck spiked. Her hands still bound together, they'd been walking in a grey, cold mist for hours, giving the horses a break from the muddied roads that sucked hooves deep into the muck.

Her look instantly swung up to Molson beside her. He continued to walk forward, his bushy eyebrows drawn together in a wicked line across his forehead. Aside from his wide nose, the man wasn't ugly, slightly attractive, even, to some misguided souls. But she didn't spare a thought on his outward appearance, for she knew the monster that salivated underneath his skin.

Her tongue curled up to the roof of her mouth and she immediately admonished herself. She was doing a dreadful job at accepting that his would be the face she would have to live with.

The face that would laugh when he cut her for sport.

The face above her in bed.

Her eyes closed, her stomach convulsing as bile ran up her throat.

She tripped, not seeing a thick root half stuck out of the mud in front of her. It sent her sprawling and unable to catch herself with her bound hands and she landed on her side in the mud.

"For fuck's sake, Evalyn." Molson dropped the reins of his horse and grabbed her arm, yanking her to her feet. "I swear if you trip over your damn feet one more time I'm going to tie you to the rump of the horse and it can drag you."

Evalyn kept her eyes downcast but lifted her bound wrists. Mud dripped off the side of her hand. "It's the rope. I cannot keep my balance when my feet are pulling from the mud."

Molson let loose an exaggerated sigh. "The horse to drag you would be a better option, but as I want your limbs working under me, that's not to happen."

"Working under you?"

A sneer carved his face. "When we reach the border and the divorce is delivered, we'll marry before we head back into England." He paused, pulling his dagger from under his coat. He lifted the blade to the side of her face and dragged it down along her cheek until the tip pressed into the flesh below her jaw. He pushed the blade upward, forcing her eyes to lift to him. "And I want you fighting me, bucking me when I stick you. I've been planning it out for a long while."

Her head went light, the blood leaving her face.

He dropped the knife from her jaw, grabbing her hand and sawing through the rough rope that had bound her wrists for three days. "We're far enough removed now that you can run, but we'll find you before anyone else does." The blade snapped the last of the rope and his eyes lifted, his look half threatening, half goading. "And I don't think you'll run, for you know what will happen if you do." He paused, a sickening sneer on his thin lips. "Then again, that may be more fun for both of us. Did I tell you I have a new whip? I think in the instance of you running, due punishment would be a lash for every step."

She held his look, not reacting. Not a recoil, not a frown, not a smile. He would have her body to do with what he wanted. But he would never have her. Not one emotion from her.

That, she'd decided. Quiet resistance. She knew well how to do it and that was how she wouldn't break.

A sneer pursed his lips and he turned, picking up his reins and starting forth again.

Evalyn rubbed her wrists, wincing at the raw bloody skin from the rub of the rope. At least she could move her arms freely again. As hard as it was to pick up her feet, she lifted her right leg, her thigh straining at the effort it took to suck her boot out of the mud. Her free arms almost gave her a sliver of hope, but with one of Molson's men in the lead with his horse, the other two trailing behind her, and the ground a mess of mud, she wouldn't get far. Probably not even to the side of the road.

A hundred more paces, and they started down the center of a wide planked bridge over the river.

Her eyes downcast, she was halfway across the bridge when Molson skidded to a stop in front of her. She bumped into his backside.

Garbled sounds behind her. Feet scuffling, boots pounding on the bridge. Grunts.

Evalyn spun around. One of Molson's men was flat on the ground just before the bridge, prone, his neck contorted unnaturally. Behind his body, two of the horses were free, hopping from one spot to the next, spooked by the scuffle. They bolted toward the nearby tree line.

A tortured wail pierced the air as Molson's other man struggled against a man in a black cloak with the hood pulled over his head, obscuring his face. He didn't see the second hooded man come behind him, a dagger flashing. The blade lifted, efficiently slitting his throat. Molson's man slumped to the ground, blood gurgling from his neck.

Highwaymen.

Panic filled Evalyn's chest, her breath gasping.

But then it struck her. Highwaymen were her way out.

If they killed Molson and his men, they might just leave her alive. Either way, those tenant families would be safe.

No matter what happened to her, it wouldn't be worse than dying a long, painful death under Molson's blade. His whip. A death that would be years in the making.

She had to get rid of their horse before Molson could escape on it.

She turned, her hand flinging out and slapping the rump of Molson's horse. The creature reared, yanking the reins from Molson, and ran forward, straight at the last of Molson's men at the far end of the bridge.

The brute jumped out of the way of the stampeding horse, losing his own reins as his mare joined the fracas.

The moment the horses thundered off the bridge, she saw two more cloaked figures with hooded heads approaching them from the opposite side of the river.

Molson's brute drew his pistol, but was too slow. One of the men rushed him, gutting him before he could even lift the barrel. Molson's last man fell, his body thunking to the wide planks of the bridge, then slumping off the side, dropping into the river below.

Her heart thundering in her chest, her initial hope sizzled out. These men were brutal. Callous with their kills.

And now they flanked her and Molson on both sides of the bridge by only twenty feet.

Why had she been so stupid as to smack the horse away? She could have mounted it before Molson had a chance and rammed past the highwaymen.

Mercy. She would have to beg for mercy.

The two cloaked men in front of her stepped forward, the one on the left casually wiping his bloody blade on the dark cloak that fell down to his knees. The one on the right lifted his head slightly, the grey hood about his face letting light into the shadow of it.

Or she would have to kiss them. Each and every one of them.

Lachlan's eyes locked with hers.

The blue streaks in his hazel irises were stormy, palpitating with rage. Rage mixed with something even more visceral—relief.

The air was blasted out of her chest in the next instant as Molson's arm brutally clamped around her waist and yanked her off her feet.

He set her to his side, the tip of his blade pressing into the hollow above her collarbone, trapping her in place.

"Don't you dare move, Evalyn," he hissed as his look skittered back and forth from one end of the bridge to the other.

Evalyn looked to the other side of the bridge. The cloaked figures had dropped their hoods. Rory. Finley. Her look swiveled back to Lachlan. He pushed his hood back, as did the man next to him. Domnall.

Her heart swelled, her chest expanded, and it sent the tip of Molson's knife digging into her skin.

They were here—here for her—but she was trapped.

"Dunhaven. I should've known." Molson scoffed a chuckle. "The baron said he'd take care of you, but I should've known the old man was worthless."

"Step away from my wife, Molson."

Molson's feet shuffled, his stance widening as a sneer carved into his face, sparking the air around him.

He looked at Lachlan. "I underestimated you, Dunhaven. I estimated your brother, right. But not you."

"What do you know of my brother?" Lachlan took a step forward with his arms at his sides, though the tip of his dirk flashed under the shadow of his cloak.

Molson snorted. "That he wanted to be a hero more than anything and I got to watch it be the death of him."

Lachlan stilled, his voice sinking to a deadly chill. "You were there?"

"I gave the order to burn down the buildings."

"Bloody devil."

"You look like your brother." A chortle snaked from Molson's lips. "I watched the fool die. Watched him run into that cottage. He thought he was a hero, but it turned out he was just a buffoon and he died for his idiocy."

"Lach—"

Molson jerked her, cutting her words and shifting her further away from Lachlan.

*Blast it.* She closed her eyes, expecting Lachlan to jump, to stupidly charge forth in anger at Molson's bait.

Nothing. Silence.

Silence and she was trapped. Trapped and the only way out was through Molson's blade. Her breathing went rapid, fear that she couldn't control flooding her veins.

Not now. Not now.

She couldn't be trapped.

She opened her eyes to find deadly fury had overtaken Lachlan's face. But he still stood at a distance.

He knew she was trapped the same as she did or he already would've charged.

Her breaths morphed into gasps. Gasps for air she couldn't get into her lungs.

Evalyn twisted, looking over the edge of the bridge. Every fiber in her being told her to jump. It was the only escape. It was the only direction away from the blade and the only place to go. She had to jump before Lachlan did something stupid—before his rage drove him forward straight into death.

Her toes moved to the rough wooden edge of the bridge.

She had to do it now—now before she lost herself to darkness for the air that couldn't make it to her lungs.

Her toes slipped to the edge of the bridge, her knees bending slightly, ready to spring. A hard swallow that sent the tip of Molson's blade deeper into her skin, and she cast one last furtive glance at Lachlan.

His eyes slightly squinted, the look in them meant to make her freeze. He shook his head slightly and the blue in his hazel eyes changed.

Shifted from fury to pleading.

Begging.

Begging her not to do it.

But it was the only escape. The only place to go. He could see that.

Why wouldn't he want her to jump?

*He knew.*

Knew she made stupid choices when she was trapped and couldn't escape.

He wanted her to be smart. To think.

She tore her look from his eyes and glanced over the edge.

The water far below foamed with anger. Churning. Frigid.

It wasn't escape.

It was death.

Lachlan knew that.

Air shot into her lungs with her next gasp.

She looked to Lachlan as her foot slid away from the edge.

His cheek twitched, a miniscule smile pulling back his lips.

His gaze left her to center on Molson, the fury instantly refilling his eyes. "I told you to step away from my wife, Molson."

A cackle left Molson's lips. "She won't be such for long. She'll be mine within a fortnight."

"You're delusional." Lachlan's ruthless voice echoed along the river.

"No. Smart." With that, Molson released Evalyn, shoving her behind him onto the planks of the bridge.

On her hands and knees, Evalyn saw Molson pull his pistol from under his coat. Heard the click of the hammer pull back. He pointed it at Lachlan.

*Bloody hell, no.*

With a vicious growl she lunged, her hands landing on Molson's back and shoving him with everything her body possessed.

It sent Molson flying, tumbling over the side of the bridge. Except for his one hand.

One hand that gripped the edge of the bridge, his knuckles popping.

She stared at that hand, willing the pads of his fingers to slip, to slide, to send him down to the waters of hell below.

One finger. Two.

A grunt, and his other hand swung up, grasping—grasping for anything and finding the edge of her skirt.

Molson's hand on the bridge slipped off, but the grip on her skirt was secure. He fell and her body dragged down with him, his weight a brick pendulum she couldn't shake.

She fought it, clawing against the wood planks, but her feet went over the edge, her legs, her hips.

Down. Down. Down so quickly she couldn't even scream.

Her waist. Her chest. Her head.

Her body jerked, snapping to a stop in midair.

A splash below.

Molson gone.

Her body swung, terrifying air surrounding her, vast nothingness below her feet.

Air everywhere except around her left wrist.

Her left wrist locked under her husband's grip.

She twisted, craning her neck to look up.

Lachlan's chest dangled fully off the edge of the bridge. His face contorted into a grimace and he slipped forward. Fingers straining, his left hand clutched the edge of the bridge, his knuckles white with the sheer force it took to hold them both from falling.

Another slip.

He growled.

"Dammit, Dom—a little help," he gritted out through clenched teeth.

Onto his belly next to Lachlan and Domnall's face appeared over the edge of the bridge, his hand extending down towards Evalyn.

"I need her higher, Lach."

With a groan escaping from the depths of his might, Lachlan's elbow bent and he lifted her with the sheer force of his arm.

High enough. Domnall gripped her forearm with both of his hands just under her husband's hold.

"I got her," Domnall grunted.

His eyes locked with hers, Lachlan let her go and pulled himself up over the edge of the planks. His belly flat on the bridge, he threw both hands down to her. "Swing your arm up to me, Eva."

Praying Domnall didn't lose his grip, she flung her right arm up to Lachlan with an awkward heave.

He caught her wrist and within a second she was hauled upward and onto the bridge with such force it sent Lachlan flat onto his back and her splayed on top of him, her limbs tangling with his.

He released her wrist and his arms wrapped around her, iron clamps about the jelly of her body.

His breathing hard beneath her, she rode the panting of his chest, flattening herself as close as she could to his body. A vicious tremble ran through him and he yanked her upward, his left hand going to the back of her head, clasping her tight over his shoulder. He tucked his face into her hair, his manic breath through her hair hot on her scalp.

"Heaven to hell, I wasn't too late. I wasn't too late." He gasped the words into her hair.

She managed to turn her face to him, her mouth next to his ear. "Lach—you were nowhere near late."

He nodded, his face burying back into her hair. Another shudder rolled through his body, shaking him from head to toe. "I couldn't be late. Not again. I couldn't lose you."

"You weren't. You made it." She wedged her hands upward, her hands clasping onto his face as she lifted herself enough to hover over him. "But how—how did you find me? After the note he made me write."

Lachlan's lip curled, his head shaking. He had to draw a deep breath to steady the frenzy that had taken over his body. "The note. That idiot Molson sent to Vinehill with the note. He broke. He broke easy. Told us exactly where you'd been and where Molson was headed with you."

Her heart stilled. "You didn't believe it? The note?"

His bottom lip pushed up in a frown. "Of course I didn't believe it, Eva. I'm not an imbecile. You may drive me to madness at times, but I'm not stupid enough to believe a half-scrawled note on crumpled paper as the end of us."

Her head dipped down, her brow landing on his chin as she exhaled, relief filling her chest. Several deep breaths passed, the sound of the churning water below filling the air. Her look popped up. "And I need to thank you."

"For?"

"For reminding me not to make stupid choices?"

His eyebrows arched.

"I make stupid choices when I'm trapped and you reminded of that."

"You were going to jump, weren't you?"

"I was." She shook her head. "I couldn't think and it was death. You made me think."

"And you reminded me not to let blind rage get the better of me and saved me from sending us all over the edge. Not to mention you saved me from that bullet." He kissed her forehead.

"But hell, Eva." His fingers tangled in the back of her hair tightened to her head as his eyes closed for a long moment. His look pained, it took seconds for him to crack his eyes open to her. "I cannot lose you. Don't ever do that to me again."

"Be coerced to leave you?" Her fingers alongside his face ran upward, diving into his brown hair, her palms along his temples. "He threatened to kill them, Lach—kill the children—I had to leave. I had to write the note."

"I know. But blast it, Eva." His eyes opened fully, his look piercing hers. "Those days without you—without knowing where you were, what was happening to you. It was utter madness." He paused, swallowing hard, his head shaking. "I love you, Eva. More than my own life. More than any man has a right to love."

Her breath caught in her throat. His words—so raw, so vehement—surged into her heart and sent a pang across her chest. "You…"

"Yes. I love you, Eva." He said the words with such simple conviction, the depth of feeling behind it vibrated his chest under her.

"Lachlan, you're not weak. I need you to know that. I never truly thought it of you. I was stupid and I said those things when I didn't believe any of them and I—"

His fingers untangled from her hair and went to her lips, silencing her words. "I know. I know what you were doing. I knew it five steps from the stable. But I was going to let you stew in it—stew in your words for hours. When what I should have done was storm back in there and make you see reality."

"Reality?"

"That you love me. But more than that, you trust me."

Her eyes widening, she smiled. "I do love you. And it is something that I never thought I could do, but I trust you. I trust you with everything I am."

"Lach." Domnall's voice cut into the thick air around them.

Both of their heads turned to Domnall standing at the end of the bridge.

"We should move. We dragged the other two bodies to the river and set them into the current. But we don't need to be seen in the area."

"And Molson?"

"We looked, but these waters are angry—they won't give him up for days."

Lachlan nodded, then sighed. "He's right." His look went to her face, concern surging in his hazel eyes. "Are you harmed? What did he do to you?"

"Nothing I couldn't survive."

Though the concern in his eyes told her he didn't like her half answer, he nodded. "I need to get you back to Vinehill."

She exhaled, relief flooding her. "There is no place I would rather be—ever again."

His eyes pinned her, a grin lifting his lips. "Deal."

# { CHAPTER 22 }

Lachlan's arms about his wife tightened, just as they'd done every five minutes during the last day of riding.

She was still in front of him, her body long and warm against his torso. Whole and solid and safe. He hadn't lost her. Hadn't been late.

His hands shifted on the leather of the reins, pulling his horse to the crossroad on the right and stopping it. Rory and Finley continued straight, each with a nod of his head as they passed, parting ways.

Domnall pulled his horse next to Lachlan's.

"Go on ahead, Dom. We'll catch up."

Domnall clicked his horse into motion and started on the last five miles to Vinehill.

Lachlan waited until Domnall crested the upcoming hill and disappeared beyond craggy rocks before he set his horse in motion.

Evalyn tensed, her back going rigid and she pulled slightly away from him. Her neck craned so she could look at him over her shoulder. "Why are we waiting?"

"I wanted you in private."

"That, I already deduced. It's the why I'm worried on."

Lachlan waited until his horse fell into an easy, smooth gait before clearing his throat. "There is one more thing we need to deal with."

Her eyebrow cocked at him. "What?"

"Your stepfather is still at Vinehill."

"He's what?" She jerked forward, twisting as fully toward him as she could without falling from the saddle.

"Still at Vinehill. Domnall learned it from one of our servants traveling through at the inn last night. Falsted knew I took off after you and he's waiting to see who I arrive back with."

Evalyn's gold-green eyes clouded, her look drifting off of him to stare at the hillsides dotted with rocky outcroppings. Her shoulders slumped, her face growing pale.

It sent his stomach churning, a storm of rage brewing. "You're scared?"

"I…" She didn't look to him, her chest lifting, then falling with a deep sigh. "How I reacted when I last saw him…"

Her head shook and her gaze shifted back to him. "I never wanted to be weak, Lachlan. I thought I had no other choice when I was under his roof. I thought I had left that behind when I escaped with you." She paused, her lips drawing inward for a long moment. "I wasn't prepared at Vinehill. I saw him and I just reacted—I just shrank and I was trapped again by him. I was weak."

Lachlan nodded, taking care to keep his words even. "And you're still scared?"

"I am, and it doesn't have anything to do with how I trust you—how I trust you to keep me safe, for I know you will." Her hands twisted together in her lap. "If we're together, then we lose everything—he will stop at nothing to ruin us and now that Molson's dead he'll do it out of pure spite. He'll do it with malice just to ruin me for the pleasure of seeing me suffer. He'll try to take away all of your land—he'll file with the courts and he'll win—he has so many connections."

"He doesn't have that much power, Eva."

"He does. I've watched it again and again with others—heard him gleefully gloat about crushing one poor soul after another. He doesn't lose, Lachlan. He doesn't."

Lachlan shrugged. "Maybe not. Or maybe you just need the right sword to stand up against him with."

"The right sword?"

A scheming smile broached his lips. "Yes. And I, my love, have the sharpest sword in the world. Let me tell you about it."

~ ~ ~

"I am here, by your side, ready to catch you." Standing next to her, Lachlan leaned down, his words a reassuring whisper in her ear. "But I know you, Eva, and you aren't going to need it."

Evalyn forced a wobbly smile, her hands smoothing the front of her cerulean woolen dress as she stared at the ancient door that closed off Lachlan's grandfather to the world. Lachlan's confidence in her was possibly misplaced, but she appreciated his words nonetheless.

Her hands lifted to her right temple, fingering the line of her hair that was lifted far higher than she ever dared wear it. Her ragged scar was showing, open to the world.

Her stepfather had never wanted to see it. He'd always come after her if the slightest hint of it was showing.

But it was time for it to see the light of day.

Swallowing hard, she closed her eyes for a long moment to draw a deep breath into her lungs. She nodded.

Lachlan opened the door, sending the heavy wood creaking on its hinges.

The marquess sat by the fire talking, chuckling. Her stepfather sat opposite him, a tumbler of brandy lifting to his lips as he joined in with his own laugh.

The sound scratched down her spine, sending all her nerves to a cringe. Of course. Of course the monster had made friends with Lachlan's grandfather. That was how he worked. Pander to the powerful, punish the weak.

At the sound of the hinges creaking closed, both men looked to the door and watched in silence as she and Lachlan walked to the center of the room.

"You." The smile slid from her stepfather's face. "Where's my man—Molson?"

"Met with an unfortunate accident." The edge of Lachlan's mouth pulled back in a terse line as he skewered Falsted with a glare. "Slipped off the side of a bridge."

Falsted's upper lip snarled. "I'll have you stripped of your title, Dunhaven. Sent to rot in Newgate."

Lachlan shrugged, his look impenetrable granite. "You can try, though all the witnesses to his death will testify to the unfortunate stumble he took."

Falsted sprang to his feet, storming toward Lachlan. "You don't know who you're dealing with."

Steeling herself, Evalyn stepped in front of Lachlan, intercepting him. "On the contrary, stepfather. It appears as though it is you that doesn't know who he's dealing with."

His feet skidding to a halt, her stepfather's look dragged away from Lachlan and his face contorted as his morose grey eyes sliced into Evalyn. "What is this insolence? That divorce decree should arrive any day, child, and you will pay for your impudence once I drag you away from here."

For the merest second, his threat struck to the heart of her, sending a tremble into her limbs. With a move so slight, Lachlan's fingers gently pressed into the small of her back.

Strength.

All of his strength behind her. Strength that buoyed her. Centered her.

She focused her gaze on her stepfather's pinched eyes. "Who is my father?"

"I'm your father, you impertinent child."

She shook her head. "I am no child and I am no daughter of yours."

"What?" His arm flew up, his hand whipping into the air and his fingers only missing her chin by the space of a feather.

She didn't flinch.

"After all the years I raised you by myself after your mother died? Clothes, food, shelter. All that and this is what you bring to me?"

"It was kind of you." Evalyn didn't blink. "Now tell me who my father is."

He took a step closer to her, the veins on his forehead throbbing as he went to his toes to lean over her. "You don't need to know that. Your mother wanted me to be your father. And be your father I have, for all the ingrate that you are now."

"I doubt that. I doubt my mother wanted me to grow up in the vile household you created for me. And I would ask you to be so kind as to not bring my mother's soul into this." She held her feet, her spine in place, refusing to cower away at his noxious overbearingness. Her voice went hard, her words vehement. "Now tell me who my father is."

His lips twisting in rage, Falsted's hand lifted, ready to strike her.

Behind her, Lachlan growled.

Falsted's look shifted to her husband and his arm stilled in midair. For eternal seconds, his forehead throbbed, blotching red as his hand swayed.

His hand dropped to his side and his head turned as he spat on the floor. Thick droplets landed on her skirts. "I don't have to take this from an ungrateful chit like you. Not after all I've done for you." He turned from Evalyn and started to stomp toward the door.

Lachlan moved quick, stepping in front of him, his hand on the hilt of the sword at his waist. "You're not allowed to leave yet, my lord."

"How dare you? Step aside, Dunhaven."

Lachlan stared at him in silence, the line of his jaw flexing.

"Who is my father?" Evalyn asked, not moving from the spot she had rooted herself in.

Falsted kept his eyes trained on Lachlan. "He was no one of consequence."

"Truly? No one of consequence?" Evalyn spun on her heel, facing him fully. "What was his given name?"

Falsted shook his head, his words sputtering. "I don't even remember, not after all these years."

"You don't?" She took two steps toward her stepfather. "That is so peculiar, for you've been managing his estate— my estate—for years."

"What?" Falsted's look jerked toward her. "What lies have you been told?"

"I have only been told the truth." Her hands went to her hips and she took a final step toward him, meeting him square on. "Edward Montclair, Viscount of Jaggerfall, owner of Swallowford lands. That is my father. I am his only heir. And you, stepfather, have used that estate for your own purposes for the last twenty years. For your own amusement. For your own sick desires." Her lips pulled back, the words vibrating from her chest. "That ends today."

Falsted turned fully to her, his hands lifting to grip her arms. "You have this all wrong, Evalyn. I never—"

She swatted his hands away before they made contact. "You never what? Never meant to do wrong by me? Never meant to steal every penny I was due so you could fill your own coffers? Never meant to sell me to Mr. Molson so he would then own the lands and you would still reap the rewards?" Her arms crossed over her chest and her head cocked to the side. "Never what, stepfather?"

"You little wretched ingrate." He charged her.

She held her ground, her toes not twitching. Her resolve steel. Let him come. He could never harm her again.

His hands lifted to choke her and a breath before his long fingers reached her, a fist swung into his face, sending him flying.

He fell, sprawling out on the floor.

The fury on Lachlan's face scared her. Scared her for the one moment it took to realize it was rage on her behalf.

He was never going to let another man harm her again. She was his. He was hers.

Swaying, her stepfather tried to lift himself up onto his hands, only to lose grip on the stones and fall back to the floor.

"Hah. Well done, Lach." Lachlan's grandfather hooted from his chair, a modicum of begrudging pride lighting his eyes. "Now that is doing, my boy."

Lachlan strode past Evalyn and grabbed Falsted's back collar. Blood splattered from her stepfather's mouth across his cheek. With a vicious jerk, he dragged him across the room to the door. For a long held breath, Lachlan paused at the door and Evalyn feared he was about to snap her stepfather's neck.

"You have five minutes to vacate these grounds, you despicable miscreant, or I find you and I kill you." Lachlan lifted Falsted, pushing his forehead back as he leaned down to see him eye to eye. "And if I ever hear your name again— in connection to Evalyn, in connection to these lands, there is no place you will be able to hide from me. Take this mercy your stepdaughter is giving you and disappear." He opened the door and with a kick and a shove, threw Falsted out.

Lachlan slammed the heavy oak planks shut, then turned back into the room. His look met Evalyn's, the blue in his hazel eyes sparking wild streaks. Vindication. Love. Pride.

Her heart swelled so violently her ribs nearly snapped.

He was across the room to her in four long strides, his arms wrapping her, lifting her up into him. His raw voice rumbled into her ear. "You were a goddess, my love. Pure lioness. Remind me never to cross you."

Evalyn laughed, the vibration of it cutting through the tears brimming in her eyes and sending them to her cheeks.

Lachlan pulled back slightly to see her face and his eyes darkened at the streaks of wetness. "What?"

"Happy. You. This." She shook her head. "Relief, that is all."

A smile, wide and filling the hard contours of his face lit up his eyes. Tugging her up higher onto him, his lips traveled her cheeks, kissing away the salt of her tears.

The sound of a cane slamming into stone broke through the air.

Both Evalyn and Lachlan's heads swiveled to his grandfather.

"Swallowford lands, eh?" The marquess shifted on his worn wingback chair, scooting to the edge and looking almost as though he would come to his feet. "So ye come with a dowry, child?"

Lachlan loosened his hold and Evalyn slipped down along his body until her toes touched the floor. Her arm threaded around Lachlan's back as she turned to his grandfather. "I apparently do, my lord."

"Her father owned the majority of the Swallowford lands next to ours, Grandfather. Everything that Falsted has been ravaging and selling off these last decades," Lachlan said, his right arm tightening about her shoulders. "But at least half of the lands are still intact. So no, we don't lose a thing with my marriage. We double in size. And not only that, the upper Swallowford lands hold the finest flocks this side of Stirling."

"Ah, good, very good." The marquess's long bony fingers stroked the stark bones of his chin as he appraised Evalyn from toe to head. "So it's not only coin ye bring, but the true blood runs through ye as well."

Evalyn's eyebrows lifted. "True blood, my lord?"

"The Viscount of Jaggerfall's mother-in-law was second cousin to my bonny Charlotte. Ye got Scot's blood in ye." He nodded and lifted his cane, then thwacked it down on the ottoman. "Well then, this changes everything. Welcome to the family, lass."

Lachlan stiffened. "Not so fast, Grandfather. This comes with conditions."

## { CHAPTER 23 }

"Conditions? What are ye talking about, Lach? What conditions?"

"My conditions."

His grandfather leaned forward in his chair, his wild eyebrows pulling together. "What cow-brained ideas do ye have rattling about in that skull of yers?"

Lachlan's arm sank away from Evalyn and he stepped toward his grandfather, pausing a foot away and looking down at him. "You stop."

"Stop what, boy?"

"Stop every single one of your machinations over my life, Grandfather. They end now." For a moment, Lachlan's hands curled into fists like they always did when dealing with his grandfather. But without thought, they relaxed, calm flowing through his limbs.

"Machinations?" The old man's withered lips pulled into a thin line and he flipped his cane in front of him, jabbing the tip into the floor and settling his hands atop. "I don't do that, Lach."

Lachlan scoffed. "You were sitting and laughing—*laughing*—with a sworn enemy, Grandfather. An enemy of our lands and our people for the last twenty years. You let him into this home—all in effort to control my life. So yes, you do do that. Is it worth it—are you willing to trade hatred for power? For your need to control everything here at Vinehill?"

"All of this I do for ye, Lach. I did it for yer brother and now I do it for ye."

"Exactly. You want me to stay and preserve the legacy of Vinehill." Lachlan sank to one knee on the floor so he was eye-level with his grandfather. "You want me to preserve the estate and the name and everything you've worked for. Your lands, your people."

His head bowed for a moment before his look lifted to his grandfather. "If you want that, if you want me to stay, then you are no longer in charge. I am. I will take from you all the wisdom you have, as it is considerable, but you are no longer in control of me. In control of Vinehill. Combined with Evalyn's lands, our estate, our name, our people have a way into the future. But it cannot be a future full of your edicts."

His look hardened, pinning the marquess. "Agree, or we leave."

The marquess's boney hands twisted on the brass handle of his cane, his knuckles glowing white in the light of the fire. "You would not dare leave here, boy."

"I would. I have spent my life willing to leave. I left to fight for the crown—all for the glory of the Vinehill name. I left to create my own lands and trade that I have scraped together to have a life outside of Vinehill. Even without Evalyn's lands, we would lead a comfortable life, free of the shackles of a four-hundred-year-old title." Lachlan paused, sighing. "Leaving one last time would be, frankly, a blessing."

His grandfather's head shook, the iron tone of his voice slipping. "But ye—ye cannot leave, Lach."

"Then give me a reason to stay. You've never once done that in your life—given me a reason to stay."

"What are ye speaking of, boy?"

Lachlan's head tilted to the side and he looked back at Evalyn, staring at her for long seconds. Her gaze focused on him with all the pride, support, and faith in the world that whatever he was doing in this moment was right and just.

That was it.

*She was it.*

What Evalyn was to him was the one thing that had been missing for so many years of his life. He'd had his brother and his sister, but this—her unconditional love—was everything.

His gaze slowly traveled back to the marquess. "I do not fancy something as grand as love from you, Grandfather. But since grandmother died, since my parents died, in all these years I would have settled for the slightest fondness from you, a mild consideration in the least. One nod, one word of affection. Something you could never bring yourself to do."

"Ye don't understand, boy." The wrinkles about his face deepening, drooping, the marquess exhaled a wheezing breath and sank back into his chair. His look went to the fire, his fingers fiddling with the tip of his cane.

He sat in silence for an extended moment before his look swung back to Lachlan, his ancient hazel eyes turned glassy with unshed tears, his words gravelly. "Ye don't understand, after yer father, after your grandmother—it—it was too much. I couldn't…" He shook his head. "How can ye love something ye ken ye'll lose?"

A heavy boulder settling into his chest, Lachlan moved to stand, his look pained as he looked down at his grandfather. At the withered man time had ravaged. "Except you never lost us, Grandfather. That is the difference. I am still here. Sloane is still here. And we deserved more. We always deserved more. We still do."

His grandfather lifted his eyes, the blue streaks in the hazel long since dulled to colorless streaks of grey. The marquess stared at Lachlan.

Judging his words, his worth.

Lachlan accepted it fully, returning the stare. Whether he walked out of Vinehill today, or stayed, it didn't matter. What mattered was the woman standing three feet behind him. What mattered was that she would be by his side. What mattered was her love.

"Fine. Fine boy." His grandfather's left hand lifted from the cane, waving in the air. "I cede the running of the estate."

No words of endearment. No pride.

But a start.

A start.

It took Lachlan a full breath to dislodge the lump in his throat. "Very well. The first order of business is to rescind that petition of divorce you sent."

~ ~ ~

Atop her horse, Evalyn looked over her shoulder past the four rolling hills they'd just traveled over. One last glance at the far-off group of cottages and barns set into a small circle.

It was the first thing she demanded to do the day after the confrontation with her stepfather. She needed to make sure the families Molson had threatened were alive and well. Lachlan had insisted he could send men to see to the task, but it wasn't enough for her.

She'd needed to see it with her own eyes. That the children were all alive and healthy. And she made sure Lachlan brought extra coin to leave with them.

It was another hour on the journey home before Lachlan broke the silence.

"Your worries are eased?" he asked from his horse next to hers. His eyes flicked back to the direction of the farm they'd spent the majority of the afternoon at.

"They are. For these families." She shook her head, her look shifting forward on the road. "But it scares me to think of the terror that my stepfather unleashed on this land. How many others were not so lucky. How many others ended with the fate of your brother and your relations."

Lachlan's gaze went to the rolling hills, an unsettling darkness creeping into his look.

His brother.

She could see it in the hazel of his eyes, the toll his brother's death still took upon him. The forgiveness he couldn't afford himself on the matter.

They traveled onward for thirty more minutes before they came upon ruins of several cottages and barns.

Her throat tightened.

All the structures had been burned to the ground some time past. Maybe in the previous summer. Maybe in the year before. Grasses had overgrown what looked like a once tidy vegetable garden centering the structures. Rectangles of five charred buildings' remains marked the footprints of what had once been modest cottages and barns.

A pit in the bottom of her stomach expanded, sinking. "We didn't pass by here on the way to the tenants."

"No. We took the long way there." Lachlan's eyes stayed oddly forward. "We stayed longer than I anticipated with the tenants, so this is the most direct way back to Vinehill."

She slowed her horse, her eyes riveted on the burnt wasteland. "This. This is what I fear—it's what I fear we'll find all across the lands." Her voice cracked.

A few strides ahead of her, Lachlan halted his horse and looked back to her. "You cannot take this on as your burden to bear, Eva—you were just as helpless against your stepfather and Molson as all the tenants."

She stopped her horse, unable to hold the weight of his stare, and she couldn't help her look from traveling over the destruction. All of it had burned to the dirt. Had to have burned for a long time. Just rubble. Ashes.

She glanced at Lachlan. His look remained fixed on her, unmoving.

It struck her then. His eyes hadn't moved toward the devastation of the buildings. Not once.

Her jaw dropped. "This—this is it. This was where…" Her eyes swept across the destruction, searching—searching for the slightest clue that this was the spot. Not finding one, she looked to her husband, pinning her gaze on him. "This was where Jacob died, isn't it?"

His jaw flexed, but he didn't look away. He nodded.

She tugged her foot from her stirrup and slid off her horse without thinking. Dropping the reins, she walked off the trail, moving onto the dark ground still scorched black.

Standing in the center of where the structures once stood, she looked at what was left of them, one by one. A long rectangle, fieldstone marking stalls. A barn. Another rectangle, small with stones that dipped into the ground. A larder house. Another barn.

And two larger rectangles on opposites sides of the clearing.

Cottages.

Her stomach rolled.

She walked to the far large rectangle.

"Stop, Eva. Stop."

She looked over her shoulder. Lachlan had dismounted and walked halfway to her. Halfway, but no farther. His face tortured.

All air left her lungs and she turned from the spot, walking toward him. She stopped an arm's length away, her look intent on him through tears welling in her eyes. "If this is not my burden to bear, Lachlan, then it isn't yours either." Her hands curled into fists at her sides. "What happened to Jacob—you cannot continue to flog yourself for not arriving in time to save him. You think you were too late, but maybe you were right on time for your life to be spared. You don't know what would have happened if you had arrived earlier than you did."

A deep-set frown dragged down his face. He glanced past her shoulder, his look settling on the black outline of the cottage for long seconds. "I know what you're saying, Eva, but the past is a vicious mistress—I will never be able to convince myself away from the belief that if I had just gotten here in time, all would be different. My brother would still be alive. I was late, and there is no changing the fact."

"Lachlan—"

He shook his head, looking to her. "But I also cannot wallow in that belief as I once did. The anger that came with it—that festered within me for too long—is not to be revisited. And nor should you let the sins of your stepfather stain your soul."

Her shoulders lifted in a heavy sigh. She could see the worry for her in his eyes, knew how desperately he wanted her to let this go. Yet it didn't lessen the guilt settling into her chest. "It is heavy in my heart, that is all."

He reached out, grabbing her shoulders and stepping toward her. "The solace in all of this is that the path led me to you, my wife, and that, I would never forsake. I cannot change the past, but I can embrace the future."

"Our future?"

He nodded. "Our future. And we can visit all the lands, check in on all the tenants, right what we can as we build what will come. That is how we need to honor those of the past that have been wronged."

A soft smile broached her lips. "I like that—it will be balm to my soul." Her eyes met his, and she lost herself in the blue strands weaving through the hazel. Lost herself like she did every time she looked at him. "You are balm to my soul. Everything I never could have hoped for, and everything I ever needed."

He smiled. "May I never disappoint, my love."

# { Epilogue }

Evalyn stepped through the door that led outside from the conservatory and inhaled the heady scent of early summer boxwoods. She was late, but it had taken far longer to get dressed than she had anticipated.

The sunlight blazing into her eyes, she lifted her hand, blocking the rays, and debated for a moment on going to retrieve a parasol.

But then a balmy breeze caught the wisps of her hair along her brow, calling her forward into the day. She moved forth, weaving along the granite pathway that led into the gardens at Vinehill.

Past the beds of roses closest to the conservatory, she veered to her left and started down the long formal walk lined with evergreen hedges. This part of the garden with roses and immaculately trimmed topiaries and shrubs stretched at least two furlongs from the castle to a rolling hill that swept down to a pond. Halfway down the grand walkway, an arm jutted out from a break in the tall evergreen hedge lining the path.

Yanked to the side, a laugh spurted from her lips as her husband spun her into him.

Her hands landed on his chest, splaying out along his crisp coat to his impossibly wide shoulders. "I am late to the party as it is. Now you are as well."

"I was already down there and they can wait." Lachlan leaned down, his lips ravaging her neck as he walked backward, dragging her farther into the alcove she hadn't ever noticed before. "And I wasn't about to pass up this opportunity to trap you. Revenge."

"Revenge? For what?" Her hands drifted up, threading into the back of his unusually neat hair.

His lips moved from her neck, dipping down along the swell of her breasts as he talked. "For that first time we met—when you trapped me in a much similar alcove wearing this exact same dress." Holding her in place, he tore his hungry mouth from her skin and took a step backward so his gaze could sweep her from head to toe. The smile carving onto his face spoke volumes—pride, love, and an inordinate amount of lust. "And you are more beautiful than ever."

Her hands sweeping along the front of her stomach, Evalyn looked down at her mother's dress. "That woman that you found to salvage this a marvel of the highest order—it was worth the year-long wait." She pointed to the line on the white fabric between her breasts where she had sliced the fabric long ago. "Her stitches are miniscule and she was flawless in recreating the pattern of the gold embroidery. One cannot even tell the horrors of what this dress survived. Blades. Bloody rabbits. Mud. Rivers."

"Stew."

She laughed.

Lachlan ran his hands down her sides, his fingers settling along her hips. "Seeing you radiant in it, this was worth the wait—and the coin."

"You're still not going to tell me what the cost was to fix it, are you? Do we need to sell some land?"

He grinned, shaking his head. "You never need know. Just trust me that it was worth it." His hand lifted, his forefinger running along the mother-of-pearl comb tucked into the side of her hair in her soft upsweep. His mother's comb. "And this, it completes it."

"It does, doesn't it?"

"The only thing more I could wish for in the moment is a bench in this alcove so I could steal you from the party long enough to do indecent things under your skirts."

She laughed and glanced down to the front of his trousers. He was more than ready for her. He always was. She glanced around the alcove, considering it for a long moment. Evergreen hedges. Green grass. Nothing else. Her bottom lip jutted up, sorry to disappoint. "I think the dress deserves one moment in the sun before grass stains it."

Lachlan groaned, his lips dipping back to her neck "Truly?"

"Yes." She chuckled, pushing him backward. "And I think a torturous walk down to the party is your punishment for trying to entice me away from it."

He straightened, clearing his throat as a lascivious smile danced on his lips. "Then it is time to join the others. But I have plans for the walk back up to the castle." He held his arm to her.

"I will hold you to that." She set her gloved hand in the crook of his elbow and they walked out of the alcove and onto the gravel pathway.

Twenty steps and they were strolling down the expansive lawn that led to the party in the shade by the pond.

"Took ye long enough to collect yer lass, lad." From his seat next to the trunk of the expansive oak, Lachlan's grandfather jutted his cane in the air at them. The thin bones of his free hand flicked out to the grass beyond the table laden with food and drink. "What would I have done had the wee one decided to crawl to the water?"

"I think you would have found your feet, Grandfather." Lachlan strolled to his cherub-faced son crawling along in the grass and swept him up into his arms. A high-pitched squeal of joy, and little Dunkin laughed, his chubby hands slapping blades of grass onto his father's cheeks.

Lachlan looked to his grandfather. "For this one, I imagine you would have found a way to run—to swim if necessary."

The marquess looked to his great-grandson and his wrinkled face twisted for a moment, then a smile cracked his face. "Aye. I believe I could have run. Wings under my feet for that one." His look snapped up to Lachlan. "But ye should not try me."

"We trust you, Grandfather." Evalyn looked at him from the table where she poured wine into three goblets.

"Aye, as ye should." The marquess's look swung to Evalyn. "Ye look quite bonny, lass. That dress brings me back to the years when my Charlotte shined."

"As it should. It is a beautiful piece of history." She brought the marquess one of the full goblets. "And it is a miracle it survived what it did. I would have worn it sooner, but I have only just been able to fit back into it since it was mended."

"Well, it is a treat for these ancient eyes." He lifted the goblet to her.

"And a treat for these young and virile eyes." Lachlan winked at her.

"You two." Evalyn shook her head, not able to hide the blush creeping into her face, nor the smile lifting her lips. "You two are more alike than either one of you would ever admit."

"Our uncanny charm?" Lachlan offered.

"Something akin to that." She handed one of the glasses to her husband, her fingers pausing soft on the side of Dunkin's face for a long moment before she turned back to the table and picked up her glass.

"We're all here." She lifted her goblet. "Shall we celebrate?"

"Remind me again what we're celebrating?" the marquess asked, his glass as high as his creaky elbow would allow.

"The day, Grandfather." Lachlan motioned with his goblet at the perfectly bright and clear day bathing them. He looked down at Dunkin, his lips going to his bairn's brow in a sweet kiss. "The sunny day. Do you need more than that?"

"A sunny day? Hmm." The marquess shook his head slightly, then tipped back his goblet of wine for a long sip. He lifted the glass again. "The wine is good, so fair enough. To the sun."

Evalyn smiled, lifting her glass. Indeed.

To the sun. To the warmth. To her family. To peace.

# ~ About the Author ~

K.J. Jackson is the USA Today bestselling author of the
*Hold Your Breath, Lords of Fate, Lords of Action,
Revelry's Tempest, Valor of Vinehill,*
and *Flame Moon* series.

She specializes in historical and paranormal romance,
loves to travel (road trips are the best!), and is a sucker for a
good story in any genre. She lives in Minnesota with
her husband, two children, and a dog who
has taken the sport of bed-hogging
to new heights.

Visit her at www.kjjackson.com

# ~ Author's Note ~

Thank you for allowing my stories into your life
and time—it is an honor!

Be sure to check out all my historical romances
(each is a stand-alone story):
Stone Devil Duke, *Hold Your Breath*
Unmasking the Marquess, *Hold Your Breath*
My Captain, My Earl, *Hold Your Breath*
Worth of a Duke, *Lords of Fate*
Earl of Destiny, *Lords of Fate*
Marquess of Fortune, *Lords of Fate*
Vow, *Lords of Action*
Promise, *Lords of Action*
Oath, *Lords of Action*
Of Valor & Vice, *Revelry's Tempest*
Of Sin & Sanctuary, *Revelry's Tempest*
Of Risk & Redemption, *Revelry's Tempest*
To Capture a Rogue, *Logan's Legends, Revelry's Tempest*
To Capture a Warrior, *Logan's Legends, Revelry's Tempest*
The Devil in the Duke, *Revelry's Tempest*
The Iron Earl, *Valor of Vinehill*

**Never miss a new release or sale!**
Be sure to sign up for my VIP Email List at
**www.KJJackson.com**

**Interested in Paranormal Romance?**
In the meantime, if you want to switch genres and check out my
Flame Moon paranormal romance series, ***Flame Moon #1***, the
first book in the series, is currently free (ebook) at all stores. ***Flame
Moon*** is a stand-alone story, so no worries on getting sucked into
a cliffhanger. But number two in the series, ***Triple Infinity***, ends
with a fun cliff, so be forewarned. Number three in the series, ***Flux
Flame***, ties up that portion of the series.

**Connect with me!**
www.KJJackson.com
kjk19jackson@gmail.com